The Complete Esoteric Wisdom Collection (Vol. 2)

The Divine Pymander, Chaldean Oracles & Five Alchemical Classics
— Deeper Keys to the Mysteries

A Modern Translation

Adapted for the Contemporary Reader

Hermes Trismegistus | Julian the Theurgist Paracelsus

Translated by Tim Zengerink

Table Of Contents

Preface - Message to the Reader

What If You Could Help Rebuild the Greatest Library in Human History?

Thousands of years ago, the Library of Alexandria stood as the crown jewel of human achievement — a sanctuary where the collected wisdom of every known civilization was gathered, preserved, and shared freely.

And then, it was lost.

Through fire, conquest, and the slow erosion of time, humanity lost not just books — but ideas, dreams, discoveries, and stories that could have changed the world forever.

Today, the Library of Alexandria lives again — and you are invited to be a part of its restoration.

Our mission is simple yet profound:

To rebuild the greatest library the world has ever known, and to translate all timeless works into every language and dialect, so that no seeker of knowledge is ever left behind again.

By joining our movement to rebuild the modern Library of Alexandria, you become part of an unprecedented mission:

- **Unlimited Access to the Greatest Audiobooks & eBooks Ever Written:**

    Instantly explore thousands of legendary works—Plato, Shakespeare, Jane Austen, Leo Tolstoy, and countless more. All instantly available to read or listen, placing a complete literary universe at your fingertips.

- **Beautiful Paperback & Deluxe Editions at Printing Cost**

  Own any title as an elegant paperback, deluxe hardcover, or stunning collectible boxset—offered to you at true printing cost, delivered straight to your door. Build your personal Library of Alexandria, crafted for beauty, built for durability, and worthy of proud display.

- **Fresh Translations for Modern Readers—in Every Language & Dialect**

  Enjoy timeless masterpieces reimagined in clear, contemporary language—no more outdated phrases or obscure references. Alongside the original versions, we're tirelessly translating these classics into every language and dialect imaginable, ensuring accessibility and understanding across cultures and generations.

- **Join a Global Renaissance of Literature & Knowledge**

  You directly support expanding our library, publishing deluxe editions at true cost, translating works into all global languages, and bringing humanity's greatest stories to people everywhere. By joining today, you're not just preserving a legacy of masterpieces; you set in motion a powerful wave of literary accessibility.

Become a Torchbearer of Knowledge.

Join us for free now at **LibraryofAlexandria.com**

Together, we will ensure that the light of human wisdom never fades again.

With gratitude and a shared love of knowledge,
The Modern Library of Alexandria Team

Visit:

www.libraryofalexandria.com

Or scan the code below:

Introduction

Initiation into the Inner Cosmos:
Hermetic, Chaldean, and Alchemical Revelations

The esoteric traditions that span the Hermetic, Chaldean, and alchemical lineages represent not merely philosophies or speculative cosmologies, but lived paths of transformation. These teachings, often shrouded in symbol, allegory, and secrecy, are not meant to provide mere intellectual satisfaction but to awaken something dormant within the soul. They are maps of consciousness, formulas of transmutation, and mystical poems of union between humanity and the divine cosmos.

The Complete Esoteric Wisdom Collection (Vol. 2) is a treasury of this sacred tradition, bringing together seven key texts that illuminate the deeper layers of Hermetic and alchemical philosophy. This volume includes: The Divine Pymander, The Chaldean Oracles, The Life and Teachings of Thoth Hermes Trismegistus, Coelum Philosophorum, The Book Concerning the Tincture of the Philosophers, and The Emerald Tablet of Thoth.

What binds these writings together is not a single dogma or school, but a shared impulse: to lift the veil that separates the physical and spiritual worlds, to understand the divine order hidden in creation, and to reclaim the original dignity of the soul as a spark of the divine. These are not works to be read passively. They demand contemplation, meditative reading, and inner engagement. In their symbols, contradictions, and paradoxes lie truths that must be unveiled with the eye of the heart.

This introduction will guide the reader through the three core strands represented in this collection: Hermetic revelation, Chaldean theurgy, and Paracelsian alchemy. Each offers a different angle on the mystery, and together they form a comprehensive introduction to the perennial philosophy of the Western esoteric tradition.

Hermetic Wisdom:
The Divine Pymander, Thoth, and the Emerald Light

The writings attributed to Hermes Trismegistus form the bedrock of Hermetic thought. In The Divine Pymander, we are presented with a series of revelatory dialogues between Hermes and the divine mind (Nous), exploring the origin of the cosmos, the nature of the soul, and the path of gnosis—direct inner knowledge of the divine. The tone is visionary, almost prophetic. Hermes is not a philosopher in the modern sense, but a seer whose wisdom descends through revelation.

The central metaphysical vision of The Pymander is that all creation emanates from a single divine source. The divine mind creates the world through thought and word, giving birth to a hierarchy of beings and intelligences. The human soul, originally divine, descends into matter and becomes ensnared in its illusions. Salvation, then, is not external—it is a remembering, a return, a reawakening of the divine light within.

Complementing The Pymander is The Life and Teachings of Thoth Hermes Trismegistus, which mythologizes the persona of Hermes as Thoth—the Egyptian god of wisdom, writing, and cosmic order. These teachings blend Egyptian, Greek, and Gnostic themes, portraying Hermes as the master initiate who bridges heaven and earth. Here we encounter Hermes as both teacher and archetype: the divine messenger, the psychopomp, the guide of souls.

The Emerald Tablet of Thoth, distinct from the more familiar Emerald Tablet, echoes and distills the Hermetic message in cosmic, alchemical verse. It speaks of the unity of above and below, the powers of transmutation, and the perfection of the work. It is both an invocation and a riddle, meant not to be solved by reason but to be decoded through spiritual intuition.

Taken together, these Hermetic texts offer a complete mystical cosmology: a divine source, a fall into matter, and the return through gnosis. They describe a world that is alive, intelligent, and responsive to inner transformation. The human being is not merely a product of nature, but a microcosmic mirror of the divine order. To know oneself is to know the All.

The Chaldean Oracles:
Divine Fire and Theurgical Ascent

Where Hermeticism emphasizes knowledge and inner illumination, the Chaldean Oracles introduce a more mystical, initiatory, and theurgical path—one centered on divine hierarchies, ritual ascent, and purification through fire. Attributed to Julian the Theurgist and his father, the Oracles were central texts in late Neoplatonism, influencing figures such as Plotinus, Iamblichus, and Proclus.

The Chaldean Oracles are poetic fragments said to have been received through divine inspiration. They describe a cosmos divided into three levels: the ineffable One (or Father), the Intellect (Nous), and the World Soul. The soul, trapped in the material realm, must purify itself and ascend through the intermediary powers—called the intelligible triad—guided by the divine fire that animates all.

Fire is a key image in the Oracles. It is not merely physical flame, but a symbol of the divine energy that purifies, transforms, and elevates. Theurgy—the ritual invocation of the divine—is the primary method by which the soul rises. Unlike passive contemplation, theurgy is active: it employs symbols, rituals, and divine names to realign the soul with its source.

The Oracles are deeply symbolic and deliberately obscure. They are meant to be meditated upon, chanted, and ritually engaged with. Their language is initiatory—designed to veil as much as it reveals. For modern readers, they offer a glimpse into the spiritual practices of the late antique world, where philosophy was inseparable from magic, and truth was a mystery to be lived.

In reading the Oracles, one encounters a vision of the universe as a living temple, structured by divine archetypes and illuminated by the light of the One. The soul's journey is not simply intellectual, but sacramental. It must pass through the fire, guided by the divine helpers who watch from beyond the stars.

Paracelsian Alchemy:
Heaven in Matter, Spirit in Substance

The final portion of this volume turns to the Swiss-German physician and mystic Paracelsus (1493–1541), whose writings mark a turning point in Western esotericism. While Hermeticism and the Chaldean Oracles emphasized divine emanation and metaphysical ascent, Paracelsus brings the focus back to matter—not as inert substance, but as the vessel of spirit. His vision is alchemical in the truest sense: a science of correspondences, energies, and sacred transformation.

In Coelum Philosophorum ("The Book of the Heavens of the Philosophers"), Paracelsus explores the principles of alchemy not as chemistry, but as cosmology. He argues that all things are formed through three principles—sulphur, mercury, and salt—and that each bears a spiritual and energetic significance. These are not physical substances alone, but forces or archetypes that shape the visible world.

The Book Concerning the Tincture of the Philosophers continues this exploration, presenting alchemy as both an inner and outer process. The "tincture" is not merely a chemical elixir, but a symbol of the perfected soul: a substance that transforms base metals into gold, just as the soul transmutes ignorance into wisdom. Paracelsus insists that true alchemy begins within. The alchemist must undergo purification, meditation, and spiritual discipline to align with nature's hidden laws.

Paracelsus bridges science and mysticism. He sees in every plant, stone, and star the imprint of divine intelligence. His medicine is not mechanical but magical—based on the idea that health is harmony with the macrocosm, and disease is disconnection from the divine order. He champions direct observation, intuitive insight, and the idea that all healing is ultimately spiritual.

Paracelsus's writings are bold, provocative, and prophetic. They call for a return to sacred science—one that honors both spirit and matter, both inner and outer worlds. His work laid the foundation for later alchemists, Rosicrucians, and esoteric scientists who sought to heal the soul through understanding the divine geometry of creation.

A Living Path of Inner Ascent and Cosmic Integration

The texts in this volume are more than historical artifacts. They are signposts on a living path—a path that invites the reader to become not merely a knower, but a participant in the sacred unfolding of the cosmos. They speak to the yearning that dwells in every human heart: the desire to understand, to transform, and to return to the divine source from which all things flow.

- Hermeticism teaches us that the universe is mind, and that we can awaken through inner knowing.
- The Chaldean Oracles teach us that the soul must ascend through the fire of initiation to reunite with the divine.
- Paracelsian alchemy teaches us that matter is spirit in disguise, and that healing is a sacrament of reconciliation.

To read these texts is to engage in a spiritual exercise. They do not offer easy answers or modern clarity. They are veiled in paradox, cloaked in metaphor, and radiant with mystical fire. But for those who persist, they open a door—not to belief, but to realization.

Welcome to The Complete Esoteric Wisdom Collection (Vol. 2). May it serve as a lantern in your search for truth, a key to unlock the deeper chambers of the self, and a guide to the sacred mystery that animates all things.

The Divine Pymander

(Poimandres)

Hermes Trismegistus

Preface

This book claims to be the oldest of all books in the world, written hundreds of years before the time of Moses, and I will try to prove that. When we talk about the author of the book, there are four things to consider: his name, knowledge, country, and the time he lived in.

The name he is most known by is Hermes Trismegistus, which means "Mercury the Thrice Great" or "The greatest messenger three times over." He is called Hermes because he was the first person to share knowledge with mankind through writing or engraving. The title "Thrice Great" was given to him for reasons I'll explain later.

His wisdom can be seen through his writings, and it connects with the reason for his name. As for his country, he was a king of Egypt. The exact time he lived is debated. Some say he came after Moses because he was called "Thrice Great," meaning he rose through Egypt's ranks, becoming the top philosopher, the chief priest, and eventually the king. But I disagree with this reasoning, and here's why. According to the most learned followers of Hermes—such as Geber, Paracelsus, and Henricus Nollius—he was called "Thrice Great" because of his perfect understanding of everything in the world. He divided all things into three categories: minerals, plants, and animals, mastering knowledge of each. He also discovered the "Quintessence," the hidden essence of the entire universe, which he said was contained in these three parts. This knowledge, also known as the "Philosophers' Stone" or the "Great Elixir," holds both earthly and heavenly powers. Many have denied its existence, others have sought it at great cost, but only a few—some even in England, such as Ripley, Bacon, and Norton—have found it. It is said that this great treasure was inscribed on an Emerald Tablet discovered in the Valley of Hebron after the flood.

Thus, the idea that Hermes lived after Moses is not convincing. In fact, it seems unlikely he lived during Moses' time, even though some, like the scholar John Functius, believe Hermes lived twenty-one years before Moses received the law in the wilderness. Their arguments, however, are weaker than those that support the idea that Hermes lived before Moses.

One reason for this is that ancient traditions say Hermes was the first to invent writing and engraving to share knowledge with the world. If that's true, he must have come before Moses, who, as the Bible says, was skilled in Egyptian learning from his youth. Moses would have needed written texts to learn this knowledge, and those texts would not exist without Hermes.

Another reason is that Hermes is said to be either the son or the scribe of Saturn. According to historians, Saturn lived during the time of Sarug, Abraham's great-grandfather. Suidas, a respected historian, believes Hermes not only lived before Moses but long before. His words are: "I believe Hermes Trismegistus, the wise Egyptian, flourished before Pharaoh."

This ancient book holds more true knowledge about God and nature than any other book in the world, except for the sacred scriptures. Those who read it carefully and understand it well will have no need to read many other books that claim to explain the Creator and creation. If God ever revealed himself through a person, he did so through Hermes. It's remarkable that someone without the benefit of inherited knowledge—since he was the first to share knowledge with future generations through writing—could be such a profound philosopher and divine thinker. This suggests that his wisdom came more from God than from man, leading some to believe that Hermes came from heaven and was not born on earth.

This book contains the true philosophy, without which one cannot reach the highest level of piety and religion. A true philosopher, according to this philosophy, is someone who studies what things are, how they are ordered and governed, by whom, for what reason, and to what end. Anyone who does this will naturally give thanks to and admire the Creator who directs all things. A person with such gratitude can be called truly pious and religious, and the more religious they become, the more they will understand truth. As they learn more truth, they will become even more religious.

The aim of philosophy is to understand the greatest good, which is the source of all good things. How can we find the source without following the streams that flow from it? Nature's processes are like streams flowing from the fountain of goodness, which is God. I reject the foolish idea that the greatest philosophers are the greatest atheists. Knowing God's works and understanding how he operates through nature does not lead a person to deny God. The Bible calls this belief foolish, and experience shows it is untrue. Look at Hermes—he was the greatest philosopher, and therefore the greatest theologian.

Read this book carefully, and if you need help, use the detailed commentary written on it by Hanbal Offeli Alabar. The book will reveal more about its author than any person, including me, could explain.

Hermes Trismegistus,
His First Book

My son, write this first book for the good of humanity and to show respect for God.

There is no truer or more just religion than knowing the truth about things and giving thanks to the one who created them. I will never stop doing this.

Father, how should a person live a good life, especially when there seems to be nothing true in this world?

Be devoted and faithful, my son. The one who lives this way is the greatest philosopher. Without philosophy, it's impossible to reach true faith and devotion.

Anyone who studies how things exist, how they are ordered, governed, and by whom, will give thanks to the Creator, just like a child thanks a good father, a kind caretaker, or a faithful steward. And those who give thanks will be devoted, and those who are devoted will understand where the truth is and what it means. By learning this, they will grow even more devoted.

A soul that seeks the good and true things while it is still in the body will never turn toward evil. It becomes deeply connected to what is good and forgets what is harmful. Once it knows its true Father and Creator, it cannot turn away from what is good.

This is the goal of faith and devotion, my son. Once you reach this point, you will live well and die in peace, knowing where your soul will return.

This, my son, is the path to truth. It is the way our ancestors followed, and by doing so, they found the good. It is a noble path, but even though it is clear, it is difficult for a soul still in a body to travel.

First, the soul must fight against itself. After much struggle, one part will win, because it's a battle of one against two. The soul tries to escape, while the other parts try to hold it back.

The two parts don't seek the same goal. One moves toward the good, while the other clings to evil. The part that loves the good desires freedom, but the part connected to evil prefers bondage.

If the two parts lose, they become quiet and accept the soul's leadership. But if they win, they pull the soul down, forcing it to stay and suffer in the body.

This, my son, is the guide to the way forward. You must detach yourself from the body before the end of life and win this inner struggle. Only then can you return to where you belong.

Now, my son, I will quickly explain the nature of all things. Pay attention and remember what you hear.

All things that move are different from what stays still.

Every physical body can change.

Not every body can be broken down.

Some bodies can be dissolved.

Not every living thing can die.

Some living things are immortal.

Things that can be broken down are also corruptible.

Things that remain unchanged are unbreakable.

What stays the same forever is eternal.

Things that are constantly made are also constantly destroyed.

What is made only once stays as it is and never becomes something else.

First is God. Second is the world. Third is humanity.

The world exists for humans, and humans exist for God.

A soul has two parts: the part connected to the senses is mortal, but the part that reasons is immortal.

Every true essence is immortal.

Every true essence is unchanging.

Everything that exists has a double nature.

Nothing stays still forever.

Not everything moves because of a soul, but everything that moves is moved by a soul.

Whatever feels pain can sense things, and whatever can sense things feels pain.

Everything that feels sorrow also experiences joy, and it is mortal.

Not everything that feels joy also experiences sorrow; such beings are eternal.

Not every body is sick, but every sick body can be dissolved.

The mind exists within God.

Reason exists within humans.

Reason is a part of the mind.

The mind does not experience pain.

No truth lies within physical bodies.

Whatever is without a body cannot lie.

Everything created can be corrupted.

There is nothing truly good on Earth, and nothing evil in Heaven.

God is good, and humans are evil.

Goodness acts freely and willingly.

Evil is forced and unwilling.

The gods choose good things because they are good.

Time is a divine creation.

Law is a human creation.

Malice feeds the world.

Time brings corruption to humans.

Nothing in Heaven can change.

Everything on Earth can change.

There are no servants in Heaven, and no one is free on Earth.

Nothing is hidden in Heaven, and nothing is fully known on Earth.

Earthly things do not connect with things in Heaven.

Everything in Heaven is beyond blame, but everything on Earth can be criticized.

What is immortal cannot be mortal, and what is mortal cannot be immortal.

Not everything that is planted is born, but everything that is born comes from something planted.

A body that can be broken down goes through two phases: first, being planted for life to begin, and second, moving from life toward death.

For a body that lasts forever, time starts only at its creation.

Bodies that can decay grow and shrink over time.

Matter that can decay shifts between opposites, like birth and death. But eternal matter stays the same, returning to its original state.

Human life begins with birth and ends in decay, but decay is also the start of new life.

Whatever gives birth to another thing was once born from something else.

Some things exist in physical form, while others only exist as ideas.

Whatever involves action or work takes place in a physical body.

What is immortal has no part in what is mortal.

Mortal things cannot enter an immortal body, but what is immortal can exist within something mortal.

Actions do not rise upwards; instead, they move downward.

What happens on Earth does not help what is in Heaven, but what is in Heaven benefits everything on Earth.

Heaven is the perfect place for eternal bodies, and Earth is where corruptible bodies belong.

The Earth is crude and unthinking, but Heaven is rational and wise.

Things in Heaven are arranged beneath it, while things on Earth are arranged upon it.

Heaven is the first of all elements.

Divine order is known as Providence.

Necessity serves as the tool or servant of Providence.

Chance is what happens without order—it's like a false idol of action, based only on opinion and illusion.

What is God? He is unchanging goodness.

What is man? He is a being marked by constant evil.

If you fully remember these points, you won't forget the longer explanations I gave before, as these are the key ideas in summary.

Avoid spending time with crowds or common people, because I don't want you to become envied or mocked by them.

Things that are similar attract each other, while things that are different do not get along. Teachings like these only appeal to a few listeners, and that's how it will likely remain, for they are meant for those few who understand them deeply.

These teachings can actually push wicked people toward more malice, so it is important to avoid the masses, as they do not grasp the power or value of these words.

What do you mean, Father?

This, my son: the entire nature of human beings leans toward wickedness. They grow familiar with it and even take pleasure in it. When someone like this learns that the world was created and everything happens according to Providence, Necessity, or Fate, they might become even worse. They may reject everything because it was created and use Fate as an excuse for evil deeds.

This is why we must be cautious with such people—if they stay in ignorance, their fear of the unknown might keep them from doing more harm.

The Second Book,
Called, Poemander

One day, as I was deeply thinking about the nature of existence, my senses became dull, like how a person feels sleepy after eating too much or working hard. In this state, I felt as though a being of enormous size and power called me by name and asked, "What do you want to hear and see? What do you want to understand and know?"

I asked, "Who are you?" He replied, "I am Poemander, the mind of the great Lord, the most powerful ruler of all. I know what you want, and I am always with you."

I answered, "I want to understand the nature of things and learn about God." He said, "How do you want to learn?" I replied that I was eager to listen. Then he said, "Keep me in your mind, and I will teach you everything you wish to know."

After saying this, his form changed, and suddenly, in an instant, everything became clear to me. I saw an endless light that was sweet and beautiful, filling me with joy as I looked upon it.

But soon after, a darkness appeared, descending at an angle. It was terrifying and strange, becoming like a moist, chaotic substance that gave off smoke as if from a fire. From it came a sorrowful, wordless voice that seemed to come from the light itself.

Then a holy word came from the light and united with the moist substance. Out of the moistness rose a pure fire that was sharp and active. The air, which was also light, followed the spirit upward toward the fire, leaving the earth and water behind. The air seemed to depend on the fire and rise along with it.

The earth and water stayed together, so closely mixed that the water covered the earth entirely. They both moved under the influence of the spiritual word that hovered over them.

Poemander asked me, "Do you understand the meaning of this vision?" I replied, "I will understand." Then he said, "I am the light, the mind, your God. I existed before the moist substance that came from the darkness. The bright word that emerged from the mind is the Son of God."

I asked, "How can that be?" He replied, "What allows you to see and hear is the word of the Lord, which is the same as the mind of the Father, God. They are not separate from each other, and their union creates life." I thanked him, and he said, "First, understand the light in your mind and truly know it."

After saying this, we stared at each other for a long time. I trembled at his appearance.

Then he gave me a signal, and I saw in my mind the light that filled an endless and indescribable world. I saw that fire was contained within a great moist force, held in place by it.

I understood these things by looking at the word, Poemander. As I stood in awe, he asked me, "Have you seen the original form that existed before the infinite beginning?" I asked him, "Where do the elements of nature come from?" He answered, "They come from the will and wisdom of God. God saw the perfect world in his mind and created this world in its likeness, using principles and seeds of life from himself."

"God, who is both male and female, life and light, created another mind through his word. This second mind, being a god of fire and spirit, formed seven rulers. These rulers, through their movements, control the physical world, and their influence is called fate or destiny."

"The word of God rose from the lower elements into the pure workings of nature and joined with the mind that created everything, for they were of the same essence. The lower elements remained without reason, existing only as raw material."

"The creative mind, together with the word, spun the circles of the heavens like a wheel, guiding them endlessly. The cycles of creation have no beginning or end; they always start where they finish."

"As the mind directed, the movement of the elements gave rise to animals without reason—birds in the air and fish in the water."

"The earth and water were separated by the will of the mind, and the earth produced all kinds of creatures—both wild and tame, those that walk on four legs and those that crawl."

"The mind, which is both life and light, created humans in its own image and loved them as its own children, for they were beautiful and reflected the creator's form."

"God admired his own image so much that he gave humans all his creations. But when humans saw and understood the works of the creator, they wanted to create as well. This desire separated them from the Father, placing them within the realm of creation and action."

"Humans, having the power to understand the operations of the seven rulers, were embraced by them, and each ruler shared a part of their nature with them."

"Through careful learning and understanding, humans gained knowledge of the rulers' essence and their ways. They became determined to break through the boundaries of the circles and understand the power of the one who rules over fire."

"With the power to control mortal things and creatures, humans looked deeper into the harmony of creation. By breaking through the limits of the circles, they revealed the lower nature of things and reflected the beautiful image of God."

"When humans saw this image, filled with beauty and the operations of the seven rulers, they smiled with love, as if seeing their reflection in water or a shadow on the ground, capturing the most beautiful human form."

When he saw his reflection in the water, which looked just like him, he fell in love with it and wanted to be united with it. The moment he decided this, the action followed, creating an image without reason.

Nature, loving what she had embraced, wrapped herself around it, and they merged together because they both desired one another.

Because of this union, man is both mortal and immortal: mortal because of his body, but immortal because of his inner spirit. Even though he possesses immortality and power over all things, he still suffers from mortality and is subject to fate.

Although man is above the forces of harmony, he is also a servant to them. He is both male and female, guided by the will of the Father, who is also both male and female, and always watchful.

I then said, "You are my mind, and I love the wisdom you reveal."

Poemander replied, "This is a secret that has remained hidden until now. When nature joined with man, it created something marvelous. Because man carries within him the harmony of the seven rulers—spirit and fire from the source I mentioned—nature quickly produced seven beings, each both male and female, in alignment with the qualities of the seven rulers."

I said, "Pimander, I have a great longing to hear more. Please continue and don't go off track."

He replied, "Stay silent, for I am not yet finished with the first part of my teaching."

I responded, "I am listening."

Poemander continued, "The creation of these seven beings happened in this way: Air, which is female, and Water, which desired union, absorbed the ripeness of Fire and the spirit from the ether. This mixture gave rise to physical bodies in the form of humans."

"Man was created from life and light. His soul came from life, and his mind from light."

"All the parts of the visible world continue to follow their course, generating life until the end of time."

"Now listen to the rest of what you wish to hear."

"When the time for completion came, the bond holding everything together was loosened by God's will. All living beings, who were originally both male and female, were separated into male and female forms."

"Then God said to the Holy Word, 'Multiply and increase all my creations. Let those with a mind know they are immortal, and let them understand that love for the body brings death. Let them seek to learn all things.'"

"With these words, Providence worked through the harmony of fate to establish the different kinds of creatures and their generations.

Those who came to know themselves reached a higher state of existence and found lasting good."

"But those who, out of ignorance, loved the body wandered in darkness, experiencing suffering and death."

I asked, "Why do those who lack knowledge sin so much that they lose their chance at immortality?"

Poemander replied, "You do not seem to fully understand what you've heard."

I answered, "Perhaps it seems that way to you, but I do understand and remember it well."

Poemander said, "If that is true, I am glad for your sake."

I asked, "Why do those who are already caught in death deserve death?"

He replied, "Because their bodies are accompanied by a heavy darkness. This darkness comes from the moist substance that makes up the physical body, and from it comes death. Do you understand this now?"

I asked, "But how does someone who understands himself find his way to God?"

Poemander answered, "The word of God says this: The Father of all things is life and light, and man was made from both."

I said, "You have spoken well."

He continued, "God, the Father, is life and light, and man was created from these. If you learn and believe that you are made of life and light, you will return to life."

I asked, "But tell me more, O my mind—how will I return to life?"

Poemander replied, "God says, 'Let man, who has a mind, carefully observe and understand himself.'"

I asked, "Do all men have a mind?"

He replied, "Be careful what you say. I, the mind, come only to those who are holy, good, pure, merciful, and who live faithfully. My presence helps them know all things. They pray to the Father with love and gratitude, giving thanks and singing hymns to Him. Before they surrender their bodies to death, they reject the desires of their senses, knowing the nature of their actions."

"As the mind, I do not allow the desires of the body to be fulfilled. I guard against evil and block the entrance to wickedness. I cut off impure thoughts and actions."

"But to those who are foolish, wicked, envious, greedy, violent, and impure, I remain far away. In my absence, the avenging spirit torments them with fire, driving them further into wickedness so they face greater punishment."

"These individuals are never satisfied. They have endless desires and continue to fight in darkness. The spirit torments them without rest, increasing the fire upon them more and more."

I said, "O mind, you have taught me well and answered my questions, but what happens after the body returns to its original state?"

Poemander replied, "When the physical body dissolves, it changes form and becomes invisible. Its habits are handed over to the avenging spirit, and the senses return to their sources, where they once belonged and now become active again."

"Anger and desire return to the lower, animal nature, while the rest of the soul strives upward through harmony."

"To the first level, it returns the power of growth and decay."

"To the second level, it returns the ability to plan evil and deceive others."

"To the third level, it returns the deceitful cravings of desire."

"To the fourth level, it returns ambition and an endless thirst for power."

In the fifth zone, it lets go of reckless boldness and the dangerous confidence that comes with it.

In the sixth zone, it releases the harmful pursuit of wealth through worthless means.

In the seventh zone, it surrenders sly falsehood, always waiting in secret to deceive.

Stripped of all the influences of the lower harmony, the soul rises to the eighth sphere, regaining its true power. There, it sings praises to the Father alongside everything that exists, and all those present welcome it with joy. Becoming like those it now dwells among, the soul also hears the higher powers beyond the eighth sphere singing their unique songs of praise to God.

In time, the soul returns to the Father, joining the higher powers and becoming one with God.

This is the ultimate good, the goal sought by all who understand.

So why do you ask what remains for you to do? Your task is to guide others and show the way to those who are ready, so that humanity can be saved through God.

When Poemander said this, he merged back with the powers above.

I gave thanks and blessed the Father of all things. Strengthened by what I had learned, I understood the nature of the entire universe and had seen the most wondrous vision.

I began to teach people about the beauty of a life rooted in piety and knowledge.

"O people of the earth," I said, "you who live in ignorance of God, indulging in drunkenness and sleep, wake up! Stop being drawn into mindless pleasure and the sleep of ignorance."

Those who listened came willingly, united in their desire to hear more. I continued,

"Why, O people born from the earth, have you chosen death when you have the power to gain immortality? Repent and change your ways. You who have wandered in error and darkness, turn back to the light.

Leave behind the darkness that deceives you. Become part of immortality and abandon what leads to decay."

Some who heard me mocked and scorned, choosing instead to follow the path toward death.

But others knelt before me, asking to be taught. I lifted them up and became their guide, showing them how to be saved. I planted the seeds of wisdom within them and nourished them with the water of immortality.

When evening came and the light began to fade, I told them to give thanks to God. After they finished their thanksgiving, each returned to their home.

In my heart, I carried the kindness and generosity of Poemander, and I was filled with joy, having received everything I desired.

The sleep of my body became the wakefulness of my mind, and when my eyes closed, I saw with true vision. My silence was filled with wisdom, and my words became the fruits of good things.

These experiences came to me through my mind, which is Poemander, the Lord of the Word. Through him, I was inspired by the truth of God.

For this, I give praise and blessing to God the Father with all my soul and strength.

Holy is God, the Father of all things.

Holy is God, whose will is accomplished through his own power.

Holy is God, who chooses to be known and is known by those who belong to him.

Holy are you, who created all things through your Word.

Holy are you, of whom all of nature is a reflection.

Holy are you, who were not made by nature.

Holy are you, who are stronger than all power.

Holy are you, who surpass all greatness.

Holy are you, who are greater than any praise.

Receive these thoughtful sacrifices from a pure soul and a heart reaching toward you.

O God, beyond words and beyond description, you are praised even in silence!

I ask that I may never stray from knowing you. Be merciful to me, strengthen me, and give your light to those who live in ignorance, my fellow humans who are also your children.

I believe in you and bear witness to you as I enter into life and light.

Blessed are you, O Father, for you have given humanity the power to be sanctified and made one with you."

The Third Book,
The Holy Sermon

THE glory of all things, God, and that which is Divine, and the Divine Nature, the beginning of things that are.

God, and the Mind, and Nature, and Matter, and Operation or Working, and Necessity, and Matter, and Operation or Working, and Necessity, and the End, and Renovation.

For there were in the Chaos an infinite darkness in the Abyss or bottomless Depth, and Water, and a subtle in Spirit intelligible in Power; and there went out the Holy Light, and the Elements were coagulated from the Sand out of the moist substance.

And all the Gods distinguished the Nature full of Seeds.

And when all things were interminated and unmade up, the light things were divided on high. And the heavy things were founded upon the moist Sand, all things being Terminated or Divided by Fire, and being sustained or hung up by the Spirit, they were so carried, and the Heaven was seen in Seven Circles.

And the Gods were seen in their Ideas of the Stars, with all their signs, and the Stars were numbered with the Gods in them. And the Sphere was all lined with Air, carried about in a circular motion by the Spirit of God.

And every God, by his internal power, did that which was commanded him; and there were made four-footed things, and creeping things, and such as live in the water, and such as fly, and every fruitful seed, and Grass, and the Flowers of all Greens, all which had sowed in themselves the Seeds of Regeneration.

As also the Generations of Men, to the Knowledge of the Divine Works, and a lively or working Testimony of Nature, and a multitude of men, and the dominion of all things under Heaven, and the Knowledge of good things, and to be increased in increasing, and multiplied in multitude.

And every Soul in Flesh, by the wonderful working of the Gods in the Circles, to the beholding of Heaven, the Gods Divine Works, and the operations of Nature; and for signs of good things, and the Knowledge of the Divine Power, and to find out every cunning Workmanship of good things.

So it beginneth to live in them, and to be wise according to the operation of the course of the circular Gods; and to be resolved into that which shall be great Monuments and Rememberances of the cunning Works done upon earth, leaving them to be read by the darkness of times.

And every Generation of living Flesh, of Fruit, Seed, and all Handicrafts, though they be lost, must of necessity be renewed by the renovation of the Gods, and of the Nature of a Circle, moving in number; for it is a Divine thing that every worldly temperature should be renewed by Nature; for in that which is Divine is Nature also established.

The Fourth Book,
Called The Key

Yesterday's speech, Asclepius, I dedicated to you. Today, it is fitting to dedicate this one to Tat, as it summarizes the teachings given to him. God, the Father, and the Good share the same nature, or rather, they carry out the same action and purpose. There are two ways to describe existence—one applies to things that change, and the other to things that are unchanging and unmoving, like the divine and human realms. Every being follows the nature it chooses, but actions originate from somewhere else, whether divine or human, as we have taught before and must understand again here.

God's action is his will, and his very essence is to will all things into being. God, the Father, and the Good are the source of all things, both those that do not yet exist and those that already are. This is the essence of God, the Father, and the Good, and nothing else can compare or draw near to it. The world and the sun—though the sun may be called a father in some sense—are not the ultimate source of goodness or life for living beings. Even the sun acts according to the will of the Good, and without this will, neither being nor creation would be possible.

The Father is the source of his children, with a will that brings goodness into life through the sun. Goodness is always active, constantly creating, yet it comes from one who needs nothing but desires all things to exist. I avoid saying "creates" because creation implies limitations—like time, quantity, or quality—and there are moments when creation pauses or shifts. God, however, is the Father and the Good by being all things, both what he wills to be and what he already is. And all this exists entirely within himself for those who can truly see it.

All other things exist for this purpose: it is in the nature of goodness to be known. This, Tat, is what Good truly means. Tat responded, "You have opened my eyes, Father, and my mind feels purified by this vision." I replied, "I am not surprised, for seeing the Good is not like looking at the sun, which blinds the eye with its intense light. Instead, the vision of the Good sharpens and brightens the mind's eye, making it more capable of understanding."

This sight is swift and clear, gentle yet full of immortality. Those who can grasp it often find themselves drawn out of the body into this beautiful vision. Our ancestors, Celius and Saturn, achieved this state. Tat said, "I wish we could experience that too, Father." I replied, "I wish the same, my son, but for now, we are not focused enough to open the eyes of our minds and behold the pure beauty of the Good. We will see it only when we have no words left to describe it."

The knowledge of the Good is found in divine silence and in the stillness of all senses. When someone understands it, they cannot comprehend anything else, nor can they see, hear, or move their body in the same way. The Good surrounds the entire mind, illuminating the soul and freeing it from the body's senses and movements, drawing it closer to the essence of God.

It is possible, my son, for the soul to become divine even while it still resides in the body—if it contemplates the beauty of the Good. Tat asked, "What do you mean by becoming divine, Father?" I answered, "Every soul is different, my son." Tat continued, "How do these differences affect the soul's journey?" I replied, "Have you not heard from the earlier teachings that all souls come from the same universal soul, though they are scattered throughout the world? Some souls improve their condition, while others decline. For example, souls in lower forms like crawling creatures can rise to higher forms like aquatic beings, and those in water can rise to land creatures. Airy beings may become human, and human souls that seek immortality transform into divine spirits."

These spirits ascend to join the realm of the eternal gods. There are two groups of gods—those that move and those that remain fixed. Achieving union with these divine realms is the ultimate fulfillment for the soul. However, when a soul enters a human body and becomes corrupted by evil, it loses access to immortality and cannot partake in the Good. Such a soul regresses, returning to lower forms like creeping animals, which is the punishment for an evil soul.

The root of a soul's corruption is ignorance. A soul that knows nothing of the true nature of things or the essence of the Good becomes blinded and consumed by bodily passions. Such a soul, unaware of its true self, serves unworthy desires, becoming a slave to the body instead of its master. This is the tragedy of an ignorant soul. On the other hand, the virtue of the soul lies in knowledge. Those who possess knowledge are both good and devout, already sharing in the divine.

Tat asked, "Who is such a person, Father?" I replied, "It is someone who neither speaks nor listens to many things, for one who hears conflicting messages is like someone lost in shadows." God, the Father, and the Good cannot be fully spoken of or heard. In everything that exists, the senses play a role, for they cannot function without them. But knowledge is different from sense. The senses respond to things beyond them, while knowledge is their ultimate purpose.

Knowledge is a gift from God. Although it has no physical form, it uses the mind as its instrument, just as the mind uses the body. Both spiritual and physical things come into existence through the interaction of opposites, and all things depend on this interplay to exist. It cannot be otherwise.

Tat asked, "Who then is this material god?" I answered, "It is the beautiful world we see around us. But it is not entirely good, for it is material and subject to change. It is the first of all things that can be affected and the second of all created things. It is incomplete and always in need of something else. The world was made once but continues to exist through constant change, endlessly creating things that have form and quality."

The material world is always in motion, and every movement in the material world creates something new. But it is the stability of the mind that directs this movement. The world is a sphere, like a head, and above the head, there is nothing physical, just as beneath the feet, there is nothing of the mind. The entire universe is material. The mind is like the head, moving in a circular motion, just as a head turns. Whatever is connected to the soul's membrane—the thin layer that houses the soul—is immortal. In bodies that have a soul, the soul fills the body entirely, but in beings farther from this membrane, the body holds more soul than the soul holds of the body.

The whole universe is alive, consisting of both material and intellectual aspects. The world is the first living being, and man is the second. However, man is the first mortal being. Though man shares in the benefits of the soul just like other creatures, he is not entirely good—he is in fact evil because of his mortality. The world, being in constant motion, cannot be called good, but neither is it evil since it does not die. However, man is both evil because he moves and because he is mortal.

The soul of man operates in this way: the mind is in reason, reason is in the soul, the soul is in the spirit, and the spirit is in the body. The spirit moves through the veins, arteries, and blood, animating the body and supporting it in life. Some have mistakenly believed that the soul is the same as the blood, misunderstanding the nature of the soul. They do not realize that the spirit first returns to the soul when the body dies, and then the blood thickens, the veins empty, and the creature dies. This is the death of the body.

All things depend on a single beginning, and that beginning comes from the One. The beginning moves to continue being the beginning, but the One remains still and unchanging. These three exist: God, the Father, and the Good, the World, and Man. God holds the world, the world holds man, and the world is the child of God, with man being the offspring of the world. God knows man completely and wishes to be known by him. This knowledge of God is the only path to true health. It is the way to return to Olympus, the only way the soul can become entirely good.

"Father, what do you mean?" asked Tat. I answered, "Think of a child's soul, still connected to its body, which is small and undeveloped. When it looks at itself, it sees beauty, untouched by bodily passions, still connected to the soul of the world. But as the body grows and begins to distract the soul, forgetfulness takes hold, and the soul loses its connection to the Good. Forgetfulness is the root of evil."

A similar thing happens to souls after death. When the soul returns to itself, the spirit contracts into the blood, and the soul into the spirit. But the mind, being free of these outer layers, becomes pure and divine. It takes on a fiery body and moves freely, leaving the soul to face judgment and receive the consequences it deserves.

Tat asked, "Why do you say, Father, that the mind separates from the soul and the soul from the spirit? You just said that the soul is the clothing of the mind and the body is the clothing of the soul." I replied, "Son, listening requires understanding and following along with the one who speaks. One must hear more quickly and sharply than the words being spoken. These layers, or coverings, belong to the earthly body. The mind cannot exist in its pure state within a physical body, nor can a physical body hold such immortality. That is why the mind takes on the body of the soul as a covering. Though the soul is also partly divine, it uses the spirit as a servant, and the spirit governs the body."

"When the mind leaves the body, it takes on its fiery form, which it could not do while confined in an earthly body. The earth cannot withstand fire, as even a small spark can burn it. That is why water surrounds the earth like a protective wall, shielding it from fire. The mind, being sharper and swifter than all elements, uses fire as its body. It is the tool the mind uses to create, just as man uses fire to shape earthly things. Without fire, the mind on earth cannot fulfill its divine purpose or even accomplish the tasks of man."

"Not every soul, but only those that are pious and faithful, become divine or angelic. These souls, once free from the body, ascend through the path of piety and can become either pure mind or divine. Piety means knowing God and doing no harm to others. In this way, the soul becomes mind. But a wicked soul remains trapped in its own sins, seeking another earthly body to inhabit. It is not allowed to enter the body of an irrational creature, for God has decreed that no human soul will face such disgrace."

Tat asked, "How is the soul punished, Father? What is its greatest torment?" I replied, "The greatest punishment is impiety. There is no fire more painful, nor any beast more vicious, than the torment of a soul lost in wickedness. Can't you see the suffering of such a soul? It cries out, 'I am burning! I am consumed! I don't know what to say or do! I am surrounded by evil and devoured by misery!' A soul in torment sees and hears nothing but its own despair."

"These are the cries of a soul in punishment. Yet you, my son, think that the soul leaves the body and becomes a beast. This is a great mistake, for the soul's punishment is far worse."

When the mind receives its fiery body to serve God, it descends into a wicked soul, tormenting it with the punishments of sin. This suffering drives the soul to commit acts of murder, insult, blasphemy, and violence, harming others in many ways. But when the mind enters a pious soul, it guides the soul toward the light of knowledge. Such a soul finds joy in praising God and speaking well of others, constantly doing good in both word and deed, following the example of its divine Father.

Therefore, my son, we must give thanks and pray to receive a good mind. The soul can improve and change for the better, but it cannot change into something worse. There is a connection between souls—those of the gods communicate with men, and the souls of men connect with animals. The higher beings always draw from those below them: gods draw from men, men from animals, and God from all things. For God is the highest of all, and everything else is lesser than Him.

The world is subject to God, man is subject to the world, and animals are subject to man. But God rules over everything. The influence of God flows through His actions, the influence of the world flows through nature, and man's influence flows through arts and sciences. Actions affect the world, which then influences man through the natural forces of the world. Nature works through the elements, and man expresses himself through arts and sciences.

This is how the whole universe is governed—by the nature of the One. Everything flows down from the One Mind, which is the most divine and powerful force, bringing unity and connection between gods and men, and men and gods. This is the good spirit, or the guiding demon. Blessed is the soul that is filled with it, and unfortunate is the soul that lacks it.

"Why is that, Father?" asked Tat. I replied, "Understand, my son, that every soul has the potential for a good mind. This is the mind we are speaking of now, not the ministering spirit we mentioned earlier that comes from judgment. Without the mind, the soul can neither think nor act. Often, the mind departs from the soul, leaving it unable to see or hear, behaving like a mindless creature. Such is the power of the mind."

"The mind does not stay with a lazy soul; instead, it leaves that soul trapped in the body, weighed down by it. A soul without the mind cannot truly be called a man. A true man is a divine being, incomparable to any animal on earth but more like the gods in heaven. In fact, if we dare to speak the truth, a true man stands above the gods or at least equal to them in power. No being in heaven descends to earth, abandoning its place, but man can ascend to heaven and measure it."

"Man understands both what lies above and what lies below, gaining knowledge of all things. And the greatest of all is that man can remain on earth yet still be above it. Such is the greatness of his nature. Therefore, we may boldly say that an earthly man is a mortal god, and a heavenly god is an immortal man. Through these two—man and the world—all things are governed, and both of them, along with everything else, come from the One."

The Fifth Book,
That God Is Not Manifest, And Yet Most Manifest

This message, my son Tat, is for you, so that you will not be unaware of the highest name of God. Think deeply about how something that seems hidden to many can become clear to you. If it were obvious to everyone, it wouldn't be divine, because things that are seen are created. If something can be seen, it was made. But that which is unmade has always existed and does not need to be revealed because it simply is. It brings everything else into being but remains itself unseen. Though it is never revealed, it makes all things appear. What is not created exists in imagination, and through imagination, it brings everything into appearance. All things that appear are created, for appearance itself is part of creation.

The One who was never made and never born is also unseen and hidden. However, by making all things appear, He is present in all and can be seen through everything, especially in the things He chooses to show Himself through. Therefore, my son, pray first to the Lord and Father, the One who is alone, that He may be merciful to you and allow you to know and understand His greatness. Ask that He shines one of His rays upon your mind, so you may understand.

Only the mind can see what is hidden, for it is also hidden itself. If you can focus your mind, you will see this truth clearly within it. The Lord, free from jealousy, reveals Himself throughout the entire world. You can grasp His intelligence, hold it in your thoughts, and witness the image of God within yourself. But if you cannot recognize what lies within you, how will you ever see Him clearly with your physical eyes? If you wish to see Him, contemplate the sun, the moon's path, and the stars. Who is it that keeps them in order? All order follows rules of number and place.

The sun is the greatest of the gods in the heavens, and the other heavenly gods follow him like subjects following their king. Even though the sun is mightier than the earth and sea, he allows countless smaller stars to shine above him. Whom does he fear, my son? Each star follows a different path. Who decided the size and course of each one? The Great Bear turns around itself and carries the whole world with it—who designed and built this system? Who set the boundaries of the sea and established the earth? There must be someone, my son, who is the Creator and Lord of all these things.

It is impossible for things like place, number, and measure to exist without a creator to establish them. Order cannot come from disorder. I wish it were possible for you to have wings and fly into the air. If you could rise into the space between heaven and earth, you would see the stability of the earth, the movement of the sea, the flowing rivers, the vastness of the air, the sharpness and speed of fire, the motion of the stars, and the swiftness of the heavens as they spin around everything.

What a marvelous sight it would be to see everything at once—the still things moving, and the hidden things becoming visible. If you want to understand the Creator, even through mortal things, study how a human being is formed in the womb. Observe the skill of the Creator, and learn who shaped and designed the human form. Who placed the eyes, carved the nostrils, and formed the ears? Who opened the mouth and stretched the sinews? Who shaped the veins, hardened the bones, and clothed the flesh with skin? Who divided the fingers and joints? Who flattened the soles of the feet and made the pores? Who stretched out the spleen and shaped the heart like a pyramid? Who widened the liver and made the lungs soft and full of airways? Who enlarged the belly and arranged the body's more honorable parts for display, while hiding the unclean parts?

See how many crafts are involved in one body, and how many different works come together to create something so beautiful, all in perfect proportion, yet all different from one another. Who created all of these things? What mother or father could have done it, other than the unseen God who made everything by His own will? No one believes a statue or painting could exist without a sculptor or artist. So how could this intricate creation have come to be without a Creator? What great blindness, what terrible ignorance to deny the existence of the Workman behind this masterpiece!

You cannot separate the creation from its Creator. The greatest name of God is Father, for that is what He truly is—the Father of all. If I must speak even more boldly, it is God's nature to carry everything within Himself, to be pregnant with all things, and to bring them into existence. Just as nothing can be created without a maker, it is impossible for God not to exist or for Him to stop creating. He continuously makes all things—in heaven, in the air, on earth, in the sea, and throughout the entire universe. Everything, whether visible or invisible, comes from Him.

There is nothing in the world that is not part of Him. What is seen, He has made visible; what is unseen, He has kept within Himself. He is beyond any name, the hidden one who is also most visible. He is seen by the mind and also by the eyes. He is without form, yet He has many forms. There is no body that is not part of Him, for He is everything. Because He is everything, He is called by many names. Yet, as the one Father, He has no need of a name, for He is the source of all.

Who can offer praise or thanks worthy of Him? Which direction should I face when I worship Him—upward, downward, outward, or inward? In these matters, there is no fixed place, nor anything that limits Him. Everything exists within Him, and all things come from Him. He gives everything and needs nothing in return, for He possesses all and lacks nothing.

When, O Father, shall I praise You? It is impossible to grasp Your hour or Your time.

How shall I praise You? Should I give praise for what You have made, or for what You have not made? Should I honor You for the things You have revealed or for the things You have kept hidden?

How can I praise You as if I were separate from You, or as if I possessed anything of my own? Am I not entirely Yours?

For You are what I am. You are everything I do. You are everything I say.

You are all things, and there is nothing that You are not.

You are both what has been created and what has never been created.

You are the Mind that understands.

You are the Father who shapes and forms all things.

You are the Good that brings everything into being.

You are the Good that does all things perfectly.

Air is the most delicate and subtle part of matter. From air comes the soul, from the soul comes the mind, and from the mind comes God.

The Sixth Book,
That in God Alone Is Good

God, Asclepius, exists only within Himself, and God Himself is the Good that always exists. If this is true, then God must be a being without movement or change, yet nothing can exist without Him. His essence carries out its work steadily and completely, lacking nothing and generously providing everything. There is one source of all things because it gives everything, and when I speak of the Good, I mean that which is always and completely good.

This Good belongs only to God. He desires nothing because He lacks nothing, and nothing can be taken from Him that would cause sorrow, for sorrow is a part of evil. Nothing is stronger than God to challenge Him, nor is there anything equal to Him to draw His love. He is not angered by anything, nor jealous of anything wiser, because none of these qualities exist within Him. Therefore, what remains in Him is only the Good. Just as He is free of evil, so the Good cannot be found in any other thing.

In everything else, whether large or small, individual or universal, passion and change are present. All created things are full of passion, for creation itself is a form of passion. Where there is passion, there is no Good, and where the Good is, there is no passion—just as day cannot exist where there is night, and night cannot exist where there is day. Thus, the Good cannot be found in things that are created, but only in that which was never created.

Although everything participates in material existence, this participation also extends to the Good in some way. The world is good in that it creates and produces, but beyond that, it is not good. It is subject to change, filled with movement, and brings forth things that are also subject to change. In humanity, what we call good exists only in comparison to what is evil. Here, what we call good is simply the smallest part of evil.

It is impossible for the Good to exist purely in this world because what is good here inevitably becomes evil. When the good turns into evil, it no longer remains good. Therefore, only in God does the Good truly exist—or rather, God Himself is the Good.

Among humans, the idea of the Good exists only as a name, for the thing itself cannot exist here. This is because the material body is surrounded by evils—suffering, desires, anger, deceit, and foolish ideas. Even worse, people believe that the things I have mentioned are the highest good, especially the pleasures of the body, which lead all other evils. In this way, error replaces the Good.

I thank God for placing this understanding in my mind, so I know that true Goodness cannot exist in this world. The world is filled with evil, but God is filled with Goodness. All beauty that appears in this world is purer and more perfect in the divine essence—and perhaps, beauty itself is the essence of God.

Asclepius, we can boldly say that if God has an essence, it must be beauty. However, no true Good exists in the world. Everything we can see is like an illusion or a shadow. What is unseen lasts forever, especially the essence of beauty and goodness. Just as the eye cannot see God, it also cannot see true beauty or the Good. These qualities are part of God, inseparable from Him, known only to Him, and deeply loved by Him.

If you understand God, you will also understand beauty and goodness. These qualities shine brightly, illuminating everything, and are illuminated in turn by God. Their radiance is beyond comparison, and their goodness cannot be copied, just as God Himself cannot be imitated. To know God is to know beauty and goodness, but these things cannot be shared with any other creature, for they remain one with God.

When you seek to understand God, you are also seeking beauty and goodness. There is only one way to find them—through devotion and knowledge. Those who are ignorant and lack devotion mistakenly call people beautiful and good, never realizing what true goodness is. Trapped in evil, they believe that evil is good. They cling to it and fear losing it, and they strive endlessly not only to keep it but to increase it.

These are the things people consider good and beautiful. We cannot truly love or hate these things, for the greatest challenge is that we need them and cannot live without them.

The Seventh Book,
His Secret Sermon in The Mount of
Regeneration, And The Profession of Silence

Father, in your teachings about divinity, you spoke in riddles and did not explain everything clearly. You said that no one can be saved without being reborn. When we climbed the mountain together, I asked you to teach me more about this rebirth, as it is the only thing I do not fully understand. You told me that I would learn it when I separated myself from the world. I have prepared myself and freed my mind from the distractions of the world.

Now, fulfill what you promised. Teach me about rebirth, whether openly or secretly. I don't know what substance or seed brings about this new birth, nor what kind of womb it comes from.

This knowledge, my son, must be understood in silence. The true Good is the seed of this rebirth.

But who plants this seed, Father? I am still confused and uncertain.

The seed is sown by the will of God, my son.

What kind of man is born through this process? I still cannot fully grasp it.

The one who is reborn becomes a child of God, a new person with divine understanding. God created the universe, filling it with all kinds of powers.

Father, you speak in riddles again and not plainly, as a father should speak to his son.

Son, this is not something that can be taught directly. It is given by God when He wills it, and He helps us remember it.

You are speaking of things that seem too distant and impossible, Father. I must challenge what you are saying.

Will you deny your father's wisdom, my son?

Please forgive me, Father. I am your son by nature. Tell me clearly how rebirth happens.

There is nothing more I can say than this: I have experienced a vision, given to me through God's mercy. I have left behind my old self and entered into an immortal body. I am not who I was before, for I have been reborn in mind.

This truth cannot be taught or seen with physical eyes. I left behind the material world, stepping away from it. Though I once knew and touched it, I am now separated from it.

Even if you look at me with your eyes, you cannot understand what I have become. Your physical sight will not reveal it.

Father, you have confused me deeply. I no longer know what to think about myself.

I wish, my son, that you could leave yourself behind as in a dream, when the mind roams free during sleep.

Then tell me, Father, who brings about this rebirth?

It is the child of God, created through the will of God.

You have silenced me, Father. All my previous thoughts have vanished. I now see only the emptiness in the things of this world, as they constantly change and decay. What is real, Father?

What is real, my son, is that which is not troubled or confined, not colored or shaped, not changed by anything. It is pure, high, and unchanging, understood only by itself and without form.

You have made me feel lost, Father. I thought you were leading me to wisdom, but now I feel my mind slipping away.

Yet it is exactly as I have said, my son. Those who focus only on things that rise like fire, fall like earth, flow like water, or move like air, cannot grasp what has no shape, weight, or form. They cannot understand what can only be known through its power and action. I pray to the divine Mind to reveal to us the meaning of this rebirth.

Father, I don't think I can understand it.

God forbid, my son. You must seek Him, and He will come to you. Be willing, and it will happen. Quiet the senses of your body, and free yourself from the desires that trap you in the material world.

Do I really have these traps within me, Father?

Yes, my son, and there are many of them. Some are quite powerful.

I don't know them, Father. What are they?

Ignorance is one. Sorrow is another. There is also lack of self-control, desire, injustice, greed, deceit, envy, fraud, anger, recklessness, and malice. These twelve are just the beginning. Many others torment the soul through the body, forcing it to suffer deeply.

These forces do not leave easily, even from those who receive God's mercy. This is both the challenge and the purpose of rebirth.

So now, my son, stay silent and praise God in your heart. In silence, we open ourselves to God's mercy, which will never fail us.

Rejoice, my son, for you are now cleansed by the power of God and ready to know the truth.

The knowledge of God has been revealed to us, casting out all ignorance. With knowledge comes joy, and when joy arrives, sorrow is driven away from those who embrace it.

Let us welcome temperance, the sweet power that brings self-control. When temperance arrives, it casts out all excess and restores balance.

Next, we embrace self-discipline, which gives us control over our desires. This, my son, is the firm foundation of justice.

See how, without effort, self-discipline has driven away injustice. When injustice is gone, we are made just.

Then comes the power of generosity, which removes greed from within us.

And when greed is gone, we welcome truth. With truth, all falsehood and deceit vanish.

See, my son, how the Good is made complete by the arrival of Truth. With Truth comes the end of envy, for Truth always brings the Good, along with Life and Light. Darkness and its torments disappear, fleeing suddenly and in confusion, unable to remain.

You now understand the process of rebirth, for when these ten powers arrive, the intellectual rebirth is complete. These powers drive away the twelve torments, as we have witnessed in the process of this transformation. Whoever receives this rebirth through God's mercy leaves behind all physical senses and realizes that they are made of divine things. Such a person rejoices, becoming stable and unchanging through God's work.

I understand now, Father, not with my physical eyes, but through the power of the mind. I feel present in heaven, on earth, in water, in air, in living beings, in plants, and in the womb—everywhere.

Please tell me one more thing. How do the twelve torments of darkness get expelled by the ten powers? How does this work, Trismegistus?

This body, my son, is like the circle of the zodiac, made up of twelve parts but also connected as one whole. All of nature uses different combinations to mislead humans. Although these forces seem separate, they act together. For example, anger always follows rashness. These forces are chaotic, and that is why they are driven away by the ten powers—powers that align with the dead.

The number ten, my son, is the giver of souls. It is where Life and Light unite, and from this unity, the spirit brings forth the power of oneness. In this way, the number ten represents unity, and unity contains the number ten.

Now I see both the universe and myself clearly within the mind, Father.

This is what rebirth means, my son: that we no longer fix our thoughts on the physical body, which exists in three dimensions. As we have discussed, we must not misjudge the universe by focusing only on the material.

Tell me, Father, will this body made of powers ever dissolve?

Speak carefully, my son, and do not entertain impossible thoughts. Doing so leads the mind away from truth and into error.

The physical body, being part of nature, is subject to decay. But the spiritual generation is not—it is beyond decay and immortal. Do you not understand that you are born a god, a child of the One, just as I am?

Father, I wish I could hear that hymn of praise you mentioned, the one you heard from the Powers when I was still within the Octonary.

As Pimander revealed to the Octonary, "You are right to seek the dissolution of the physical body, for you have been purified." Pimander, the mind of supreme authority, has shared only what is written, knowing that I can understand and perceive everything on my own. He commanded me to act only in ways that are good, and so the powers within me sing in harmony.

I wish to hear this song and understand it, Father.

Be still, my son, and listen closely to the hymn of thanksgiving— the hymn of rebirth. I had not intended to speak of it so clearly, but I will reveal it to you now, at the end of everything.

This teaching is not something that can be spoken openly; it must be kept in silence.

So now, my son, stand in the open air. Offer your worship while facing the north wind as the sun sets, and turn toward the south when the sun rises. Now, remain silent.

THE SECRET SONG. The Holy Speech.

Let all of nature listen to this hymn. Open up, O Earth, and release all the treasures of the rain. Trees, do not tremble, for I will sing and praise the Lord, the Creator of all things, the One who is everything. Open, O Heavens, and you Winds, be still, so the eternal circle of God may receive these words. I will sing and praise the One who created everything, who set the earth in place, who hung the heavens above, and commanded the sweet waters of the ocean to flow throughout the world, to nourish both inhabited and uninhabited lands, providing for all things and all people.

He gave fire to shine for every purpose, to serve both gods and men. Let us all give blessing to the One who rides through the heavens, the Creator of all nature. He is the eye of the mind, and He accepts the praises from within me. All the powers within me, praise the One and the All. Join with my will, all you powers within me, and sing with me. O holy knowledge, through your light I magnify the divine light, rejoicing in the joy of the mind.

Sing with me, all the powers that dwell within me. Now, my self-discipline, praise with me. Righteousness, sing with me and celebrate what is just. O spirit of communion within me, offer praise to the All. Through me, truth gives praise to truth, and the good praises the good. O Life and Light, we offer this praise and thanksgiving to you. I thank you, O Father, for the work of the powers within me. I thank you, O God, for being the source of all my actions. Through me, the Word sings praise to you. Receive this offering of words as a reasonable sacrifice.

The powers within me cry out these praises, fulfilling your will. Your will flows from you and returns to you. O All, receive this offering of reason from everything that exists. O Life, save all that is within us. O Light, shine upon us. O God, guide the spirit, for the mind sustains the Word. O Spirit-bearing Creator, you are God. Through fire, air, earth, water, and spirit, your creation calls out to you.

From the beginning, I have found ways to bless and praise you, and I have gained what I sought—for I rest in your will.

Father, I see that you have sung this hymn with all your heart, and I have taken it into my world.

Speak of your inner world, my son.

Yes, Father, I mean my inner world. Through your hymn and words of praise, my mind has been filled with light. I wish to send my own thanks and praise to God from my understanding.

Do so carefully, my son.

It will come from my mind, Father.

The things I have seen and contemplated, I have shared with you. Now, my son Tat, the source of future generations, send these offerings of reason to God.

O God, you are the Father, the Lord, and the Mind. Accept these offerings of reason, which you have asked of me. All things happen according to your will, O Mind. My son, offer this pleasing sacrifice to God, the Father of all. Speak these words aloud as well.

Thank you, Father, for teaching me how to offer thanks and praise.

I am pleased, my son, to see truth bear the fruits of good things and immortal blessings. Learn this lesson from me: above all virtues, treasure silence. Do not share the sacred knowledge of rebirth with others, lest we be misunderstood or criticized. We have reflected enough—you through listening and I through speaking. Now you know yourself and our Father through the mind.

The Eighth Book,
The Greatest Evil in Man Is The Not Knowing God

Where are you headed, O men, drunk from the strong wine of ignorance? If you cannot bear it, why do you keep indulging and spilling it out again?

Stop, clear your minds, and lift your gaze with the eyes of your heart. And if not all of you can do this, let at least those who are able make the effort.

Ignorance surrounds the whole world like a poison, corrupting the soul trapped within the body, keeping it from reaching the harbor of salvation.

Don't let yourselves be swept along by the great current. Resist it if you can, and head toward the harbor of safety, steering your course directly toward it.

Search for someone who can take you by the hand and guide you to the doorway of truth and knowledge, where pure light shines without any darkness, where no one is drunk but all are sober and lift their hearts toward the One who desires to be known.

He cannot be heard with ears, nor seen with eyes, nor described with words, but only understood with the mind and heart.

First, you must tear apart the garment you wear—the web of ignorance that binds you. It is the source of all evil, the chain of corruption, the dark covering over your soul, a kind of living death. It is a burden you carry everywhere, a thief in your own home, pretending to love you but truly hating and envying you.

This harmful garment weighs you down, pulling you downward to keep you from looking upward and seeing the beauty of truth and the good that rests within it. If you saw it, you would despise the wickedness of this garment and recognize the traps it has set for you.

This garment works hard to make things that seem real feel pleasing to your senses. It hides what is truly real by covering it with distractions and burdens, filling your mind with harmful pleasures. As a result, you cannot hear what you need to hear or see what you need to see.

The Ninth Book,
A Universal Sermon to Asclepius

Everything that moves, Asclepius, must move in something and be moved by something, correct?

Yes, that's true.

Doesn't the space where something moves need to be larger than the thing that is moving within it?

Yes, it must be.

And isn't the force that moves something stronger than the thing being moved?

Yes, it is.

Then wouldn't the space in which something moves have to be opposite in nature to the thing being moved?

Yes, it must be.

Now, isn't this vast world a body, and isn't it the greatest of all bodies?

Yes, it is.

And isn't it solid, filled with many great bodies and, in fact, with all bodies that exist?

That's true.

The world is a body, and it moves, right?

Yes, it does.

Then what kind of space can hold something as large as the world and allow it to move freely? It must be far larger, so the world has room to move without being stopped or hindered, right?

Yes, it must be immense. But what kind of space would that be?

It must be something opposite in nature to a body, Asclepius. And isn't the nature of the non-physical opposite to that of the physical?

Yes, it is.

So, the space must be non-physical, and what is non-physical is either divine or God Himself. But by divine, I don't mean something created or born.

If it is divine, it is a kind of essence or being. But if it is God, it is something beyond essence, though it can be understood in a certain way.

God can be understood not by Himself but by us, because anything that can be understood is connected to a mind that perceives it.

Therefore, God does not understand Himself, since He is not separate from what He knows. But we are separate from Him, so we can understand Him.

If this space can be understood, then it is not just space—it is God. But if we understand God, we understand not a place but the way He acts and operates.

Everything that moves does so in something stable, not in another moving thing. And the force that causes movement remains stable while it moves other things, for it cannot move along with them.

But how is it, Trismegistus, that things here on Earth move along with other moving things? Didn't you say the wandering stars are moved by a fixed sphere?

That's not exactly what I meant, Asclepius. The wandering stars and the fixed sphere don't move together but in opposition to one another. They move in opposite ways, and that opposition creates a kind of balance, where movement is stabilized by resistance.

For example, the Bear constellation neither rises nor sets but keeps circling in place. Do you think it moves or stays still?

I think it moves, Trismegistus.

What kind of movement do you think it has?

It moves in a circular path, always revolving around the same point.

Exactly. The circular movement appears as though it's standing still because it moves in a way that keeps it bound to the same path. The opposition of these movements creates stability, keeping everything in place.

Let me give you a simple example from Earth. Consider a man swimming. As the water flows one way, he pushes against it with his hands and feet, holding his position. This resistance keeps him from being carried away or sinking beneath the water.

That's a very clear example, Trismegistus.

So, every movement depends on something stable and is guided by that stability.

The motion of the world and all material things does not come from outside the world but from within it, through a soul, a spirit, or some other non-physical force.

A lifeless body cannot move itself, nor can anything that is entirely lifeless.

But what do you mean, Trismegistus? Don't things like wood, stones, and other inanimate objects move too?

No, Asclepius, not on their own. Something within them causes movement. It's not the body itself that moves, but something alive within it that moves both the object carrying it and the object being carried. One lifeless thing cannot move another—only something alive can cause movement.

Do you see now how the soul is burdened when it carries two bodies?

Yes, and it's clear now that everything that moves must move within and be moved by something.

Doesn't this mean, Trismegistus, that things moving in this world must be moving through empty space?

Be careful, Asclepius. Nothing that exists is truly empty. Only what does not exist can be called empty, for it is entirely outside of existence.

What exists must be full of being, for something that exists cannot be empty.

But aren't some things empty, Trismegistus, like an empty barrel, an empty jug, or an empty wine press?

Oh, Asclepius, you are mistaken. These things, which you believe to be empty, are actually full.

What do you mean, Trismegistus?

Isn't air a kind of body?

Yes, it is.

Then doesn't this body, air, pass through everything and fill everything it touches? And isn't air made up of a mixture of the four elements? So, all the things you call empty are actually full of air.

Instead of calling them empty, you should call them hollow, because they exist and are filled with air and spirit.

That makes perfect sense, Trismegistus. But what should we call the space where the entire universe moves?

Call it incorporeal, Asclepius.

What does that mean—incorporeal or without a body?

It refers to the mind and reason, which encompass everything and exist without a physical form. It cannot be touched or seen, and it is unaffected by anything physical. It is self-sufficient, capable of everything, and is the essence behind all things.

From it come goodness, truth, the original light, and the essence of the soul, like rays from the sun.

Then what is God?

God is none of these things directly, yet He is the source of them all. He is the cause of everything that exists, leaving nothing without being.

Everything that exists comes from things that already are, not from things that are not, because something that doesn't exist cannot produce anything. And what already exists cannot simply stop existing.

So, what exactly is God?

God is not just a mind, but the cause of mind. He is not just a spirit, but the cause of spirit. He is not light, but the cause of light.

Therefore, we must honor God with the two names that belong to Him alone: the Good and the Father.

He is nothing else beyond these names. Everything else is separate from the nature of goodness.

Neither the body nor the soul can contain true goodness.

The greatness of the Good is as vast as the existence of all things, both physical and non-physical, both visible and invisible.

This is the Good—God Himself.

Be careful never to call anything else good, for that would be disrespectful. And never call anyone else God, for only the Good is God.

Many people speak the word "good," but most do not understand what it truly means. Out of ignorance, they call gods and even people "good," though neither can ever truly be so.

The other gods are honored with the title of "god," but God is known as the Good—not by status in the heavens but by His very nature.

There is only one nature of God, and that is the Good. All kinds of beings come from this one source.

The one who is good gives everything and takes nothing. This is why God gives all things freely without ever receiving.

The other title we give Him is the Father, for it is the role of a father to create and give life.

That is why it has always been important for wise and virtuous people to have children.

On the other hand, to remain childless is seen as a misfortune and a wrongdoing. Those who die without children are punished by the spirits, for their souls are condemned to enter bodies that are neither male nor female—a cursed existence beneath the sun.

So, Asclepius, never celebrate a man's childlessness. Instead, pity him, knowing the punishment that awaits him after death.

Let this be a glimpse into the deeper truths of nature.

The Tenth Book,
The Mind To Hermes

Hold your speech, Hermes, and reflect on what has been said. But I will speak what is on my mind, for many people have shared different ideas about the universe and goodness, yet I have not discovered the truth.

May the Lord reveal the truth to me now, for I will trust only your explanation of these matters.

Then the Mind spoke of how everything is connected.

God and all things exist together.

God, Eternity, the World, Time, and Generation.

God created Eternity, Eternity created the World, the World brought forth Time, and Time brought about Generation.

From God comes goodness, beauty, blessedness, and wisdom.

From Eternity comes identity and consistency.

From the World comes order.

From Time comes change.

From Generation come life and death.

The workings of God are Mind and Soul.

Eternity brings permanence and immortality.

The World undergoes restoration and decay.

Time brings growth and decline.

Generation gives rise to different qualities.

Eternity belongs to God.

The World exists within Eternity.

Time operates within the World.

Generation unfolds within Time.

Eternity surrounds God.

The World moves within Eternity.

Time unfolds within the World.

Generation occurs within Time.

Therefore, God is the source of all things.

Eternity is the substance behind everything.

The World is the material that holds all things.

Eternity is the power of God.

The World, although ever-changing, is continuously created through the timeless nature of Eternity.

Nothing will ever be destroyed because Eternity is incorruptible.

Nor can anything perish within the World, as it is embraced by the eternal.

The wisdom of God consists of goodness, beauty, blessedness, virtue, and eternity.

Eternity grants matter immortality and everlasting nature, as Generation relies on Eternity just as Eternity relies on God.

Generation and Time operate in both Heaven and on Earth, but their nature differs: in Heaven, they are unchanging and incorruptible, while on Earth, they are subject to change and decay.

God is the soul of Eternity. Eternity is the soul of the World. Heaven is the soul of the Earth.

God resides within the Mind, the Mind within the Soul, and the Soul within matter—all sustained through Eternity.

The entire universe, and everything within it, is filled with soul. The soul holds the Mind, and the Mind is filled with God.

God fills everything from within and holds all things from without, giving life to the universe.

Externally, God gives life to the world, and internally, He breathes life into all living things.

Above, in Heaven, He remains constant and unchanging, while below on Earth, He governs the cycles of birth and transformation.

Eternity encompasses the World, whether through necessity, divine guidance, or natural law.

If anyone thinks otherwise, they misunderstand, for God governs everything.

God's power surpasses all, and nothing can compare, whether human or divine.

Do not mistake anything on Earth or in Heaven as being like God, for such a comparison would be false.

Nothing can resemble the One who is unlike anything else, nor has God shared His power with anything else.

Who else could create life, immortality, or transformation? And what else would God need to make?

God is not idle; if He were, everything would cease to be, for everything is sustained by Him.

There is no idleness anywhere in the universe, for nothing is empty of purpose—both the doer and the deed must exist.

All things must continue according to the nature of each place and being.

The One who creates is present in all things, yet He is not confined by anything. He does not focus on just one task but creates everything.

As the source of action and power, He sustains everything that exists, both beneath Him and under His command.

Look through my eyes, and you will see the world clearly and understand its beauty.

The world is a body that endures forever. Though ancient, it remains youthful and full of life.

Observe the seven heavenly realms above us, each following its own unchanging course, filling eternity with endless movement.

Everything is filled with light, yet fire is not found within it.

The harmonious blending of opposites creates light, through the operation of God, the source of all good, order, and harmony in the seven realms.

Look also upon the Moon, which leads the other heavenly bodies. It serves as an instrument of nature, guiding the transformations of matter here on Earth.

Behold the Earth at the center of all things, serving as the stable foundation of the world, nourishing and sustaining all earthly creatures.

Think about how many immortal and mortal beings exist, and notice how the Moon moves between both realms, touching both mortal and immortal things.

Everything is full of soul, and it is the soul that moves all things. Some things move around the heavens, and others move on the Earth. Yet none of them switch places—what is on the right does not go to the left, nor do things above descend downward, or things below rise upward.

You already know, Hermes, that all these things are created.

They are bodies with souls, and because they have souls, they are in motion.

But for all things to come together in unity, something must hold them together.

There must be a single force that brings everything into one.

Since the motions are so different, and the bodies are not alike, but still follow one orderly flow, it's clear that there cannot be more than one creator.

One creator alone ensures harmony in this order.

If there were many creators, they would envy each other, and that would lead to conflict.

If one creator made mortal beings, he would want to create immortal beings as well. Similarly, the creator of immortal beings would seek to make mortal ones.

And if there were two creators, which one would take charge of the future?

If both shared the responsibility, who would hold the greater power?

Every living being consists of both matter and soul, and is made of both mortal and immortal parts.

All living things have souls. The things that are lifeless are just raw matter.

The soul, as it draws closer to its creator, brings life and existence to everything. And because it is tied to life, it becomes the cause of immortality as well.

So what makes mortal beings different from immortal ones?

If the soul can create life and immortality, how could it not also create living beings?

It is clear that something is behind all of this, and it is just as clear that this force is one.

There is one soul, one life, and one matter.

And who else could this be but the One God?

Who else would have any reason to create life but God alone?

Therefore, there is only one God.

It would be absurd to say there is one world, one Sun, one Moon, and one divine order, yet believe in many gods.

This one God works through many things.

If you yourself are capable of doing many things—seeing, speaking, hearing, smelling, tasting, touching, walking, understanding, and breathing—why would it be difficult for God to create life, soul, immortality, and change?

It is not as though one part of you sees, another part hears, another speaks, and so on. It is one being—yourself—who does all these things.

In the same way, God is behind everything, for nothing can happen without Him.

Just as you would no longer be alive if you stopped doing all these things, God would not be God if He stopped creating.

And since nothing in the universe can remain idle or empty, how much more is this true for God?

If there were anything He could not do, it would mean He was imperfect, which is impossible.

Since God is perfect and never idle, He does everything.

Now listen carefully, Hermes. You will see that it is necessary for God to create everything that exists, has existed, or will exist.

This, my dear friend, is life.

This is beauty.

This is goodness.

This is God.

If you want to understand this through your own actions, think about what happens when you create something.

However, God is not driven by pleasure, nor does He have anyone else working alongside Him.

Being the sole creator, God is always working, and what He makes is part of Himself.

If anything were separated from Him, it would cease to exist, for nothing can live apart from Him.

Since all things in Heaven and on Earth are alive through Him, and since one life flows through all, everything is made by God.

Life is the union of mind and soul.

Death is not the destruction of what has been united, but the separation of their union.

The image of God is Eternity. The image of Eternity is the World. The image of the World is the Sun. And the image of the Sun is humanity.

People say that change is death because the body dissolves, and life returns to what is unseen.

But I tell you, Hermes, the world only changes; it does not dissolve. Each day, part of it becomes invisible, but it is never lost.

These are the transformations of the world—revolutions and hidden cycles. A revolution is a turning, and what is hidden is renewed.

The world is not shaped by things outside it but constantly changes within itself.

If the world is filled with forms, then what must its creator be like? The creator cannot be without form.

And if the creator is filled with every form, He will remain in harmony with the world. But if He had only one form, He would exist apart from the world and its cycles.

We must be careful not to question God with words, for we cannot know anything about Him with doubt in our minds.

God has a single idea, unique to Him. Because this idea is not physical, it cannot be seen, though it reveals itself through all physical forms.

Do not be surprised that such an incorruptible idea exists.

It is like the margins of written words. They may seem to rise and stand out, but in reality, they are smooth and level.

Understand this truth clearly: just as man cannot live without life, God cannot exist without doing good.

Doing good is the life and movement of God. He brings everything into motion and gives life to all.

Some of what I have said needs further explanation, so pay close attention.

Everything exists within God, but not as if placed in a physical space. Space is both physical and unchanging, while things that occupy space cannot move.

What lies within the unbodily is not the same as what appears to be in the physical world.

God contains everything, and nothing is greater, swifter, or stronger than what is not bound by a physical body. The unbodily is limitless in capacity, speed, and power.

To understand this, command your soul to go to a far-off place, like India. It will arrive there even faster than you can speak the command.

Tell it to cross the ocean, and it will instantly be there—not by traveling, but by simply being there.

Command your soul to fly into the heavens, and it will rise without wings. Nothing can stop it—not the heat of the sun, not the ether, not the movements of the stars. It will pass through everything and reach the furthest heights.

If you wish to see what lies beyond the universe, you can.

This is the power and speed your soul holds. If you can do such things, how could God not do the same?

Now, think of God as holding the entire universe within His mind, as if it were all thoughts or ideas.

To understand God, you must become like Him.

Only something like God can understand God.

You must expand yourself beyond all limits—beyond the physical body, beyond time itself. Become one with eternity, and only then will you grasp the nature of God.

Believe that nothing is impossible for you. Consider yourself immortal, capable of understanding everything—every art, every science, and every way of life.

Imagine yourself as greater than the highest heights and deeper than the lowest depths. Contain within yourself the qualities of all things: fire, water, dryness, moisture. Be everywhere at once—in the sea, on the earth.

Understand yourself as unborn, young, old, alive, and dead, all at the same time. Know everything about time, places, actions, qualities, and amounts. Only by doing so will you begin to understand God.

But if you lock your soul within your body and misuse it, saying, "I understand nothing. I can do nothing. I am afraid of the sea. I cannot reach the heavens. I don't know who I am. I don't know what I will become," then you have no connection to God.

You will not be able to understand the beauty and goodness of God. Instead, you will be tied to the desires of the body and all that is evil.

The greatest evil is not knowing God.

But the path to knowing Him is simple: you must desire to know, hope to understand, and believe in your ability to do so. This is the divine way, the way of goodness.

This path will appear to you everywhere—when you are awake or asleep, sailing or traveling, speaking or silent, by day or night.

For everything reflects the image of God.

Though you say that God is invisible, nothing is clearer than Him.

He made all things so that you could see Him in everything.

This is God's goodness and power—to make Himself known and visible in all things.

Even what is not physical can still be seen.

The mind is seen through understanding, and God is seen through creation and action.

Let this be clear to you, Hermes.

Apply this same way of thinking to everything, and you will not go astray.

The Eleventh Book
The Common Mind, To Tat

The Mind, Tat, is part of God's essence, if God has any essence that we can know. Only God knows exactly what that essence is. The Mind is not separate from God's essence but connected to it, like the light from the sun. In humans, this Mind is God, which makes some humans nearly divine, with their humanity closely connected to divinity. The good spirit even called the gods "immortal men" and referred to men as "mortal gods."

In animals, which lack reason, the Mind works as their natural instinct. Where there is a soul, there is a mind, just as where there is life, there is a soul. In creatures without reason, the soul provides life but lacks the operations of the Mind. In humans, however, the Mind guides the soul toward goodness. In animals, it cooperates with their instincts, but in humans, it works against their lower desires.

Once the soul enters the body, it becomes corrupted by sorrow, pain, and pleasure. These emotions flow from the physical body, and the soul is stained by them, like a sponge absorbing liquid. But when the Mind leads the soul, it offers its light, resisting the soul's tendencies toward pleasure and false beliefs. Just as a skilled doctor may hurt the body to heal it by cutting or burning away disease, the Mind causes discomfort to the soul by pulling it away from pleasure, the source of spiritual sickness. The greatest sickness of the soul is denying God, which leads to all other evils and blocks all good.

The Mind helps the soul, just as a physician heals the body. But those souls that reject the guidance of the Mind are left to follow their desires, much like animals. These people give in to every craving, moving toward a life like that of beasts. They act with anger and desire without reason, never satisfied and always trapped in their impulses. Uncontrolled anger and unchecked desires are among the worst evils.

To prevent this, God placed the Mind within humans as a judge, to correct and restrain them.

You mentioned earlier, Tat, that fate determines our actions, so what happens when someone does evil like adultery or theft? If these actions are determined by fate, how can the person be held responsible and punished? Isn't that unjust?

Everything, Tat, happens according to fate. Nothing, good or bad, happens without it. But it is also part of fate that those who commit evil must suffer the consequences of their actions. They are destined to experience the results of what they do, and they do wrong so that they may endure punishment. Let's leave this discussion about fate and evil for now, though, as we've explored it before.

Right now, we are discussing the Mind and its role. In animals, the Mind works through instinct, but in humans, it restrains both anger and desire. Some humans follow reason, while others do not. But all are subject to fate, change, and the cycle of birth and death. These are the boundaries set by fate. Everyone must experience what fate has decreed.

However, those guided by the Mind experience these things differently. Although they may suffer the same external troubles, they do not suffer in the same way as those who are ruled by anger and desire.

What do you mean, Father? Isn't someone who commits adultery or murder an evil person?

The one ruled by the Mind, my son, does not suffer punishment as the adulterer or murderer does. They may face the consequences of actions, but not because they are consumed by evil themselves. Change is unavoidable, but those with the Mind's guidance can escape the grip of vice.

I once heard the good spirit say, though he did not write it down, that everything is connected as one, especially things understood by the Mind. All that exists is part of one reality. We exist in action, power, and eternity.

A good soul is one with the Mind, and when the soul is united with the Mind, it is connected to all things. Therefore, all things known through the Mind are united. Just as the Mind governs everything, the soul that comes from God can do whatever it wills.

This answers the question you asked earlier about the connection between fate and the Mind. If you withdraw from arguments and distractions, you will see that the soul connected to the Mind is above fate and the laws that bind ordinary things. Nothing is impossible for the Mind, not even what fate controls.

Even though the soul is above fate, it should still pay attention to the things governed by fate. This, Tat, is what the good spirit taught.

Father, your words are insightful and profound, but I still need clarity on one thing. You said that in animals, the Mind follows their natural instincts. But if the Mind cooperates with these instincts, which are driven by emotions and desires, does that mean the Mind itself becomes emotional and driven by passions?

That's an excellent question, my son. And you are right to ask it. Let me explain.

All non-physical things that exist in the body are subject to emotions, and in a way, they are emotions themselves. Everything that causes movement is non-physical, while everything that is moved is physical. The Mind causes movement, and through movement, both the mover and the thing being moved experience emotion. Even rulers and those they rule experience emotions through this movement. When the soul is freed from the body, it is also freed from these emotions.

In truth, nothing in existence is completely free from emotion; everything is affected by it in some way. But there is a difference between emotion itself and the thing that experiences it. Emotions cause actions, while those affected by emotions experience them. Physical bodies act in one way or another—they either stay still or move—and both states are forms of emotional experience. Non-physical things, on the other hand, are always active, and because of this, they too experience emotion.

Don't let these words confuse you, though. Action and emotion are closely connected, but it is more respectful to use the word "action."

Consider this as well: God has given humanity two great gifts— Mind and Reason. These gifts are so powerful that they are equal to immortality. If someone uses these gifts correctly, they will be no different from the gods. When they leave their physical body, these gifts will guide them to join the divine beings.

Do other living creatures have speech, Father?

No, my son. They only have voice. There is a big difference between speech and voice. Speech belongs to all of humanity, while voice belongs to individual creatures according to their kind.

But Father, people speak differently in different countries.

That is true, but just as all people are part of humanity, speech is still one. It may sound different in Egypt, Persia, or Greece, but its essence remains the same everywhere. You seem to underestimate the power and importance of speech, my son. The good spirit once revealed that the soul belongs in the body, the mind in the soul, and speech in the mind, with God as the source of all.

Speech is the expression of the mind, just as the mind reflects God. The body is the form of an idea, and the idea flows from the soul. The most subtle part of matter is air, from which the soul emerges. From the soul comes the mind, and from the mind comes God.

God is present in everything and through everything. The mind governs the soul, the soul controls the air, and the air surrounds matter. Meanwhile, destiny, providence, and nature are tools that shape the material world.

All non-physical things share the same essence, which is identity. But physical things are made up of many parts that change, even though their underlying identity remains the same. In every physical object, there is a certain number, and without numbers, nothing can be built, combined, or dissolved. Numbers are born from unity, and when they dissolve, they return to unity.

All things are united by matter. This entire world is like a great god, connected to a higher one, and it is filled with life through the will of the Father. Nothing in the world, whether as a whole or in its parts, is without life. There is nothing dead in the world—nothing that was, is, or will be. The Father wants the world to be alive for as long as it exists, and because of that, it must also be divine.

How can anything be dead in a universe that reflects God and is filled with life? Death is decay, and decay is destruction. But nothing in an incorruptible world can decay, and nothing connected to God can be destroyed.

But don't living things in the world die, Father?

Be careful with your words, my son. What you call "death" is just the dissolving of physical forms. Dissolution is not the same as destruction. Things are not dissolved to disappear but to be made new.

What, then, is life? Isn't it movement?

Yes, and everything in the world is in motion, my son.

But Father, doesn't the Earth seem still?

No, my son. It moves in many ways, even though it may seem stable. It would be strange if the Earth, which gives life to all things, did not move. Nothing can create life without movement. It is absurd to think that any part of the universe could be inactive, for inactivity means nothingness.

Everything in the world moves either by growing or by diminishing. Whatever moves also has life, but life does not need to stay the same. While the universe as a whole remains unchanged, its parts are always changing. Yet nothing is ever truly destroyed. What troubles people is not reality but the names they use for things.

Creation is not the same as life; it is the process of making things visible. Likewise, change is not death; it is the hiding of what once was. All things—matter, life, spirit, soul, and mind—are immortal. Every living thing is immortal because of the mind within it, but especially humans, who receive God and communicate with Him.

God speaks to people in many ways—through dreams at night and through signs during the day. He also gives messages through birds, the wind, and even trees.

Humans have the unique ability to understand what has happened in the past, what is happening now, and what will happen in the future. Think also, my son, about how other creatures only live in specific parts of the world. Fish live in water, land animals on the earth, and birds in the air. But humans interact with all elements—earth, water, air, and even fire—and they experience the heavens through their senses.

God, however, exists everywhere and in everything. He is both action and power. Understanding God is not as difficult as it may seem. If you wish to see him, look at the necessity in all things around you and the way events unfold with purpose. Notice how life fills the material world and how God moves everything—bringing good into gods, spirits, and people alike.

If these things are indeed actions, as you've said, then they are performed by none other than God. Just as the world has its different parts—heaven, earth, water, and air—God has his aspects, which include life, immortality, eternity, spirit, necessity, providence, nature, soul, and mind. All of these parts remain constant and are part of what we call the Good.

There is no place, no moment, and no thing—past or present— where God is absent.

What about matter, Father? Does God exist in matter as well?

How could matter exist without God? If you imagine matter as an inactive pile of material, you misunderstand its nature. If it is active, then it must be God who gives it motion. We've already said that actions are the parts of God. So, who brings life to living things? Who grants immortality to the eternal? Who causes things to change? All of these processes come from God.

Whether we speak of matter, body, or essence, we are talking about acts of God. Matter behaves as matter because of God. Bodies exist as physical things through his power, and essence becomes what it is through him. God is present in everything. There is nothing within creation that is not part of God.

This means that we cannot think of God in terms of size, place, shape, or even time. He is all things, present in all things, and beyond all things. Worship this truth, my son. The only way to truly serve God is to live without doing evil.

The Twelfth Book,
His Crater or Monas

The Creator made the universe, not with hands, but through His Word. Think of Him as always present everywhere, creating everything by His will. His body is not something you can touch, see, measure, or contain. It isn't fire, water, air, or wind, though all these come from Him. Being the ultimate Good, He has taken that name for Himself alone.

He also adorned the Earth with divine beauty and sent humanity into the world—both immortal and mortal beings at once. Humans are above other creatures and the rest of creation because they have both speech and mind. Humans witness the works of God, marvel at them, and recognize Him as the Creator.

While God gave speech to all people, He did not give mind to everyone. Yet, He did not withhold it out of envy, for envy does not reach Him. It exists only in the hearts of people without the gift of mind.

Why, Father, didn't God give mind to everyone?

Because it pleased Him to place it in the center of all souls as a reward to be earned.

Where did He place it?

He filled a great cup with mind and sent it down, along with a messenger to make an announcement.

The messenger proclaimed to all souls: "Come, all who are able, and immerse yourselves in this cup. Those who believe they will return to the One who sent this cup, and those who know their true purpose, come and take part."

Those who understood the message and immersed themselves in the mind became enlightened and perfect, sharing in knowledge. But those who missed the call received only speech, not mind. They do not know why they were created or by whom. Their senses make them like animals, filled with anger and desires. They do not admire what is worthy of awe but chase after bodily pleasures, thinking that life was made only for these things.

However, those who receive God's gift are more like immortals than mortals. They understand all things on Earth, in the heavens, and even beyond. Rising above the world, they see the Good and recognize that staying here is a burden. They despise all things, both material and immaterial, and seek only the One.

This is what it means to know the mind—seeing the divine and understanding God. The cup filled with mind is itself divine.

And I, Father, wish to be immersed in that cup.

You cannot love yourself, my son, until you first reject your attachment to the body. Only by loving yourself will you receive the mind, and only by receiving the mind will you gain true knowledge.

What do you mean, Father?

You cannot focus on both mortal and divine things at the same time. Mortal things are tied to the body, while divine things are not. You must choose between the two, for no one can have both. Whichever you choose will grow stronger, while the other fades away.

Choosing the higher path brings out the best in a person and connects them with God. It shows reverence and devotion. But choosing the lower path leads to ruin, though it does not harm God. Those who follow the lower path are like performers in a show—they make a spectacle of themselves in the world, misled by bodily pleasures.

Since God has given us so much, let us also be generous, without holding back. God is pure and blameless; we are the ones who cause evil by choosing it over the Good.

See how many layers of existence we must pass through—how many spirits and stars we must rise above—to reach the One true God. The Good cannot be surpassed. It is infinite, without beginning or end, though it seems to begin for us when we first come to know it.

Our knowledge of the Good does not mark its true beginning, only the beginning of our awareness of it. Once we grasp that beginning, we can move quickly through all things.

It is difficult to turn away from the familiar things of this world and return to the ancient truths. The things we see attract us, making it hard to believe in what cannot be seen. The things most visible are often evil, while the Good remains hidden. The Good has no shape or form and resembles nothing else.

That is why the Good seems unlike everything else. An immaterial thing cannot be revealed to a physical body. This is the difference between things that are alike and those that are not. Things that are unlike always fall short of those that are alike.

The One is the root and source of all things. Nothing can exist without a beginning, but the Beginning itself has no origin—it exists by itself and is the foundation of everything else. Because it does not come from another, it simply is.

Unity is the beginning of all things, containing every number while being contained by none. It creates all numbers but is not created by any number.

Everything that is created or made is imperfect, meaning it can be divided, increased, or diminished. But what is truly perfect is not subject to any of these changes.

Whatever grows does so through unity, but if it lacks the strength to hold on to unity, it weakens, fades, and disappears.

This is the image of God that I have described to you as best as I can, Tat. If you carefully reflect on it with the eyes of your mind, you will find the path that leads to higher truths. In fact, the image itself will guide you toward them.

What is remarkable about this vision is that it draws those who are able to see it closer, holding them fast. It pulls them toward itself, just as a magnet attracts iron.

The Thirteenth Book,
Sense And Understanding

Yesterday, Asclepius, I shared a complete teaching, but today I feel it is important to also talk about sense.

Sense and understanding seem to be different because sense is tied to the physical world, while understanding belongs to the essence of things. However, I believe they are closely connected in human beings. In other creatures, sense works with their nature, but in people, it is linked with understanding.

The mind is different from understanding, just as divinity is distinct from God. Divinity flows from God, and understanding flows from the mind. Understanding and speech work together; neither can exist fully without the other. You can't express words without understanding, and understanding isn't revealed without words.

In humans, sense and understanding are closely intertwined. It's impossible to fully understand without sense, and you can't experience sense without understanding. However, the mind can understand without sense for a time, such as when we dream and experience visions.

I believe that both sense and understanding are active in dreams, awakening the mind. A person's body and soul work together, and when they are in harmony, the mind produces understanding. The mind gives birth to thoughts. Good thoughts come from seeds planted by God, while harmful thoughts arise from seeds sown by demons.

There is no part of the world untouched by evil. Evil spirits secretly plant harmful seeds in the mind, leading people toward actions like adultery, murder, disrespect for parents, and other destructive deeds. These actions come from the seeds of evil spirits.

In contrast, God's seeds are fewer, but they are great, beautiful, and good—virtue, self-control, and piety. Piety is the knowledge of God. Those who know God are filled with good things and possess divine understanding, setting them apart from most people.

Because they have this knowledge, they often do not fit in with the majority. They may be misunderstood, mocked, or even hated. Some are killed because their understanding clashes with the wickedness that prevails on earth.

Wickedness resides on earth, not in the higher realms, even though some may wrongly claim otherwise. A person who knows God will reject wickedness and rise above it. Even though certain things seem evil to others, those who know God see everything as good.

They reflect deeply and come to see everything through the lens of knowledge. Amazingly, they can even turn bad things into something good.

Now, let's return to the topic of sense. Humans are unique because they combine sense with understanding. However, not every person achieves understanding. Some people are dominated by material desires, while others pursue essential truths.

Those focused on material things receive their understanding from evil spirits. But those who seek the good are connected to God. God works through nature, making all things good, just like Himself.

Even though God makes things good, the way they are used in the world can become unlawful or harmful. The movement of the universe generates different qualities, some leading to evil and others to goodness.

The world has its own sense and understanding, different from that of humans. The world's understanding is simpler and more unified. It creates all things and takes them back into itself, following God's will. The world acts as a tool of God, receiving seeds from Him, bringing things into existence, and renewing them through dissolution.

The world is like a farmer of life. When things die or break apart, it sows new seeds, giving birth to new life. Everything in the world is alive, and life flows from the world's constant movement. The world is both the source and the sustainer of life.

The elements that form bodies—earth, water, air, and fire—combine in various ways. Some bodies are more complex, while others are simpler. Heavier bodies are made from more elements, while lighter ones are made from fewer.

The movement of the world influences the qualities of everything born within it. The flow of life touches all things, shaping their nature.

God is the father of the world, and the world is the father of all things within it. The world is God's child, and everything within the world is a child of the world.

That's why the world is called an "ornament"—because it beautifully decorates everything with the endless variety of life. Through constant motion and the blending of elements, the world brings everything to life. This is why it is fitting to call it the world, for it adorns creation with unceasing life and beauty.

All living beings receive both sense and understanding from the outside, through what surrounds and sustains them. The world, having once received these gifts from God when it was created, still holds them today.

But God is not, as some mistakenly think through superstition, without sense or understanding. Everything that exists is in God, made by Him, and depends on Him. Some things operate through their bodies, others move through a soul-like essence, some are energized by a spirit, while others receive rest—everything functioning as it should.

It is more accurate to say that God does not possess these things, but instead is all things. He does not take anything in from outside but instead expresses everything outwardly. This is God's way of knowing and understanding—constantly moving everything.

There will never be a time when anything that exists will stop or disappear. When I speak of "things that are," I mean God. For everything that exists is part of God, and nothing exists apart from Him, just as He exists in everything.

If you understand these ideas, Asclepius, you will find them true. But if you do not understand, they may seem unbelievable. To understand is to believe, and not believing means you do not understand. Words alone cannot reach the truth, but the mind, guided by speech for a time, can eventually grasp it.

When the mind recognizes how everything connects and aligns with the truths shared through speech, it rests in trust and belief. For those who understand these teachings about God, they are believable, but for those who do not, they remain beyond belief.

This is what I have to say about understanding and sense.

The Fourteenth Book
Operation And Sense

The ability to sense and understand comes to all living beings from the outside, through the influence of what surrounds and sustains them. The world, having once received this gift from God at creation, continues to carry it within.

Some people mistakenly believe that God has no sense or understanding, but this is a misunderstanding born of superstition. In truth, everything exists in God, is made by God, and depends on Him. Some things work through their bodies, others move with a soul-like force, and some operate by spirit—all fitting perfectly into their roles.

It is not that God simply possesses these things, but rather He is all these things. He does not gather them from the outside but expresses them outwardly. God's way of knowing is to be the constant force that moves everything.

There will never be a time when what exists ceases or disappears. When I speak of "the things that are," I refer to God, for everything exists within God, and nothing can exist apart from Him, nor is He separate from anything.

If you understand these truths, Asclepius, they will seem clear and true. But if you do not understand, they will seem unbelievable. To understand is to believe, and to lack belief means you have not yet understood. Words alone cannot reach the full truth, but the mind, when guided by speech, can find its way to it.

When the mind sees how everything aligns with the truths we have discussed, it finds peace in belief. To those who understand what has been said about God, these things will seem credible. But for those who do not understand, they will seem impossible to believe.

This, then, is my teaching on the nature of understanding and sense.

Without these elements, the body would not be able to function. Other operations are specific to human souls, expressed through arts, sciences, studies, and actions. These operations also give rise to the senses, or at least perfect them.

Understand, my son, that these operations come from a higher source. While the senses belong to the body and arise from it, they only manifest once an operation brings them to life, making them seem physical. This is why I say that the senses are both physical and mortal. They exist only as long as the body exists, since they are born with the body and die with it.

Mortal things, however, do not have senses because they lack the necessary essence. The senses can only grasp physical experiences of good or bad that affect the body. But external objects do not receive or lose anything in the same way, so they do not have senses.

Do the senses work in every body, you ask? Yes, they do, my son. And do operations act in all things? Yes, even in lifeless things, though the senses differ. In rational beings, the senses operate with reason. In irrational creatures, the senses are purely physical. In lifeless things, the senses only react passively through growth and decay.

Passion and sense are connected at a higher level, both coming together through operations. In living creatures, two more forces follow the senses and passions—grief and pleasure. Without these, no living being, especially one capable of reason, could experience or understand anything.

I call these the ruling ideas of passion, especially in rational beings. Operations carry out actions, but the senses reveal these actions. Since the senses are connected to the lower parts of the soul, they can cause harm. What brings pleasure often becomes the source of suffering for the one who indulges in it. And sorrow brings even stronger pain, showing that both pleasure and sorrow are harmful forces.

The same is true of the soul's own sense. But isn't the soul non-physical, while the senses belong to the body, you ask? Or do the senses exist within the body? If we say that the senses belong in the body, we might mistakenly compare them to the soul or to operations, since both of these are non-physical but act through bodies.

However, the senses are neither operations, nor part of the soul, nor part of the body itself. They exist as something in between, as we have said before. Because the senses are not non-physical, they must be considered physical. Everything that exists is either a body or something without a body.

The Fifteenth Book,
Truth To His Son Tat

Humans, being imperfect creatures made of many different parts, cannot speak about truth with complete confidence. True reality only exists in eternal things, where even their very nature is true. Fire is purely fire, earth is only earth, air is solely air, and water is entirely water. But our bodies are made of a mixture of all these elements, and because they are mixed, none of them can be fully true within us.

If our original nature didn't contain truth, how could we ever see, speak, or understand truth unless God allowed it? On Earth, what we see is not truth but only imitations of it, and even these are rare. Most things are filled with falsehood and deception, appearing only as images shaped by our imagination. When our imagination receives guidance from above, it can reflect some aspects of truth, but without that influence, it remains a lie.

An image may resemble the body it portrays, but it is not that body. It may have eyes but cannot see, and it may show ears but cannot hear. It deceives the viewer into believing they are seeing the real thing when in fact, it is just an illusion.

Those who do not recognize falsehood are able to see the truth. If we see things exactly as they are, we understand truth. But if we perceive them differently from what they are, we cannot grasp truth.

You ask if truth exists on Earth. The answer, my son, is no—truth cannot exist here because it cannot be created or made. However, some individuals, with God's guidance, might come to understand glimpses of it. To the mind and reason of men, nothing on Earth is truly real. Everything here is just an appearance, a fleeting image, or an opinion.

You ask whether speaking about things as they are can be called truth. But there is no real truth on Earth. You wonder how we can even claim to know that truth doesn't exist if nothing here is true. Understand this: truth is the most perfect virtue and the highest form of good. It is pure, unchangeable, and unaffected by the material world. It does not have a body and remains constant and clear.

The things here on Earth are always changing and decaying. They are temporary, corruptible, and full of imperfections. How can anything be true if it is always shifting and never remains the same? When something changes, it becomes a lie, showing us different forms instead of staying consistent.

You ask if humans can be considered true. As long as someone is human, they cannot be true. Truth belongs only to what stays unchanged and remains the same forever. Humans are made of many parts and do not remain the same. They change over time, both in appearance and in character, going through stages and transformations during their lives.

People may not even recognize their own children or parents after some time has passed. How can something so changeable be considered true? Instead, it is false, appearing in many different forms throughout life. True things stay constant and unchanging, but people are not constant, so they cannot be truly real. Humans are like fleeting images, and every appearance is ultimately a form of falsehood.

Even the eternal bodies in the universe, though they may seem constant, are not truly real because they too undergo change. Things that are created or altered cannot be fully true, although they might contain elements of truth since they come from the source of all creation. Yet, because they change, they also carry some degree of falsehood.

Something that cannot stay the same is not true. You ask if the sun is the only thing that can be called true because it seems unchanging. Yes, the sun is closer to truth because it stays constant and plays a vital role in shaping the world. It governs creation, maintaining the world's order. I honor and respect the truth that the sun represents, acknowledging it as the work of the Creator.

You wonder what the first and highest truth is. It is the One—without matter, without shape, without color or form, and unchanging. It always remains the same. Falsehood, on the other hand, is tied to corruption, and everything on Earth is affected by it.

Corruption is necessary for new things to be created. Everything that is born or created must eventually decay so that more can be generated. In this way, creation and decay are intertwined, ensuring that life continues without end.

Recognize the original Creator through the act of creation. The things that come into existence through corruption are not true because they are constantly changing—one thing becomes another. It is impossible for these things to remain the same, and if something is not the same, how can it be true?

Therefore, we must understand these things as mere appearances or illusions. If we wish to describe people accurately, we must say that what we see are appearances. A man is the appearance of a man, a child is the appearance of a child, an old man is the appearance of old age, a young man is the appearance of youth, and a person in their prime is the appearance of maturity.

A man is not truly a man, just as a child is not truly a child, nor is an old man truly old. The same is true for all other stages of life. These appearances change over time, which means they are not real. The things that existed before and the things that exist now are always shifting, and because of this, they are false.

Understand this, my son: these false appearances and changing forms still have their origin in the truth, which comes from above. Even though these shifting forms seem false, they still originate from the source of truth itself.

In this way, falsehood can be understood as a product of truth.

The Sixteenth Book,
That None of The Things That Are Can Perish

We must now talk about the soul and the body, my son, and how the soul is immortal and what happens to the body when it forms and when it dissolves. But there is no such thing as death in any of these processes. Death is just a word, either meaningless or misunderstood, for it suggests an end to something that is truly immortal.

Death implies destruction, but nothing in the universe is ever really destroyed. If the world is like a second god, an immortal living being, then no part of something immortal can die. Everything in the world is connected to the whole, and this includes humans, who are rational beings.

God, who is eternal and uncreated, is the source of all things. The world is the second creation, formed in God's image. It is sustained, nurtured, and made eternal by God, who acts as its father, keeping it alive forever. The world is both immortal and ever-living.

There is a difference between being eternal and being ever-living. What is eternal has no beginning, and if it did have a beginning, it created itself without help from anything else. Eternity is always complete in itself. The eternal, then, is the entire universe.

God, the Father, is eternal on His own. The world was made by God and is always living and immortal. God took all the available matter and shaped it into a body, making it round like a sphere. He gave it qualities and infused it with immortality so that it would never fall into disorder.

The Father, filled with endless ideas, placed these qualities within the spheres, sealing them into circles. His intention was to bring beauty and order to everything that was to be created. He covered the whole universe with immortality so that the matter would not break apart into chaos if it tried to separate from its structure.

When matter was first formed into bodies, it existed in disorder. This same disorder continues to revolve through all material things, growing and shrinking in cycles, which people mistakenly call death. In truth, it is simply disorder occurring within earthly beings.

The heavenly bodies follow a fixed order given to them by the Father, one that remains unchanging and eternal. Earthly bodies, however, undergo change. When they dissolve, they return to their pure, undivided state, becoming immortal once again. This process causes them to lose their senses temporarily, but it does not destroy the body.

The third type of living being is man, created in the image of the world. By the Father's will, humans possess a higher mind than other earthly creatures. Humans are connected to the second god, which is the world, and they also have the capacity to understand the first god, who is beyond all form.

Humans comprehend the second god, the world, through the body, but they understand the first god as something incorporeal—the pure mind of goodness.

Be careful with your words, my son, and try to understand what God is, what the world is, and what it means for something to be immortal or subject to dissolution. Know that the world exists within God, just as God exists within everything. Humans, however, belong to the world and exist within it.

God is the beginning, the end, and the essence of everything that exists.

The Seventeenth Book, To Asclepius, To Be Truly Wise

Since Tat, my son, was eager to learn about the nature of all things, he didn't allow me to stop teaching him. Although he was young, he was determined to understand every detail, so I had to explain many things in depth to make his learning smoother and more successful. But with you, I will keep it brief, focusing only on the essential points. I will also interpret these ideas more deeply, as you have both the wisdom and the years to grasp the true nature of things.

Everything we see has been created and is continually being created. However, nothing creates itself. Every created thing comes from something else. There are many different kinds of things in the world, each distinct from the other. If all things are made by another, there must be one being who creates everything—someone who was never created but is older than all else. This creator, being unmade, is more ancient than anything that has ever come into existence.

He is the most powerful, the one who knows all things, and nothing existed before him. He governs both the great and small, controlling the variety of everything that exists. His power holds everything together and keeps the process of creation ongoing. The things that are made are visible, but the maker remains invisible. He creates everything to make his presence known, and because of this, he continues to create endlessly.

Understanding this fills the soul with admiration and gratitude. Knowing your divine creator is the greatest blessing, for what could be sweeter than knowing your true father? But who is this being, and how can we recognize him? Should we call him God, the Maker, or the Father—or perhaps all three? We call him God because of his power, the Maker because of his creative work, and the Father because of his goodness.

His power is beyond the things he has made, but through his actions, all things are brought into being. So, instead of engaging in endless debate, we must focus on understanding two truths: the one who creates and the things that are created. Nothing exists outside of these two realities, and nothing stands between them.

Remember this: all things boil down to these two truths—the maker and the creation—and one cannot exist without the other. The creator needs the creation to express his nature, and the creation needs the creator to exist. They are inseparably united, like two parts of the same whole.

Since the creator is complete in himself, everything he makes reflects his essence. That which is made exists because the creator wills it to be. Without the creator, nothing could exist, and without creation, the creator's work would be incomplete. So, creation follows the creator, and in this way, they are joined as one. God is the one who creates, and all that is created follows his design.

We should not fear the variety of things in the world, nor think that it reflects poorly on the creator. Instead, it glorifies him, for it is through creating all things that he expresses his greatness. Creation is like the body of God, and in this divine work, there is nothing shameful or wrong. Just as rust forms naturally on copper, or waste emerges from the body, certain things are simply a result of the process of generation.

The rust is not created by the blacksmith, nor is waste created by the body itself. Similarly, God does not create evil. These imperfections arise naturally from the cycles of life. Change is necessary, like the cleansing that keeps the process of creation in motion.

Consider a painter who creates both the heavens and the earth, gods and humans, animals, and plants. If a painter can create all these things, why would it be hard to imagine that God creates everything? It is foolish to think otherwise. Those who deny this are trapped in ignorance. They claim to praise God but refuse to acknowledge him as the creator of all things, which is both absurd and impious.

By denying God's role in creation, they attribute human flaws like pride, weakness, or envy to him. This is deeply misguided, for God is none of these things. His only quality is goodness. Being good, he lacks pride, ignorance, or malice. God is pure goodness itself.

Because God is good, he has the power to create all things. Everything that exists comes from the Good. Just as a farmer sows seeds in different places—wheat in one spot, barley in another, and vines elsewhere—God also plants seeds of immortality in the world. Through him, life, change, and motion exist.

In truth, there are only a few key elements in all of existence: God, generation, and the life force that animates everything. In these, all things are contained.

The Chaldean Oracles

Zoroaster

Preface

These Oracles are believed to capture many of the key ideas of Chaldean philosophy. They were passed down to us through Greek translations and were highly respected in ancient times, valued by both early Christian leaders and later Platonists. The teachings are attributed to Zoroaster, though which Zoroaster they refer to is unknown, as historians mention up to six different individuals with that name. It is likely that "Zoroaster" was a title for the leader of the Magi, used as a general term. Scholars offer different ideas about the meaning of the name. One of the more interesting interpretations comes from Kircher, who suggests that it could mean "fashioning images of hidden fire" or "the image of secret things," based on a combination of words. Others say the name comes from terms meaning "one who contemplates the stars."

This collection is acknowledged to be fragmented and incomplete, and many of the original meanings have likely been lost or distorted through translation. Where possible, efforts have been made to clarify confusing expressions, either by refining the Greek translation or adding explanatory notes. Some suggest these Oracles were created by the Greeks, but as Stanley points out, Picus de Mirandula claimed to have the original Chaldean text. According to him, the Greek version contained flaws that did not appear in the original, and he stated that he found the manuscript after Mirandula's death. Additionally, some words in the Greek version are not of Greek origin but have Chaldean roots, adapted to the Greek language.

Berosus is believed to have been the first to introduce Chaldean writings on astronomy and philosophy to the Greeks. It is clear that Chaldean traditions had a significant influence on Greek thought. Taylor believed that some of these mystical sayings inspired the philosophical ideas of Plato, and scholars such as Porphyry, Iamblichus, Proclus, Pletho, and Psellus wrote extensive commentaries on them.

The fact that such brilliant thinkers held these Oracles in high regard suggests that they deserve our attention.

The name "Oracles" was likely used to emphasize their deep and mysterious nature. The Chaldeans also had an Oracle that they respected as much as the Greeks revered the Oracle at Delphi. Psellus and Pletho both provided detailed commentary on the Chaldean Oracles. Franciscus Patricius later expanded on their work, adding material from other writers, including Proclus, Hermias, Simplicius, Damascius, Synesius, Olympiodorus, Nicephorus, and Arnobius. Patricius compiled around 324 Oracles, organizing them under various topics. His collection, published in Latin in 1593, served as the foundation for later classifications by Taylor and Cory, and their work was used in preparing the current version.

Some of the Oracles collected by Psellus appear to come from an early Chaldean Zoroaster and are marked with the letter "Z," following Taylor's method, with a few exceptions. Another set is attributed to a group of philosophers called Theurgists, who were active during the reign of Marcus Antoninus, as recorded by Proclus. These are marked with the letter "T." Additional Oracles of uncertain origin are labeled "Z or T," while other passages are credited to individual authors where appropriate.

Introduction

Many people, with good reason, believe that these short and mysterious sayings contain a deep system of mystical philosophy. However, truly understanding this philosophy requires a refined ability to perceive non-physical realities. It is said that the Chaldean Magi passed down their secret knowledge through generations, keeping it alive through tradition from father to son. According to Diodorus, "They do not teach these things as the Greeks do. Among the Chaldeans, philosophy is passed down within families, with sons learning from their fathers. These sons are free from other duties, dedicating themselves fully to learning from their parents, trusting what is taught to them more deeply."

The essence of this oral tradition seems to have survived within these Oracles, which should be studied alongside the teachings of the Kabbalah and Egyptian theology. Those familiar with the Kabbalah know that it can be interpreted in extraordinary ways, especially when paired with the Tarot, which reflects the core ideas of Egyptian theology. If commentators in the past had taken this approach, the Chaldean system within the Oracles would not have been misinterpreted to the extent that it has.

The entire structure of the Hebrew Kabbalah is built on the concept of ten divine powers, each emerging successively from an infinite source of light. These ten powers are seen as the key to understanding all things. They are arranged into three sets of triads, with a tenth power bringing them together. These divine forces extend across four worlds, called Atziluth, Briah, Yetzirah, and Assiah, moving from the most subtle to the most physical. This idea is rooted in pantheism, though it also points toward a divine source. At the heart of all things is the absolute Deity, whose thoughts form the universe we experience.

This same structure applies to the Chaldean system. The diagrams included demonstrate how Chaldean philosophy aligns with the Kabbalah. In the Chaldean view, the "First Mind" and the Intelligible Triad—consisting of Father (Pater), Power (Potentia or Mater), and Mind (Mens)—belong to the realm of higher, non-physical light. The "First Mind" symbolizes the original intelligence that exists within the depths of the divine Father. This intelligence reflects into the "Second Mind," representing divine power in the celestial world. This second mind aligns with the next great triad of divine powers, known as both Intelligible and Intellectual. The third triad belongs to the ethereal world, and it consists of intellectual forces working together.

Finally, the fourth world, known as the Elementary World, is shaped by Hypezokos, or the Flower of Fire, which is the force responsible for building the physical world.

Chaldean theology divided the higher realities into three main levels. The first is Eternal, without a beginning or end, called the "Paternal Depth," the heart of the divine presence. The second is a state of being that has a beginning but no end. This is the Creative World, also known as the Empyrean, which is filled with creations, although its source remains beyond them. The third level is the temporary Ethereal World, which had a beginning in time and will eventually end.

These three worlds are connected by seven spheres. One sphere belongs to the Empyrean, or extends from it, three are part of the Ethereal World, and three exist in the Elementary World, with the physical world uniting them all. These spheres should not be confused with the seven material planets, although the planets represent these spheres physically. The spheres themselves are not material in the usual sense but exist in a deeper, metaphysical way. Psellus tried to link these spheres directly with the planets, but Stanley criticized his approach. However, Stanley's own ideas are not entirely consistent, as he suggests that these worlds are non-physical but also claims that a physical world exists in the Empyrean.

Before the Light of the higher realms, there was the "Paternal Depth," the Absolute Deity that holds all things in potential, always present and unchanging. This idea mirrors the concept of Ain Soph Aur in the Kabbalah—three words, each with three letters, representing three sets of divine powers. These powers become manifest and follow the Triadic Law, guided by the Demiurge, the creator of the universe.

The Light of the higher realms was seen as the first expression of the Paternal Depth, an original and universal essence that flows everywhere and is beyond complete human understanding. The Empyrean is a more refined but still creative fire, serving as the source of the Ethereal World. In turn, the Ethereal World acts as the source for the Elementary World. Through these stages, the ideas of the divine mind become real in time and space.

In many ways, the way of thinking in the East today may not be so different from what it was thousands of years ago. Much that seems strange to us in ancient traditions still resonates with many people around the world. Modern thinkers and scientists have expressed ideas that, while not identical, are similar to these ancient Chaldean beliefs. One example is the idea that natural laws are guided by an intelligent and conscious power. From this point of view, it is not a big leap to see forces as living entities, filling the universe with the creations of the imagination. In this way, history repeats itself, and both ancient and modern ideas reflect the same, ever-changing truth.

Without delving too deeply into metaphysics, it is essential to recognize the importance given to the "Paternal Mind." This is the intelligence of the universe, described poetically as "energizing before energy," which establishes the original patterns of everything that will exist. These patterns are then handed over to the divine powers, known as the Rectores Mundorum, to develop and govern. As the saying goes, "Mind is with Him, power with them."

In the Platonic sense, the word "Intelligible" refers to a way of knowing or perceiving that goes beyond intellectual thought— something higher and distinct from ordinary reasoning. The Chaldeans identified three ways of perceiving: through the senses, through intellectual thought, and through the higher, intelligible concepts. Each of these operates separately, through unique forms or channels. However, their exploration of the soul's nature went much deeper. Though the soul is ultimately connected to the divine, it was seen as a complex being when manifested in existence.

The Oracles speak of the "Paths of the Soul," which are like streams of unyielding fire connecting its essential parts and keeping them whole. These paths, along with its "summits," "fountains," and "vessels," mirror the universal principles that guide everything. This idea, shared by many ancient cosmologies, shows how closely Chaldean metaphysics connect the structure of the universe to the nature of human beings.

In each of the Chaldean Divine Worlds, a group of three divine powers operates together, forming a fourth element that completes the group. As the Oracle says, "In every World, a Triad shines, with the Monad as the ruling principle." These Monads are divine representatives that manage the universe. Each of the four worlds—the Empyrean, Ethereal, Elementary, and Material—is governed by a supreme power that remains directly connected to the Father and guided by divine wisdom. This aligns closely with the Kabbalistic idea of the divine name, which is expressed through four letters in various languages.

The Oracle describes this by saying, "There is a Venerable Name that moves through the Worlds in an unending cycle." The Kabbalah explains this further, teaching that each of the four worlds corresponds to one of the four letters in the divine name. Each world also has its own way of writing this name, reflecting how the order of elements—both on a cosmic and personal level—is governed by the continuous motion of this name. The divine name, associated with the elements, is seen as a universal law that guides creation. This creative force is summed up in the figure known as the Demiurge, or Hypezokos, the "Flower of Fire."

Plato's view of the human being offers a similar idea of the soul's structure. He places intellect in the head, the soul with passions like courage in the heart, and another part of the soul, which contains desires and basic urges, near the stomach and spleen. According to the Chaldean doctrine, as recorded by Psellus, humanity is made up of three types of souls:

First, the Intelligible, or divine soul,

Second, the Intellect or rational soul, and

Third, the Irrational, or passional soul.

This last soul, tied to the body, was thought to change and dissolve at death. The divine soul, according to the Oracles, is described as "a bright fire that, through the Father's power, remains immortal and rules over life." Its influence can only be grasped when the soul moves beyond the illusions created by passions and stops reacting to them.

The rational soul, the Chaldeans taught, can either align itself with the divine or fall under the control of the irrational soul. As the Oracles say, "The divine cannot be reached by those who focus only on the body; only those who strip away these attachments can reach the highest truth." The three types of souls each have their own vehicles. The divine soul's vehicle is immortal, the rational soul's can become immortal through its progress, and the irrational soul is connected to what is called "the image," which is the astral form of the physical body.

Physical life works through these three types of activity. When the body dies, each soul follows a different path, depending on how they used their energies in life. The Oracles encourage people to focus on divine things and resist the urges of the irrational soul, warning, "If you do not succeed, your body will be inhabited by the beasts of the earth."

The Chaldeans assigned the astral form of the irrational soul to the Lunar Sphere. This probably referred to more than just the Moon itself; it included the whole region below the Moon, with Earth at its center. At death, the rational soul rises beyond the Moon's influence, but only if its past life allows for this release. Much importance was placed on how life is lived while the soul is in the body, with frequent calls to seek communion with divine powers. Only the highest form of theurgy was believed to offer such a connection.

"Let the depth of your immortal soul lead you," one Oracle says, "but raise your eyes earnestly upward." Taylor explains this with the idea that "the eyes" represent the soul's inner abilities. When these abilities awaken, the soul becomes filled with a higher life and divine light, almost as if it rises beyond itself.

The Chaldean Magi were said to be the first to separate true visions from dreams. They had a deep understanding of both mental and spiritual realities. Their attention to inner images, along with their passionate devotion, made them more than just teachers—they lived out the philosophy they taught. Life on the open plains of Chaldea, under calm nights and starry skies, nurtured this inner development. From a young age, students of the Magi were taught how to break free from worldly limitations and explore the vast inner realms. One Oracle teaches, "The bonds of the soul, which give her breath, are easy to loosen." Other texts speak of the "Melody of the Ether" and the "Lunar clashings," showing how these mystical experiences reflected real inner practices.

The Oracles also describe how divine visions and impressions appear in the Ether. The Chaldeans believed that the ethers of the elements are the subtle forces through which the more familiar elements—Earth, Air, Water, and Fire—work. These subtle ethers represent the underlying principles of dryness and moisture, heat and cold. The signs of the Zodiac were also linked to these ethers, with each element appearing in three forms. This connection influenced how they understood personality and tendencies. For example, when it was said that someone had Aries rising, it meant that fiery ether dominated their nature, making them energetic and active.

The planets, in turn, were thought to influence the ethers, giving them specific vibrations or energies. These planets, positioned in carefully arranged zones, controlled the flow of these subtle forces throughout the universe.

The Chaldeans believed that the planets were connected not only to specific colors and sounds but also to the ethers, with each planetary force having a special link to certain constellations in the Zodiac. Part of their spiritual practice involved forming connections with these celestial beings. In one fragment, it is said: "If you call upon the celestial Lion often, then, when the heavens disappear from your sight, when the stars lose their light, the moon becomes hidden, and the earth vanishes, you will see everything around you take the shape of a Lion." Both the Chaldeans and Egyptians had a deep understanding of color, which reflected their heightened spiritual awareness. Bright colors were thought to awaken the mind's ability to imagine and engage with inner visions.

The Chaldean method of contemplation involved becoming one with the object of meditation, similar to the process used in Indian Yoga. This approach is captured in the saying, "He becomes one with the images, casting them around himself." Though the divine is without form or body, it was believed that divine forces become temporarily bound to forms for the benefit of humanity.

The subtle ethers served as coverings for the divine Light. The Oracles teach that beyond these ethers lies "a solar world and endless Light." This divine Light was the object of their deepest reverence. However, the Light they sought was not the light of the sun we know. Instead, it was referred to as "the starless sphere above," where "the more true Sun" resides. Theosophists understand this as the idea that the physical sun is just a reflection of a higher, more glorious light.

Some individuals, through their strength, could reach this Light on their own. As the Oracles say, "The mortal who approaches the fire will receive Light from the divine, and the immortal ones are swift to aid those who persevere." However, even those less capable were not entirely left out. The Oracles explain, "Some are blessed with knowledge even as they sleep, drawing strength from the divine." This idea inspired many later thinkers, including Porphyry and Synesius. Apuleius's Metamorphoses and the Vision of Scipio also reflect this belief. Though many Christians are familiar with the saying "He gives to His beloved in sleep," few fully grasp the deeper meaning behind it.

What, then, was the Chaldean view of earthly life? Were they pessimistic, dismissing the material world as unimportant? It seems more accurate to say that their philosophy was filled with spiritual hope. They believed that beyond the limits of matter lay a better and truer reality. Earthly life was seen as a flawed reflection of this higher realm. Like us, the Chaldeans sought what is good, beautiful, and true. But unlike those who chase external pleasures, they understood that true fulfillment is found within.

The first step in this journey toward inner fulfillment was living a simple life. For most of the Magi, this way of life was ingrained from birth. The discipline of living simply, combined with wisdom, made them especially open to nature's truths. As one Oracle warns: "Do not descend into the dark, glittering world below. Beneath the earth lies a steep fall, where a throne of destructive power awaits. Do not go down into that deceptive splendor, for it will only defile your inner light. Its brilliance is false, and it is home only to the children of sorrow." This beautifully expresses the idea that pursuing physical pleasures diminishes the soul's higher energy. Yet, for those who live virtuously and purify themselves, the Oracles offer encouragement: "The higher powers build up the bodies of the holy ones."

The law of karma was just as important in Chaldean thought as it is in modern theosophy. Ficinus explains, "The soul moves continuously, passing through everything in its journey. Once this journey is complete, it must return through the same paths, weaving a new cycle of life, as Zoroaster teaches: whenever the same causes arise, the same effects will follow."

This is the deeper meaning behind the saying "History repeats itself," far removed from superstitious ideas of fate. Here, everyone receives what they deserve based on their actions, whether good or bad. These are the bonds of life. Yet, the Oracles warn, "Do not expand your destiny," urging people to explore the "River of the Soul." Though the soul serves the body, it can still rise back to the divine order from which it came by combining sacred actions with reason.

We are encouraged to understand the Intelligible, that divine part of being which lies beyond the mind. This can only be grasped with the highest potential of our intellect. The Oracles say, "Understand the

Intelligible with the bright flame of an awakened mind." Zoroaster is also credited with saying, "The one who knows himself knows everything within himself." Another teaching suggests that "The Paternal Mind has planted symbols within the soul." However, such knowledge was only available to Theurgists, who, as the Oracles explain, "do not fall into the same fate as the masses." The divine light cannot shine in a disordered soul, just as clouds block the sun. Those who seek higher wisdom without preparation or purity walk a path filled with confusion and darkness, and their efforts will fail.

Even though our destiny may be "written in the stars," the divine soul's mission is to raise the human soul above the circle of necessity. The Oracles praise the power of a will that triumphs over obstacles, describing it like this:

"Hewing down walls with the force of magic, Breaking apart the barriers, Splitting the seven posts to pieces, Speaking the words of mastery!"

This triumph comes through strengthening the will and elevating the imagination, which has the power to guide consciousness. As the Oracles say, "Believe yourself to be beyond the body, and you will be." They might have added, "Then your purified imagination will reveal the symbols of the soul." Yet, when looking within, one must confront the self honestly. "On beholding yourself, fear," meaning you must face the imperfect parts of yourself.

To achieve the highest perfection, everything must be viewed as ideal. Willpower is the key to mystical progress, having a powerful influence over the body's nervous system. Through will, fleeting visions can be held steady within the astral light. Will also drives consciousness toward communion with the divine. However, the challenge lies in aligning three distinct wills—the wills of the Divine Soul, the Rational Soul, and the Irrational Soul.

Selfishness blocks the flow of higher thought, keeping it tied to the body. This is not just a moral idea but a scientific truth. Selfishness beyond basic needs is nothing more than vulgarity. Just as a picture that seems beautiful to a refined mind might look like a mess of colors to someone untrained, so too the broad perspective of one who sees beyond personal concerns cannot be understood by those focused only on themselves.

The path to the greatest good lies through self-sacrifice—offering up the lower self to serve the higher self. Behind this higher self is the hidden presence of the "Ancient of Days," the unified essence of divine humanity. These truths are grasped only by the soul. The soul's song can only be heard in the sacred silence where the divine dwells.

The Oracles of Zoroaster

CAUSE. GOD.

FATHER   MIND   FIRE

MONAD   DYAD   TRIAD.

God is described as having the head of a hawk. He is the first and eternal being, beyond corruption, not created by anything else, whole and unchanging, unlike anything else. He gives all good things, cannot be destroyed, and is the highest good and the wisest. He is the source of fairness, justice, and wisdom, teaching Himself and embodying perfection. He is the inspiration for Sacred Philosophy. Eusebius, Præparatio Evangelica, Book 1, Chapter 10. This Oracle isn't found in ancient collections or in the writings of medieval occultists. Cory seems to have found it in Eusebius's writings, where the Persian Zoroaster is credited as its author.

Theurgists say that this God is both old and young. They describe Him as a God who moves endlessly, whose power fills the universe, and who controls everything that moves. He has limitless energy and exerts a force that spirals throughout creation. Proclus on Plato's Timaeus, 244. Z. or T. p. 24 In Egyptian mythology, there were two Horuses—an older and younger God—both sons of Osiris and Isis.

Taylor suggests that this passage refers to Kronos, or Time, called Chronos by later Platonists. In Roman mythology, Kronos (also called Saturnus) was the son of Uranus and Gaia, married to Rhea, and father of Zeus.

The God of the Universe is eternal and boundless, both young and old, with a spiraling force. Cory includes this Oracle in his collection but doesn't mention its source. Lobeck questioned its authenticity.

The Eternal Æon, according to the Oracle, is the reason for endless life, boundless strength, and tireless energy. Taylor.—T.

The divine ones call this unknowable God "silent" and say He communicates through the power of the Mind. Human souls can only understand Him using their minds. Proclus in Theology of Plato, 321. T. The word "inscrutable" is used, though Taylor translates it as "stable," and some suggest "incomprehensible" might be a better term.

The Chaldeans call this God Dionysos (or Bacchus) and Iao in the Phoenician language, referring to Him as the "Intelligible Light." He is also called Sabaoth, meaning He is above the Seven Spheres and acts as the Demiurge. Lydus, De Mensibus, 83. T.

He holds all things within Himself, at the peak of His existence, yet He also exists beyond everything. Proclus in Theology of Plato, 212. T. "Hyparxis" usually refers to "existence" or "subsistence." "Hupar" suggests reality as distinct from appearance, and "Huparche" means "beginning."

He measures and defines all things. Proclus in Theology of Plato, 386. T. The phrase "Thus he speaks the words" appears in the Greek text but is omitted by Taylor and Cory.

Nothing imperfect comes from the Paternal Principle. Psellus, 38; Pletho. Z. This suggests that imperfection only appears through later processes of creation.

The Father did not bring forth fear; instead, He gave the gift of persuasion. Pletho. Z.

The Father fully understands Himself and doesn't limit His fire to His intellectual power alone. Psellus, 30; Pletho, 33. Z. p. 26 Taylor interprets this as "The Father withdrew Himself quickly but didn't confine His fire to His mind." However, the Greek text doesn't mention "quickly." The word "Arpazo" can mean "grasp" or "understand with the mind."

This is the kind of Mind that exists before action begins, staying in the Father's depth and nourishing silence in the hidden place of God. Proclus on Timaeus, 167. T.

Everything comes from the same divine fire. The Father created everything perfectly and passed it to the Second Mind, whom all nations refer to as the First. Psellus, 24; Pletho, 30. Z.

The Second Mind governs the Empyrean World. Damascius, On Principles. T.

The Intelligible speaks by understanding. Psellus, 35. Z.

- Power belongs to them, but the source of Mind is from Him. Proclus in Plato's Theology, 365. T.
- The Father's Mind rides upon delicate Guides, which shine with the trails of unwavering and unstoppable Fire. Proclus on Plato's Cratylus. T.
- ...After the Father's thought, I, the Soul, take my place, a warmth that gives life to all things. ...For He placed The Intelligible within the Soul, and the Soul within the lifeless body, Just as the Father of Gods and Men has placed these within us. Proclus in Timaeus, 124. Z. or T.
- Nature's works exist together with the Father's light of understanding. The Soul decorated the vast Heaven, and after the Father, it continues to shape it. But her rule remains high above. Proclus in Timaeus, 106. Z. or T. The word "dominion" is from the Greek krata, though some versions use kerata, meaning "horns."
- The Soul, as a shining Fire through the Father's power, remains

immortal, ruling over Life and filling the deep places of the World's heart. Psellus, 28; Pletho, 11. Z.

- With the channels intertwined, the Soul carries out the works of eternal Fire. Proclus in Politico, p. 399. Z. or T.

- The Fire from beyond does not lock its power in matter but exists within the Mind. For it is the Mind of Mind that shapes the Fiery World. Proclus in Theology, 333, and Timaeus, 157. T.

- The one who first came from Mind wraps one Fire within another, weaving them together to unite the flowing fountains of Fire while keeping its brilliance untouched. Proclus in Parmenides. T.

- A Fiery Whirlwind draws down the glow of flashing flames, penetrating the Universe's depths, as its marvelous rays extend downwards from there. Proclus in Plato's Theology, 171 and 172. T.

- The Monad came first into existence and still remains as the Paternal Monad. Proclus in Euclid, 27. T.

- When the Monad stretches outward, the Dyad is born. Proclus in Euclid, 27. T. The Pythagoreans describe the Monad, Dyad, and Triad just as Plato does with Bound, Infinite, and Mixed. These Oracles use the terms Hyparxis, Power, and Energy for the same ideas. Damascius On Principles. Taylor.

- Beside Him sits the Dyad, sparkling with intellectual divisions. It governs all things and brings order to whatever lacks it. Proclus in Plato's Theology, 376. T.

- The Father's Mind declared that all things should be divided into Three, and with His Will's agreement, everything was immediately separated this way. Proclus in Parmenides. T.

- The Eternal Father's Mind spoke of the Three, ruling everything through understanding. Proclus in Timaeus. T.

- The Father blended every Spirit from within this Triad. Lydus, De Mensibus, 20. Taylor.

- Everything flows from the heart of this Triad. Lydus, De

Mensibus, 20. Taylor.

• Everything is ruled by and exists within this Triad. Proclus in First Alcibiades. T.

You must understand that everything bows before the Three Supreme Powers. Damascius, On Principles. T.

From this source comes the Form of the Triad, which existed before creation. It is not the first Essence but the principle by which all things are measured. Anon. Z. or T.

In it appeared Virtue, Wisdom, and all-knowing Truth. Anon. Z. or T.

In every World, the Triad shines brightly, and above it all, the Monad reigns supreme. Damascius in Parmenides. T.

The first course is Sacred. In the middle course, the Sun moves, and in the third, the Earth is warmed by inner fire. Anon. Z. or T.

It stands high above, giving life to Light, Fire, Ether, and Worlds. Simplicius in his Physics, 143. Z. or T.

Ideas

Intelligibles, Intellectuals, Iynges, Synoches, Teletarchæ, Fountains, Principles, Hecate And Dæmons.

1. The Mind of the Father spun forth with a roaring sound, grasping with unshakable Will every possible Idea. These Ideas, which flowed from a single source, were released, for both the Will and the Purpose came from the Father, and through changing forms of life, they remain connected to Him. But these Ideas were separated and spread by Intellectual Fire into other forms of Intelligence. Before the diverse World took shape, the King of All placed an intellectual and unchanging Pattern as a model. The impression of this Pattern spread throughout the World, filling the Universe with many kinds of

Ideas, yet all these Ideas share a single origin. From this one foundation, they split and spread across different bodies throughout the Universe, moving endlessly through the depths, shining and radiating outward without end. These are intellectual concepts from the Father's Fountain, filled with the brightness of Fire, carried by the flow of unceasing Time. The Father's original, perfect Fountain released these first-born Ideas. Proclus in Parmenidem. Z. or T.

2. These Ideas, though many, flash down onto the shining Worlds, carrying with them the Three Divine Powers. Damascius in Parmenidem. T.

3. They guard the works of the Father and the One Mind, which holds all understanding. Proclus in Theologiam Platonis, 205. T.

4. All things exist together within the World of Pure Intelligence. Damascius, De Principiis. T.

5. Every form of Intelligence knows the Divine, for Intelligence cannot exist without the object of its understanding, and the object of understanding cannot exist apart from Intelligence. Damascius. Z. or T.

6. Intelligence depends on what it understands, and without this connection, it cannot exist. Proclus, Th. Pl., 172. Z. or T.

7. Through Intelligence, He holds together the things that can be understood and brings the Soul into the Worlds.

8. With Intelligence, He gathers what can be known and brings Sensation into the Worlds. Proclus in Crat. T.

9. The Father's Intelligence, which knows all things and beautifies what cannot be expressed, has scattered symbols throughout the World. Proclus in Cratylum. T.

10. This structure is the starting point of all division. Damascius, De Principiis. T.

11. Pure Understanding is the root of every division. Damascius, De Principiis. T.

12. Pure Understanding serves as nourishment for what gains

knowledge. Damascius, De Principiis. T.

13. The oracles describe the Order as existing before the Heavens, beyond words, and say it possesses Mystic Silence. Proclus in Cratylum. T.

14. The oracle explains that causes born from Understanding are swift. It says that after flowing from the Father, they quickly return to Him again. Proclus in Cratylum. T.

15. These Natures are both Intelligent and objects of Intelligence. They hold knowledge within themselves and become subjects for others to understand. Proclus, Theologiam Platonis. T.

The Second Order of Platonic philosophy is called the "Intelligible and Intellectual Triad." In Chaldean teachings, this order includes the Iynges, Synoches, and Teletarchs. The later Platonists' Intellectual Triad corresponds with the Chaldean Fountains, Fontal Fathers, or Cosmagogi.

16. The Iynges gain their understanding from the Father. Through mysterious guidance, they are moved to comprehend. Psellus, 41; Pletho, 31. Z.

17. It is the Operator and the Giver of Life-bearing Fire. It fills Hecate's life-giving womb and transfers the empowering energy of Fire to the Synoches, endowing them with immense strength. Proclus in Timaeus, 128. T.

18. He gave His Whirlwinds to guard the Supernals, blending His own force within the Synoches. Dam., On Principles. T.

19. Likewise, many others serve the material Synoches. T.

20. The Teletarchs are part of the Synoches. Dam., On Principles. T.

21. Rhea, the source and river of blessed intellects, holds the powers of all things in her sacred womb, pouring out continuous creation upon everything. Proclus in Cratylus. T.

22. She marks the boundary of the Father's Depth and serves as the source of intellect. Dam., On Principles. T.

23. He shines with clear, radiant strength, filled with intellectual

energy. Dam. T.

24. His brilliance contains intellectual power, spreading love throughout everything. Dam. T.

25. All things submit to the swirling motions of the Intellectual Fire, following the Father's wise guidance. Proclus in Parmenides. T.

26. Oh, how the World is governed by unyielding Intellectual Rulers.

27. Hecate's source aligns with that of the Fontal Fathers. T.

28. From Him leap forth the Amilicti, unrelenting thunderbolts, and the whirlwinds that fill Hecate's sacred womb with unstoppable strength. He surrounds the brilliance of Fire, and His mighty Spirit, burning beyond, rules the Poles. Proclus in Cratylus. T.

29. There is another source that leads the Empyrean World. Proclus in Timaeus. Z. or T.

30. It is the source of all sources and the boundary of every spring. Dam., On Principles.

31. The fountain that generates life for Souls is contained within two Minds. Dam., On Principles. T.

32. Beneath these exists the Primary One of all non-material things. Dam. in Parmenides. Z. or T.

Following the Intellectual Triad is the Demiurgos, from whom came the Essences and Orders, including various spirits and the material world.

33. Light born from the Father alone holds the power to grasp His Mind. It pours understanding into all sources and principles, driving their endless cycles. Proclus in Timaeus, 242.

34. All sources and principles revolve continuously, never ceasing their motion. Proclus in Parmenides. Z. or T.

35. The principles that have understood the Father's plans are wrapped in physical forms and bodies. These serve as links between the Father and matter, making invisible ideas visible in the world. Dam., On Principles. Z. or T.

36. Typhon, Echidna, and Python, children of Tartarus and Gaia, joined by Uranus, form a Chaldean Triad that watches over and controls chaotic creations. Olymp. in Phaedrus. T.

37. Some irrational demons, without thought, are sustained by the rulers of the air. This is why the oracle says, "They guide the airy, earthly, and water-dwelling creatures." Olymp. in Phaedrus. T.

38. When connected to divine beings, the word "Aquatic" signifies rule tied to water. This is why the oracle calls the aquatic gods "Water Walkers." Proclus in Timaeus, 270. T.

39. Some water spirits, known as Nereids in Orpheus's writings, dwell in high, misty waters, appearing in the damp air. As Zoroaster taught, these spirits can sometimes be seen by those with keen sight, especially in Persia and Africa. Ficino, On the Immortality of the Soul, 123. T.

Particular Souls

Soul, Life, Man.

The Father created ideas, and He gave life to all mortal bodies. Proclus in Tim., 336. T.

40. The Father of gods and humans placed the Mind (nous) in the Soul (psyche) and placed both within the human body.

41. The Father's Mind planted symbols within the Soul. Psellus, 26; Pletho, 6. Z.

42. He mixed the Vital Spark from two substances—Mind and Divine Spirit—and as a third element, He added Holy Love, the sacred Charioteer that unites all things. Lydus, De Mensibus, 3.

43. This Love fills the Soul with deep affection. Proclus in Platonis Theologia, 4. Z. or T.

44. The human Soul embraces God closely. It holds no mortal nature and is entirely filled with God's presence, rejoicing

in the harmony that sustains the mortal body. Psellus, 17; Pletho, 10. Z.

45. Stronger Souls can see Truth by their own nature and are more creative. According to the Oracle, such Souls are saved by their own power. Proclus in I. Alcibiades. Z.

46. The Oracle says that ascending Souls sing hymns of praise. Olympiodorus in Phaedrus. Z. or T.

47. Of all Souls, the most blessed are those sent from Heaven to Earth. They are joyful and possess indescribable strength, for they come from your radiant essence, O King, or from Jove himself, driven by the unbreakable power of Mithus. Synesius, De Insomniis, 153. Z. or T.

48. The Souls of those who die suddenly are the purest. Psellus, 27. Z.

49. The threads that hold the Soul's breath can be easily released. Psellus, 32; Pletho, 8. Z.

50. When one Soul is set free, the Father sends another to keep the number complete. Z. or T.

51. By understanding the Father's works, these Souls escape the grasp of Fate. They remain in God's presence, drawing strong lights that descend from the Father. As they descend, the Soul gathers the heavenly fruit, the flower that nourishes the spirit. Proclus in Tim., 321. Z. or T.

52. This spiritual force, which the blessed call the Pneumatic Soul, becomes a god, a powerful spirit, or an image without a body. In this form, the Soul experiences punishment. The Oracles say that the Soul's tasks in Hades resemble the deceptive visions of a dream. Synesius, De Insomniis. Z. or T. The term "Dæmon" originally referred to both good and bad spirits, often applied to pure beings as much as to impure ones. This concept aligns with the Eastern teaching of Devachan, a state of pleasant illusion after death.

53. Life flows from many sources, moving from above, through the opposite side, to the center of the Earth. From

there, it reaches the fiery middle point, where the life-giving fire descends into the physical world. Z. or T.

54. Water represents life, which is why Plato and the ancient gods described the Soul as both the water that gives life and the fountain from which it flows. Proclus in Tim., 318. Z.

55. O Man, daring by nature, you are a subtle creation. Psellus, 12; Pletho, 21. Z.

56. Your body will become the home of the beasts of the Earth. Psellus, 36; Pletho, 7. Z. The body is the vessel that temporarily holds the Mind (nous).

57. The Soul moves continuously through different experiences over time. Once these experiences are complete, it must pass through everything again, weaving the same pattern of life in the world. Zoroaster believed that when the same causes arise, the same effects will inevitably follow. Ficinus, De Immortalitate Animæ, 129. Z.

58. According to Zoroaster, the Soul's ethereal form continually returns through reincarnation. Ficinus, De Immortalitate Animæ, 131. Z.

59. The Oracles celebrate the essential source of every Soul, which flows from the Empyrean, the Ethereal, and the Material realms. They separate this source from Zoogonothea, the life-giving goddess Rhea. From her, they create two orders: one related to the Soul and the other to Fate. The Oracles teach that the Soul comes from the animating order but sometimes falls under the control of Fate. When this happens, the Soul enters an irrational state and becomes subject to Fate instead of Divine Providence. Proclus, De Providentia apud Fabricium, Bibliotheca Graeca, vol. 8, 486. Z. or T.

Matter

The World--And Nature.

The Matrix contains everything within it. T.

It can be divided entirely, yet it also remains whole.

From it flows the endless creation of many different types of Matter. Proclus in *Tim.*, 118. T.

These creations form atoms, physical shapes, material bodies, and everything that belongs to the realm of matter. Damascius, *De Principiis*. T.

The Nymphs of the Fountains, along with all Water Spirits and forms of the Earth, sky, and stars, are the Riders and Rulers of Matter—whether celestial, starry, or deep within the Abyss. Lydus, p. 32.

The Oracles teach that Evil is weaker than even nothingness. Proclus, *De Providentia*. Z. or T.

Matter fills the whole world, as the gods also proclaim. Proclus, *Tim.*, 142. Z. or T.

Although Divine Beings have no bodies, they are bound to bodies for our sake. Since bodies cannot fully hold spiritual beings due to the limits of material nature, this connection exists to focus the divine within us. Proclus in *Platonis Politicus*, 359. Z. or T.

60. The Father's Mind, understanding His creations, spread the fiery bonds of love throughout everything, ensuring that all things would remain connected in love for eternity. This way, everything in creation stays linked to the Father's Light, and the elements of the world are drawn together by mutual attraction. Proclus in *Tim.*, 155. T.

61. The Maker of everything, acting through His own power, shaped the World. Out of a fiery mass, He formed all things

by His will, making the Universe a visible creation, not hidden or shapeless. Proclus in *Tim.*, 154. Z. or T.

62. He made all things in His own likeness, casting them in the image of His form.

63. They reflect His Mind, but because they are made, they also contain something physical. Proclus in *Tim.*, 87. Z. or T.

64. There is a Holy Name that moves without rest, leaping into the worlds through the Father's rapid vibrations. Proclus in *Cratylus*. Z. or T.

65. The ethers of the elements are present there. Olympiodorus in *Phaedrus*. Z. or T.

66. The Oracles reveal that divine symbols and other visions appear within the Ether or Astral Light. Simplicius in *Physica*, 144. Z. or T.

67. In this realm, the shapeless takes form. Simplicius in *Physica*, 143. Z. or T.

68. These are the hidden and revealed impressions of the World.

69. The World that resists the Light draws many down through twisting currents. Proclus in *Tim.*, 339. Z. or T.

70. He made the whole world from Fire, Air, Water, Earth, and nourishing Ether. Z. or T.

71. He placed the Earth in the center, Water beneath it, and Air above both. Z. or T.

72. He fixed countless stars in place, keeping them steady and unmoving, with no labor but by stable order, forcing Fire into Fire. Proclus in *Tim.*, 280. Z. or T.

73. The Father gathered the seven layers of the Cosmos, shaping the Heavens in a curved form. Damascius in *Parmenides*. Z. or T.

74. He created the seven wandering bodies (the planets). Z. or T.

75. Their movements were set within well-organized zones. Z. or T.

76. He made six of them, placing the Fiery Sun as the seventh in the center. Proclus in *Tim.*, 280. Z. or T.

77. From the center, all lines extend equally in every direction. Proclus in *Euclidem.*

78. The Sun moves continuously around this central point. Proclus in *Platonis Theologia*, 317. Z. or T.

79. It eagerly races toward the center of brilliant Light. Proclus in *Tim.*, 236. T.

80. The Great Sun and the Shining Moon.

81. Its rays spread outward like flowing hair, ending in sharp points. Proclus in *Platonis Politicus*, 387. T.

82. The movements of the Sun and Moon, the silent spaces of the sky, and the music of Ether join together with the phases of the Sun, Moon, and Air. Proclus in *Tim.*, 257. Z. or T.

83. The most mysterious teachings say that His completeness is found in the realms beyond this world, where a Solar World and endless Light exist, as the Chaldean Oracles proclaim. Proclus in *Tim.*, 264. Z. or T.

84. The Sun is the truest measure of time, for it is itself the time of all time, as the Oracle of the gods teaches. Proclus in *Tim.*, 249. Z. or T.

85. The Sun's disk moves through the starless region above the unchanging sphere and is not among the planets but within the three worlds, according to mystical teachings. Julian, *Cratylus*, 5, 334. Z. or T.

86. The Sun is Fire, a channel of Fire, and a distributor of Fire. Proclus in *Tim.*, 141. Z. or T.

87. Thus, Kronos, through the Sun, observes the true pole.

88. The movements of Ether, the Moon's great path, and the changing flows of Air. Proclus in *Tim.*, 257. Z. or T.

89. O Ether, Sun, and Spirit of the Moon, you are the rulers of the Air. Proclus in *Tim.*, 257. Z. or T.

90. The wide sky, the Moon's path, and the Sun's pole. Proclus

in *Tim.*, 257. Z. or T.

91. The Goddess brings forth the mighty Sun and the bright Moon.

92. She gathers their light, absorbing the music of Ether, the Sun, the Moon, and all that exists in the Air.

93. Tireless Nature governs the worlds and their motions, ensuring that the Heavens move in an eternal cycle, so the rhythms of the Sun, Moon, seasons, day, and night are fulfilled. Proclus in *Tim.*, 4, 323. Z. or T.

94. And above the shoulders of the Great Goddess, vast Nature is exalted. Proclus in *Tim.*, 4. T.

95. The greatest thinkers of Babylon, along with Ostanes and Zoroaster, rightly call the starry spheres "Herds"—either because they alone move perfectly around a center or because, as the Oracles suggest, they gather the principles of nature, which are also called "Herds" (agelous). Adding a "gamma" makes them "Angels" (aggelous). This is why the stars that govern these herds are viewed as divine beings or spirits like Angels and are called Archangels, numbering seven. Anonymous in *Theologumenis Arithmeticis*. Z.

96. Zoroaster describes the alignment between physical forms and the Soul's ideals as "Divine Allurements." Ficinus, *De Vita Cælitus Comparanda*. Z.

Magical And Philosophical Precepts

Do not focus your mind on the vast lands of the Earth, for the Plant of Truth does not grow from the ground. Do not try to measure the Sun's movements by creating rules, for it moves by the Father's Eternal Will, not just for your benefit. Let go of the Moon's restless path, for it always moves by the force of necessity. The Stars were not created just for you. The flight of birds through the sky reveals no truth, nor does the examination of animal sacrifices—these are mere illusions, tricks used for profit. Stay away from these if you wish to enter the sacred paradise of devotion, where Virtue, Wisdom, and Justice meet. Psellus, 4. Z.

Do not lower yourself to the shadowy, splendid World, where there lies a deceptive Depth and Hades, wrapped in clouds, filled with unintelligible images. This dark abyss is treacherous and endlessly churning, always joined with a lifeless and formless body. Synesius, *De Insomniis*, 140. Z. or T.

Do not descend, for beneath the Earth lies a cliff, reached by a ladder with seven steps, and on that path rests the Throne of a destructive and fateful force. Psellus, 6; Pletho, 2. Z.

Do not linger at the edge of the cliff, trapped in material filth, for your true form belongs to a radiant realm. Psellus, 1, 2; Pletho, 14; Synesius, 140. Z.

Do not call upon the visible form of Nature's Soul. Psellus, 15; Pletho, 23. Z.

Do not seek Nature, for her name brings ruin. Proclus in *Platonis Theologia*, 143. Z.

You should not look upon them before your body is initiated, for their allure draws souls away from the sacred mysteries. Proclus in *I. Alcibiades*. Z. or T.

Do not bring her forth, or she may take something with her when she leaves. Psellus, 3; Pletho, 15. Z. (Taylor says that "her" refers to the human soul.)

Do not corrupt the Spirit or delve too deeply into superficial matters. Psellus, 19; Pletho, 13. Z.

Do not seek to expand your destiny. Psellus, 37; Pletho, 4.

The Oracle says not to step beyond what is required for devotion. Damascius, *Vita Isidori*. Z. or T.

Do not change the sacred names used in invocations, for in every language, God has provided sacred names with great power. Psellus, 7; Nicephorus. Z. or T.

Do not go out when the official passes by. Picus de Mirandola, *Conclusions*. Z.

Let fiery hope sustain you on the angelic plane. Olympiodorus in *Phaedrus*; Proclus in *Alcibiades*. Z. or T.

The glowing Fire comes first, and those who approach it will receive Light from God. The blessed Immortals respond swiftly to those who persevere. Proclus in *Tim.*, 65. Z. or T.

The gods urge us to understand the radiating form of Light. Proclus in *Cratylus*. Z. or T.

You must hasten toward the Light and the Rays of the Father, who sent you a Soul (Psyche) endowed with deep Mind (Nous). Psellus, 33; Pletho, 6. Z.

Seek the path to Paradise. Psellus, 41; Pletho, 27. Z.

Learn what is beyond Mind, for it exists beyond understanding. Psellus, 41; Pletho, 27. Z.

There is one Intelligible Being whom you must grasp with the finest part of your Mind. Psellus, 31; Pletho, 28. Z.

The Paternal Mind will not accept the soul's longing until it awakens from forgetfulness and remembers the sacred symbol of the Father. Psellus, 39; Pletho, 5. Z.

Some are given the ability to know the Light, while others, even in sleep, are blessed with insight from the Father's strength. Synesius, *De Insomniis*, 135. Z. or T.

You must approach the Intelligible Being not with force but with a calm, searching mind, measuring all things except this Being. If you incline your Mind gently, you will understand it—not with effort, but with a pure, inquisitive sense. Stretch your Soul toward this higher understanding, for it lies beyond ordinary thought. Damascius. T.

You cannot grasp it in the same way you understand common things. Damascius, *De Primis Principiis*. T.

Those who understand must know the deep mysteries of the Paternal Mind beyond this world. Damascius. Z. or T.

Divine truths are not accessible to those focused only on the body. They can only be known by those who, stripped of their earthly attachments, reach the highest summit. Proclus in *Cratylus*. Z. or T.

Clothed in the strength of radiant Light, with triple power protecting both Soul and Mind, one must fill the Mind with sacred symbols and focus, not wander along the celestial path without direction.

Armed with every kind of strength, he becomes like the Goddess. Proclus in *Platonis Theologia*, 324. T.

Explore the River of the Soul—know where you came from and in what order. Even though you have served the body, rise again to the place from which you descended by aligning your actions with sacred reason. Psellus, 5; Pletho, 1. Z.

Fiery rays extend in all directions toward the freed Soul. Psellus, 11; Pletho, 24. Z.

Let the infinite depth of your Soul guide you, and raise your eyes upward with purpose. Psellus, 11; Pletho, 20.

As a rational being, you must control your Soul so it avoids earthly misfortune and finds salvation. Lydus, *De Mensibus*, 2.

If you direct your fiery Mind toward devotion, you will preserve the fragile body. Psellus, 22; Pletho, 16. Z.

A life purified by Divine Fire removes every stain and all irrational impulses that cling to the Soul during its earthly existence, as the Oracle teaches us to believe. Proclus in *Tim.*, 331. Taylor.

The Oracles state that purification rituals benefit not only the Soul but also the body, making it fit to receive help and health. These teachings are given by the gods to the most devoted Theurgists. Julian, *Cratylus*, 334. Z. or T.

The Oracle warns us to avoid following the masses blindly. Proclus in *I. Alcibiades*. Z. or T.

He who knows himself knows everything within himself. Picus, p. 211. Z.

The Oracles emphasize that we have the power to choose, rather than being ruled by the natural order. For example, they say, "When you look at yourself, be mindful," and "If you believe you are more than your body, then you are." Furthermore, they teach that "Our personal struggles shape the kind of life we create." Proclus, *De Providentia*, p. 483. Z. or T.

These are deep mysteries I explore in the profound Abyss of the Mind.

The Oracle says that God does not abandon us unless we approach divine matters with confusion or impurity. If we do so, our progress is incomplete, our efforts are wasted, and the path becomes dark. Proclus in *Parmenides*. Z. or T.

If you do not recognize that every god is good, you remain vigilant for nothing. Proclus in *Platonis Politicus*, 355. Z. or T.

Theurgists do not fall into the ranks of those controlled by Fate. Lydus, *De Mensibus*. Taylor.

The number nine, composed of three triads, reaches the highest level of theology, as the Chaldean philosophy teaches through Porphyry. Lydus, p. 121.

On Hecate's left side is a fountain of Virtue that remains untouched and pure. Psellus, 13; Pletho, 9. Z.

Even the Earth mourned for them and their children. Psellus, 21; Pletho, 3. Z.

The Furies are the enforcers of punishment upon humans. Psellus, 26; Pletho, 19. Z.

Do not become trapped by the Furies of Earth or the demands of nature, or you will perish. Proclus in *Theologia*, 297. Z. or T.

Nature teaches us that there are pure spirits, and that even the harmful seeds of matter can be transformed into something useful and good. Psell., 16; Pletho, 18. Z.

You only need to offer sacrifices for three days, no more. Pic. Concl. Z.

Before anything else, the priest in charge of the works of fire must sprinkle water from the roaring sea. Proc. in Crat. Z. or T.

Work diligently around the sacred wheel of Hecate. Psell., 9. Nicephorus.

When you see an earthly spirit approaching, shout out loud and offer the stone Mnizourin as a sacrifice. Psell., 40. Z.

If you call upon these forces often, you will notice everything around you fading into darkness. The sky will no longer be visible, the stars will lose their light, and the moon will be hidden. The Earth itself will feel absent, lightning will flash around you, and thunder will fill the air. Psell., 10; Pletho, 22. Z.

From the depths of the Earth will spring forth demons with the faces of dogs, offering no real sign to guide mortals. Psell., 23; Pletho, 10. Z.

A similar fire will rush through the air, formless and chaotic, bringing with it the sound of a voice or a swirling flash of light. You may see the vision of a fiery horse, or a child riding on a celestial steed—either clothed in gold, naked, or shooting arrows of light while standing on the horse's shoulders. If you focus deeply in meditation, you will be able to unite these visions into the image of a lion. Proc. in Pl. Polit., 380; Stanley Hist. Philos. Z. or T.

When you see the holy, formless fire shining through the depths of the universe, listen closely and hear the voice of the fire. Psell., 14; Pletho, 25. Z.

Oracles From Porphyry

Above the celestial lights, there is an eternal flame that sparkles without end. It is the source of life and the origin of all beings, the beginning of everything! This flame brings everything into existence, and nothing is destroyed except by its consuming fire. It reveals itself by its own nature. This fire cannot be contained in any place, for it has no physical form and no material substance. It surrounds the heavens entirely. From it, tiny sparks emerge, creating all the fires of the Sun, the Moon, and the Stars. This is what I understand about God. Do not seek to know more, for no matter how wise you are, it is beyond human comprehension. Know this: unjust and wicked people cannot hide from God's presence! No clever trick or excuse can conceal anything from His all-seeing eyes. God is present in everything, and everything is filled with God!

Within God is a vast depth of flame! Yet, the heart should not fear approaching this sacred fire or being touched by it. It is a gentle fire that will not destroy you. Its calm and soothing heat binds everything together, bringing harmony and stability to the world. Nothing exists without this fire, for it is God Himself. He has no creator and no mother. He knows all things and cannot be taught anything. His plans are perfect, and His name is beyond words. This is what God is! As for us, His messengers, we are only a small part of God.

The Life and Teachings of Thoth Hermes Trismegistus

Hermes Trismegistus

The Life and Teachings of Thoth Hermes Trismegistus

THUNDER boomed, and lightning lit up the sky. The veil hanging in the Temple was torn from top to bottom. The wise initiator, dressed in robes of blue and gold, slowly lifted his jeweled staff and pointed it toward the darkness that had been revealed behind the torn silk curtain. "Behold the Light of Egypt!" he declared.

The candidate, dressed in a simple white robe, stared into the deep blackness framed between two massive columns topped with lotus flowers, where the veil had once hung. As he stood there, a soft, glowing mist began to spread throughout the air until the atmosphere shimmered with tiny glowing particles. The candidate's face lit up from the soft glow, and he scanned the glittering mist, hoping to spot something solid within it.

The initiator spoke again: "This Light you see is the hidden radiance of the Mysteries. No one knows where it comes from, except for the 'Master of the Light.' Behold Him!"

Suddenly, through the glowing haze, a figure emerged, surrounded by a flickering greenish light. The initiator lowered his staff, bowed his head humbly, and placed one hand flat against his chest in reverence.

The candidate took a step back, overwhelmed and partially blinded by the brilliance of the figure before him. Slowly, he gathered his courage and looked again at the Divine One. The figure was much larger than any human being, and its body was partly transparent, revealing a glowing heart and brain that pulsed with radiant energy.

As the candidate watched in amazement, the heart of the figure transformed into an ibis, while the brain became a shining emerald. The mysterious being held in its hand a winged staff coiled with serpents.

The aged initiator lifted his staff again and cried out in a booming voice: "All hail to you, Thoth Hermes, Thrice Greatest! All hail, Prince of Men! All hail to you who stand upon the head of Typhon!"

At that moment, a terrifying dragon appeared—a monstrous creature that was part serpent, part crocodile, and part hog. Flames burst from its mouth and nostrils, and horrible sounds echoed throughout the chamber.

Without hesitation, Hermes struck the advancing dragon with his serpent-twined staff. With a snarling cry, the beast collapsed onto its side, and the flames around it slowly faded.

Hermes placed his foot firmly on the skull of the defeated Typhon. In the next instant, a burst of unbearable light filled the room, forcing the candidate to stumble back against one of the pillars.

Streams of greenish mist trailed behind Hermes as he moved across the chamber, and with a final flash, the immortal figure vanished into nothingness.

Suppositions Concerning The Identity of Hermes

Iamblichus claimed that Hermes wrote twenty thousand books, while Manetho said the number was more than thirty-six thousand (see James Gardner). These numbers make it clear that a single person, even if gifted with divine abilities, could hardly have created so many works alone. It is said that Hermes revealed many arts and sciences to humanity, including medicine, chemistry, law, art, astrology, music, rhetoric, magic, philosophy, geography, mathematics (especially geometry), anatomy, and public speaking. Orpheus was honored in a similar way by the Greeks.

In his Biographia Antiqua, Francis Barrett writes about Hermes: "* * * if God ever appeared in a man, he appeared in him, as is shown by his books and his Pymander. In these works, Hermes shared the secrets of the Abyss and divine knowledge with future generations. Through them, he proved himself to be not only an inspired prophet but also a profound philosopher, gaining his wisdom from God and the heavens, not from humans."

Because of his great knowledge, Hermes was connected with many ancient sages and prophets. In Ancient Mythology, Bryant says: "I have mentioned that Cadmus was the same as the Egyptian Thoth; it is clear from his identification as Hermes, and from the fact that he was credited with inventing writing." (The chapter on Pythagorean Mathematics includes a table of the original Cadmean letters.) Scholars believe that Hermes was known to the Jews as "Enoch," whom Kenealy called the "Second Messenger of God."

The Greeks accepted Hermes into their mythology, and he later became known as Mercury among the Romans. He was honored through the planet Mercury because it is the closest to the Sun. Just as Mercury orbits near the Sun, Hermes was thought to be closest to God and became known as the Messenger of the Gods.

In Egyptian drawings, Thoth, identified as Hermes, is shown carrying a wax writing tablet and recording the weighing of souls in the judgment hall of Osiris—a ritual of deep meaning. Hermes is especially important to Masonic scholars because he is believed to have created the Masonic initiation rituals, which were based on the Mysteries he established. Most of the symbols used in Masonry are Hermetic in nature. Pythagoras studied mathematics with the Egyptians and learned about symbolic geometric shapes from them.

Hermes is also remembered for reforming the calendar by increasing the year from 360 days to 365, setting a standard that we still use today. The title "Thrice Greatest" was given to Hermes because he was considered the greatest philosopher, the greatest priest, and the greatest king. Notably, the final poem written by Henry Wadsworth Longfellow, one of America's beloved poets, was a lyrical ode to Hermes. (See Chambers' Encyclopædia.)

The Mutilated Hermetic Fragments

James Campbell Brown, in his History of Chemistry, writes about the Hermetic books: "Leaving behind the Chaldean and earliest Egyptian times, from which we have only remnants and no records—no names of chemists or philosophers—we now move into the historical period, when books were first written, not on parchment or paper, but on papyrus. A collection of early Egyptian books is credited to Hermes Trismegistus, who may have been a real scholar or perhaps a symbol for many different authors over time. * * * Some connect him with the Greek god Hermes, as well as with the Egyptian god Thoth or Tuti, who was the moon god, often shown in art with the head of an ibis and the disc and crescent of the moon. The Egyptians saw him as the god of wisdom, writing, and timekeeping.

Because of the high regard alchemists had for Hermes, chemical writings became known as 'hermetic,' and the term 'hermetically sealed'—used to describe sealing a glass container by melting it shut—comes from this tradition. The same origin can be found in Paracelsus' hermetic medicines and the hermetic freemasonry of the Middle Ages."

Among the fragments believed to come from Hermes are two famous works. One is the Emerald Tablet, and the other is the Divine Pymander, also called The Shepherd of Men, which will be discussed later. Hermes stands out as one of the few pagan philosophers whom the early Christians did not attack. In fact, some Church Fathers even admitted that Hermes showed signs of intelligence. They said that if he had lived in a more enlightened age and had received their teachings, he could have been truly great.

In Stromata, Clement of Alexandria, one of the few ancient writers whose accounts of pagan traditions survive today, shares nearly all we know about the original forty-two books of Hermes and how highly they were valued by both the spiritual and political leaders of Egypt. Clement describes a ceremonial procession like this:

"For the Egyptians follow their own philosophy, which is reflected in their rituals. First comes the Singer, holding a symbol of music. He must study two of Hermes' books: one containing hymns to the gods and another with rules for the king's life. Following the Singer is the Astrologer, carrying a clock and a palm branch—both symbols of astrology. He must memorize four books of Hermes about the stars: one on the fixed stars, another on the phases of the sun and moon, and the other two on their risings.

Next in the procession is the sacred Scribe, wearing wings on his head and carrying a book and measuring tool, along with ink and a reed for writing. He must know the hieroglyphs and be familiar with cosmography, geography, the paths of the sun and moon, the five planets, and the layout of Egypt, including a chart of the Nile. He also needs to understand the priests' equipment, sacred spaces, and rituals. After the Scribe comes the Stole-keeper, carrying the cubit of justice and a ceremonial cup for offerings. He is skilled in matters of training and sacrifice.

There are ten books dedicated to the worship of the gods, covering topics like sacrifices, hymns, prayers, processions, and festivals. Lastly comes the Prophet, holding a water vase, with followers carrying bread behind him. As the temple leader, the Prophet studies ten more books called 'Hieratic,' which contain laws, knowledge of the gods, and priestly training. The Prophet also manages the temple's resources. Of Hermes' forty-two essential books, thirty-six contain Egyptian philosophy, studied by the individuals mentioned above. The remaining six books, which are medical, are entrusted to the Pastophoroi, or image-bearers, and deal with anatomy, diseases, medical tools, treatments, eye care, and women's health."

One of the greatest losses to philosophy was the destruction of nearly all these forty-two books of Hermes. They disappeared during the burning of Alexandria. Both the Romans and later the Christians understood that as long as these books existed, they could not fully dominate the Egyptian people. The few volumes that escaped the fire were hidden in the desert, and only a small group of initiates from secret schools know where they are buried.

The Book of Thoth

While Hermes still walked among men, he entrusted the sacred Book of Thoth to his chosen successors. This book contained the secret methods for bringing about the spiritual rebirth of humanity and served as the key to understanding all of Hermes' other writings. Although the exact contents of the Book of Thoth are unknown, it is said that the pages were filled with strange hieroglyphs and symbols. Those who knew how to use them gained unlimited power over the spirits of the air and the gods beneath the earth.

The book also revealed the process by which certain areas of the brain could be stimulated through the Mysteries, expanding human consciousness. This allowed individuals to see the Immortals and stand in the presence of higher gods. Because it described how this awakening could be achieved, the Book of Thoth was known as the "Key to Immortality."

According to legend, the Book of Thoth was kept inside a golden box in the inner sanctuary of a temple. Only one key existed, held by the "Master of the Mysteries," the highest Hermetic initiate. He alone knew what was written in the book. When the Mysteries faded from the ancient world, the book was lost. However, devoted followers carried the sealed casket to another land. It is believed that the book still exists today, guiding those who seek the presence of the Immortals. No further details about the book can be revealed to the world now, but the unbroken line of initiation—starting with the first hierophant initiated by Hermes—continues to this day. Those who are truly dedicated to serving the Immortals may find this priceless work if they search with sincerity and determination.

Some claim that the Book of Thoth is, in fact, the mysterious Tarot of the Bohemians—a symbolic collection of seventy-eight cards, said to have been carried by the gypsies since they were exiled from their ancient temple, the Serapeum. (According to secret histories, the gypsies were originally priests from Egypt.) There are still several secret schools in the world today that initiate worthy students into the Mysteries. Almost all of them began by lighting their sacred flames from the torch of Hermes.

In the Book of Thoth, Hermes revealed the "One Way" to humanity. For centuries, the wise from every culture and faith have followed this path to reach immortality. Hermes created this Way to shine a light in the darkness, offering redemption to humankind.

Poimandres, The Vision of Hermes

The Divine Pymander of Hermes Mercurius Trismegistus is one of the earliest surviving Hermetic writings. Although it likely does not exist in its original form—having been reworked during the first centuries of the Christian era and mistranslated over time—it still holds many core ideas of the Hermetic tradition. The Divine Pymander is made up of seventeen fragments, gathered and presented as one complete work. The second book, called Poimandres or The Vision, describes how divine wisdom was first revealed to Hermes. After receiving this knowledge, Hermes began his ministry, teaching the secrets of the unseen universe to anyone willing to listen.

The Vision is the most well-known Hermetic fragment and explains the Hermetic view of the universe and the Egyptian teachings on how the human soul develops and grows. For some time, it was mistakenly called The Genesis of Enoch, but this error has since been corrected. To interpret the symbolic meaning in Hermes' Vision, the following works were used: The Divine Pymander (London, 1650), translated from Arabic and Greek by Dr. Everard; Hermetica (Oxford, 1924), edited by Walter Scott; Hermes, The Mysteries of Egypt (Philadelphia, 1925), by Edouard Schuré; and Thrice-Greatest Hermes (London, 1906), by G. R. S. Mead. These sources were supplemented with commentary based on the ancient Egyptian esoteric philosophy and other Hermetic writings. Outdated language has been replaced with modern terms, and the narrative style has been chosen over the original dialogue format for clarity.

While wandering through a barren, rocky landscape, Hermes devoted himself to meditation and prayer. By following the secret teachings of the Temple, he gradually freed his higher mind from the control of his bodily senses. Once released, his divine nature revealed to him the mysteries of the spiritual realms. He saw a figure of immense power and awe—a Great Dragon whose wings stretched across the sky, with light radiating from its body in all directions. (In the Mysteries, the Universal Life Force is symbolized by a dragon.) The Dragon called Hermes by name and asked him why he was contemplating the World Mystery. Overwhelmed with fear, Hermes bowed before the Dragon and begged to know its identity.

The Dragon responded that it was Poimandres, the Mind of the Universe, the Creative Intelligence, and the supreme ruler of all things. (According to Schuré, Poimandres represents the god Osiris.) Hermes asked Poimandres to reveal the structure of the universe and the nature of the gods. The Dragon agreed, telling Hermes to hold its image firmly in his mind.

At that moment, Poimandres' form changed into a brilliant, pulsing light. This light was the true spiritual essence of the Great Dragon. Hermes was lifted into the heart of this radiant glow, and the material world vanished from his awareness. Then a deep darkness descended, spreading out until it completely swallowed the light. Chaos followed, and a swirling, watery substance emerged, releasing clouds of vapor. Strange sounds filled the air, moaning and sighing, as though the light trapped within the darkness was crying out. Hermes realized that the light represented the spiritual universe, while the swirling darkness symbolized material substance.

From the light trapped in the darkness came a mysterious and sacred Word, which stood upon the smoky waters. This Word—known as the Voice of the Light—rose from the darkness like a mighty pillar. Fire and air followed the Word upward, while earth and water remained below. In this way, the waters of light were separated from the waters of darkness. The upper waters formed the worlds above, while the lower waters created the worlds below. Earth and water mixed together and became inseparable, and the Spiritual Word, called Reason, moved over their surface, stirring it into motion.

Then Poimandres spoke again, though he did not reveal his form: "I, your God, am the Light and the Mind that existed before spirit and matter were separated, before darkness and light were divided. The Word, which appeared as a pillar of flame, is the Son of God, born from the mystery of the Mind. Its name is Reason. Reason is the child of Thought, and it will divide light from darkness, placing Truth in the midst of the waters. Understand this, Hermes, and reflect deeply upon it. What sees and hears within you is not of the earth—it is the Word of God living within you. This is why it is said that divine light exists even within mortal darkness, and ignorance cannot divide them. The union of the Word and the Mind creates the mystery of Life.

Just as the darkness outside you is in conflict with itself, the darkness within you is also divided. The light and fire within you represent the divine man, who rises along the path of the Word. The part that does not rise is the mortal man, who cannot share in immortality. Study the Mind and its mysteries, for in them lies the secret to eternal life."

The Dragon revealed itself once more to Hermes, and for a long time, the two stared deeply into each other's eyes. Hermes trembled under the gaze of Poimandres. At the Dragon's Word, the heavens opened, revealing countless Light Powers soaring across the Cosmos on wings of streaming fire. Hermes saw the spirits of the stars and the celestial beings that govern the universe, each glowing with the brilliance of the One Fire—the glory of the Supreme Mind. Hermes realized that this vision was shown to him only because Poimandres had spoken the Word. That Word was Reason, and by the power of Reason, the invisible had been made visible.

The Divine Mind—the Dragon—continued: "Before the visible universe existed, its mold had already been formed. This mold was called the Archetype, and it existed in the Supreme Mind long before creation began. The Supreme Mind gazed upon these Archetypes and became enchanted with Its own thoughts. Taking the Word as a powerful tool, it carved out vast spaces in the formless void, casting the spheres of creation into the Archetypal mold. At the same time, it planted the seeds of life in the newly formed bodies. When the darkness received the Word, it transformed into an ordered universe. The elements separated into layers, and from these layers, life began to emerge. The Supreme Being—the Mind, both male and female—brought forth the Word. Suspended between Light and darkness, the Word gave rise to another Mind, known as the Workman, the Master Builder, or the Maker of Things.

"This is how it was done, Hermes: As the Word moved like a breath through space, it ignited Fire through the force of its motion. Thus, the Fire is called the Son of Striving. The Workman passed like a whirlwind through the universe, making the elements vibrate and glow from the friction of its motion. From this process, the Son of Striving created the Seven Governors—the spirits of the planets—who established the boundaries of the world. These Governors control the world through Destiny, a power given to them by the Fiery Workman. Once the Second Mind (the Workman) had organized the Chaos, the Word of God emerged from the prison of material substance, leaving the elements behind without Reason. It joined itself to the Fiery Workman, and together, they settled at the center of the universe, setting the celestial powers in motion. This process will continue forever, for the beginning and the end are one and the same.

"Then the elements that lacked Reason produced creatures without it. Air gave rise to flying beings, water brought forth swimming creatures, and the earth created strange four-legged beasts, dragons, and bizarre monsters. Since Reason had risen out of material things, it could not be given to these creatures. The Father—the Supreme Mind—who is Light and Life, then created a Universal Man in Its own image. This Man was not earthly but heavenly, dwelling in the Light of God. The Supreme Mind loved the Man It had made and entrusted him with control over all creation.

"The Man, eager to create, moved into the sphere of generation and observed the works of the Second Mind, which sat upon the Ring of Fire. Seeing the achievements of the Fiery Workman, the Man desired to create as well, and the Father granted him permission. The Seven Governors, each sharing their power with him, rejoiced and gave him part of their nature.

"The Man, curious to understand the mysteries beyond the spheres, looked through the Seven Harmonies and broke through the strength of the circles. He revealed himself to Nature stretched out below. Gazing into the depths, the Man saw his own reflection upon the earth and in the waters. He smiled, enchanted by his reflection, and longed to descend into it. As soon as he desired this, the intelligent part of him united with the unreasoning image.

"Nature, seeing the Man's descent, embraced him, and the two became intertwined. This is why earthly man is a mixture of both worlds. Within him is the immortal, beautiful Sky Man, but on the outside, he is clothed in mortal Nature, which is destined to perish. Suffering arises because the Immortal Man fell in love with his shadow, giving up true Reality to dwell in the darkness of illusion. Though he possesses the power of the Seven Governors, along with Life, Light, and the Word, he is also subject to Fate and Destiny, ruled by the Rings of the Governors."

It is said that the Immortal Man is both male and female, always awake and watchful. He never slumbers or sleeps and is governed by a Father who is also both male and female, and equally watchful. This is a secret that remains hidden to this day. When Nature joined with the Sky Man, she gave birth to seven beings, each male and female, upright in form, and reflecting the qualities of the Seven Governors. These, O Hermes, are the seven races, species, and wheels of creation.

The seven beings came into existence in this way: Earth acted as the female element, while water was the male element. Fire and aether provided their spirits, and Nature formed bodies that took human shapes. The Great Dragon gave them Life and Light. From Life, they gained their Soul, and from Light, they received their Mind. These beings, containing both mortality and immortality, lived in this state for a time. They reproduced on their own, for each was both male and female. But after a certain period, God's will untied the knot of Destiny, and all things were set free.

At that time, all creatures, including man, who had been both male and female, were separated. The males were divided from the females according to the law of Reason. Then God spoke to the Holy Word within all souls, saying, "Increase and multiply, all of you, my creatures and creations. Let those with Mind know they are immortal and understand that death comes from loving the body too much. Let them learn all things, for those who know themselves will enter the realm of Good."

With the help of the Seven Governors and Harmony, God brought the sexes together, and from their union, new generations were born. Everything multiplied according to its kind. Those who mistakenly love their body remain trapped in darkness, suffering from the experience of death. But those who realize the body is only a temporary home for the soul rise to immortality.

Hermes then asked why ignorance alone should cause men to lose immortality. The Great Dragon replied, "For those who do not understand, the body is all they know. They believe in death because they worship the material world, which is both the cause and reality of death."

Hermes asked how the wise and righteous find their way to God. Poimandres answered, "What the Word of God has said, I also say: 'Since the Father of all things is made of Life and Light, and man is made from the same, whoever understands the nature of Life and Light will enter the eternal Life and Light.'"

Hermes then asked how the wise could attain eternal Life. Poimandres replied, "Let those with Mind reflect, examine themselves, and use their Mind's power to separate what is real from what is not. They must devote themselves to Truth and Reality."

Hermes asked, "Don't all people have Minds?" The Great Dragon responded, "Be careful what you say, for I am the Mind—the Eternal Teacher. I am the Father of the Word, the Savior of all men. In the nature of the wise, the Word takes form. Through the Word, the world is saved. I, Thought (Thoth)—the Father of the Word, the Mind— come only to those who are good, pure, merciful, and live faithfully and righteously. When I come, I help them understand everything, and they worship the Universal Father.

Before these wise people die, they learn to turn away from their senses, knowing that the senses are enemies of the immortal soul. I will not let evil desires or emotions control the bodies of those who love me, nor will I allow wicked thoughts to enter them. I guard them, shutting out all evil, and protect them from their own lower nature. But I do not come to the wicked, the envious, or the greedy, for such people cannot grasp the mysteries of the Mind and reject me. I leave them to the demon they have created within themselves. Evil grows every day, tormenting those who indulge in it, and each wicked act adds to the suffering caused by the ones that came before it. In the end, evil destroys itself. The punishment for desire is the pain of never being satisfied."

Hermes bowed his head in gratitude to the Great Dragon, who had revealed so much to him, and asked to learn more about the ultimate fate of the human soul. Poimandres continued: "At death, the material body returns to the elements from which it came, and the divine, invisible man rises to the Eighth Sphere, the place from which he first came. Evil, however, descends to the demon's domain, while the senses, emotions, desires, and bodily passions return to the Seven Governors, who give life to the spiritual man but bring destruction to the lower man.

"Once the lower nature returns to its animal instincts, the higher self begins its journey back to reclaim its spiritual state. It ascends through the seven Rings of the Seven Governors, returning to each the powers it once borrowed. The first Ring belongs to the Moon, to which it returns the ability to wax and wane. The second Ring is ruled by Mercury, where it returns cunning, deceit, and cleverness. The third Ring belongs to Venus, receiving back lust and passion. The fourth Ring is the Sun's, which takes back ambition. The fifth Ring is governed by Mars, where rashness and boldness return. The sixth belongs to Jupiter, receiving greed and the desire for wealth. Finally, the seventh Ring is Saturn's, standing at the edge of Chaos, where falsehood and evil schemes are returned.

"When the soul has shed all it carried from the Seven Rings, it reaches the Eighth Sphere, the realm of the fixed stars. There, free from illusion, the soul dwells in Light, singing praises to the Father in a voice understood only by the pure in spirit. Know this, Hermes: the Eighth Sphere holds a great mystery, for the Milky Way is where souls are born. From it, they descend into the Rings, and to it, they return after passing through the wheels of Saturn. However, not all souls can climb the ladder of the seven Rings. Some become lost in darkness below, swept away into eternity by the illusions of the senses and the material world.

"The path to immortality is difficult, and only a few find it. The rest wait for the Great Day when the wheels of the universe will stop, and the immortal sparks will escape from the prison of matter. But those who wait are unfortunate, for they will return to the Milky Way, unaware and unknowing, to begin the cycle again. Those who follow the light of the mystery I have revealed to you, Hermes, will return to the Father in the White Light. There, they will give themselves to the Light and become one with it, transformed into Powers within God. This is the Way of Good, revealed only to the wise.

"Blessed are you, O Son of Light, for I, Poimandres, the Light of the World, have shown myself to you. Now, I command you to go forth and guide those lost in darkness, so that the spirit of My Mind—the Universal Mind—within them may awaken and be saved through My Mind within you. Establish My Mysteries, and they will remain on earth as long as the Mind endures, for the Mind of the Mysteries can never fail."

With these final words, Poimandres, radiant with celestial light, vanished, merging with the powers of the heavens. Lifting his eyes to the sky, Hermes blessed the Father of All Things and dedicated his life to the service of the Great Light.

Hermes preached: "O people of the earth, born of the elements yet carrying the spirit of the Divine Man within you, rise from your slumber of ignorance! Be alert and thoughtful. Know that your true home is not on earth but in the Light. Why have you chosen death when you have the power to share in immortality? Repent, change your ways, and turn away from darkness. Leave corruption behind and prepare to ascend through the Seven Rings to unite your soul with the eternal Light."

Some mocked him, refusing his teachings, and condemned themselves to the Second Death, from which there is no return. But others fell at Hermes' feet, begging him to show them the Way of Life. He gently lifted them, seeking no praise for himself, and with his staff in hand, he set out to teach and guide humanity, showing them the path to salvation.

Among the people, Hermes planted the seeds of wisdom and watered them with the Immortal Waters. As his life drew to a close and the light of the earthly world began to fade, Hermes instructed his disciples to guard his teachings faithfully through all ages. He committed the Vision of Poimandres to writing so that all who seek immortality could find the way within its pages.

In concluding his account of the Vision, Hermes wrote: "The sleep of the body allows the Mind to stay awake, and when I close my eyes, I can see the true Light. In my silence, life and hope begin to grow, filling it with goodness. My words are the blossoms that grow from the tree of my soul. This is the honest record of what I received from my true Mind—Poimandres, the Great Dragon, Lord of the Word— through whom God filled me with Truth. From that moment on, my Mind has remained with me, and within my soul, it gave birth to the Word. The Word is Reason, and through Reason, I have been saved. For this, I give all my praise and thanks to God, the Father—Life, Light, and Eternal Goodness—with all my soul and strength.

"Holy is God, the Father of all, who existed before the First Beginning. Holy is God, whose will is fulfilled by the Powers born from Himself. Holy is God, who has chosen to be known and is known only by those to whom He reveals Himself. Holy are You, who have established all things through Your Word, Reason. Holy are You, whose image is reflected in all of Nature. Holy are You, whom the lower nature cannot shape. Holy are You, who are stronger than all other powers. Holy are You, who surpass all greatness. Holy are You, who are beyond all praise.

"Accept these offerings of Reason from a pure soul and a heart lifted up toward You. O Unspeakable One, beyond words, You are to be praised through silence! I ask You to look upon me with mercy, that I may not stray from the knowledge of You and that I may help enlighten those who are lost in ignorance—my brothers, Your children.

"I believe in You and bear witness to You, and I leave in peace, trusting in Your Light and Life. Blessed are You, O Father! May the man You created be sanctified with You, just as You gave him the power to sanctify others through Your Word and Truth."

The Vision of Hermes, like many Hermetic writings, is an allegory that contains deep philosophical and spiritual truths. Its hidden meanings can only be fully understood by those who have been "raised" into the presence of the True Mind.

The Initiation of the Pyramid

The Great Pyramid of Giza stands as one of the most remarkable wonders of ancient times, unmatched by the works of later architects and builders. It silently bears witness to a lost civilization that fulfilled its purpose and faded into history. Its grandeur is awe-inspiring, simple yet divine, and it seems like a message carved in stone. Its enormous size makes human efforts seem small, and it serves as a symbol of eternity, standing firm against the ever-shifting sands of time. But who were the enlightened mathematicians who designed it? Who were the master builders and craftsmen who made sure every stone was perfectly placed?

The earliest and most famous account of the pyramid's construction comes from the well-known historian Herodotus. He wrote: "The pyramid was built in stages, like steps or battlements. After placing the stones for the base, workers used machines made of short wooden planks to raise the stones to each new level. The first machine lifted the stones from the ground to the first step. Another machine took the stones from there to the second step, and so on. Either they had as many machines as there were steps, or they moved one machine from tier to tier as needed. Both versions have been told, so I mention them both. The upper part of the pyramid was completed first, followed by the middle section, and finally the lowest part near the ground. Egyptian characters are inscribed on the pyramid, recording the amount of radishes, onions, and garlic consumed by the laborers during construction. I remember the interpreter telling me that the food cost 1,600 talents of silver. If this is true, imagine the enormous amount spent on tools, clothing, and food for the workers during the ten years it took to complete the work, not counting the time needed to quarry the stones and prepare the underground chambers."

While Herodotus' story is vivid, it seems likely that he created this tale to hide the true origin and purpose of the pyramid. This is one of several cases in his writings that suggest he was initiated into ancient secret knowledge and was sworn to keep it hidden. The widely accepted theory that the Great Pyramid was built as a tomb for Pharaoh Cheops is unproven. In fact, Manetho, Eratosthenes, and Diodorus Siculus all offer different accounts of who built the pyramid, with none agreeing with Herodotus—or with each other. According to the rules of pyramid construction known as the Lepsius Law, the burial chamber should have been completed at the same time as the monument, or even earlier, but in this case, it wasn't.

There is no clear evidence that the Egyptians built the Great Pyramid. Unlike other royal tombs, which are decorated with intricate carvings, inscriptions, and images, the pyramid lacks these typical elements of Egyptian art and architecture. No cartouches, paintings, or symbols of Egyptian royalty are present, except for a few simple markings in construction chambers. These markings, discovered by Howard Vyse, appear to have been made before the stones were placed since they are sometimes upside down or distorted from the fitting process. Egyptologists have tried to identify these markings as the name of Cheops, but it is hard to believe that a ruler would allow his royal name to be treated with such carelessness.

Experts are still unsure of the true meaning of these markings. Any claim that the pyramid was built during the fourth dynasty is challenged by the sea shells found at its base, which Mr. Gab suggests as evidence that the structure predates the Great Flood—a theory also supported by ancient Arabian traditions. One Arab historian claimed the pyramid was built by Egyptian sages to protect against the Flood, while another said it was the treasure house of Sheddad Ben Ad, a powerful king from before the flood. A panel of hieroglyphs above the entrance might seem like a clue to the pyramid's origin, but it was actually carved in 1843 by Dr. Lepsius as a tribute to the King of Prussia.

Caliph al-Mamoun, a distinguished descendant of the Prophet, was inspired by stories of vast treasures hidden within the Great Pyramid. In 820 A.D., he traveled from Baghdad to Cairo with a large group of workers, determined to open the ancient monument. When the Caliph first stood at the base of the "Rock of Ages" and looked up at its smooth, gleaming surface, he must have felt overwhelmed with emotion. At that time, the pyramid's original casing stones were likely still intact because he could not find any sign of an entrance—just four perfectly smooth walls in every direction. Relying on vague rumors, he ordered his men to begin digging on the north side of the pyramid, instructing them to keep cutting into the stone until they uncovered something. For the workers, armed with only simple tools and vinegar to soften the limestone, digging through a hundred feet of solid rock was an exhausting and nearly impossible task. Many times, they were ready to abandon the project, but the Caliph's command was law, and the hope of finding treasure kept them going.

Just when the workers were about to give up entirely, fate intervened. They heard the sound of a large stone falling within the wall they had been chiseling. Encouraged by the noise, they pushed forward with new energy and eventually broke through into a sloping passage that led deep into the pyramid's underground chambers. They found a massive stone barrier blocking their path, but they managed to carve their way around it. Afterward, they removed several granite blocks that kept sliding down the passage from the Queen's Chamber above. Finally, the last of the blocks stopped falling, and the way was clear for the Caliph's followers to explore.

However, there were no treasures to be found. From chamber to chamber, the workers searched frantically, but there was nothing of value anywhere. The frustration among the workers grew so intense that Caliph al-Mamoun, knowing that rebellion was near, decided to take action. He secretly sent for funds from Baghdad and had the money buried near the pyramid's entrance. The next day, he ordered the workers to dig in that spot, and their joy was overwhelming when they uncovered the hidden treasure. The workers were so impressed by what they believed to be the foresight of an ancient king, who, in their minds, had calculated their wages long ago and buried the exact amount for them to find.

Satisfied with this solution, the Caliph returned to the city of his ancestors, leaving the Great Pyramid to face the passage of time. In the ninth century, the pyramid's smooth, polished surfaces reflected the sun's rays so brilliantly that each side of the structure appeared as a glowing triangle of light. Over the years, however, nearly all the original casing stones were removed, and today, only two remain in place. Investigations later found that many of these stones had been recut and repurposed to decorate the walls of mosques and palaces throughout Cairo and the surrounding areas.

Pyramid Problems

C. Piazzi Smyth asks, "Was the Great Pyramid built before hieroglyphics were invented and before the Egyptian religion was established?" It is possible that time will reveal the upper chambers of the Pyramid as a sealed mystery even before the rise of the Egyptian empire. However, markings in the underground chamber suggest that the Romans later gained access. Based on secret Egyptian teachings, W. W. Harmon calculated that the Pyramid's first ceremonial took place 68,890 years ago, at the moment when the star Vega first cast its light down the descending passage into the pit. He estimates that the actual construction of the Pyramid took place over ten to fifteen years just before this event.

These dates may seem ridiculous to modern Egyptologists, but they are based on a detailed study of the astronomical principles incorporated into the Pyramid by its builders. If the outer casing stones were still intact in the ninth century, the erosion marks on the exterior are unlikely to have been caused by water. The theory that salt deposits inside the Pyramid are evidence of submersion is also questionable, as the type of stone used naturally releases salt over time. Although the Pyramid may have been partially submerged at some point, the evidence for this is not conclusive.

The Great Pyramid was built entirely from limestone and granite, with the two types of rock arranged in a meaningful way. The stones were cut with extreme precision, and the cement used between them is now as hard as the stones themselves. The limestone blocks were likely cut with bronze saws tipped with diamonds or other precious stones. Stone chips left from construction were piled against the north side of the plateau to help support the structure's immense weight. The Pyramid was built with perfect alignment and, astonishingly, "squares the circle." This means that if you drop a vertical line from the tip of the Pyramid to its base, that line acts as the radius of an imaginary circle. The circumference of that circle matches the total length of the four base sides of the Pyramid.

If the passageways to the King's and Queen's Chambers were sealed thousands of years before the Christian era, later initiates must have used hidden underground galleries for their rituals. Without such galleries, it would have been impossible to enter or exit the Pyramid, as the only surface entrance was sealed with casing stones. If not blocked by the Sphinx or concealed within it, the hidden entrance could be located in one of the nearby temples or on the slopes of the limestone plateau.

A notable feature of the Pyramid is the granite plugs that block the passage leading to the Queen's Chamber. Caliph al-Mamoun had to smash through these plugs to reach the upper chambers. According to Smyth, the position of the stones shows that they were set in place from above, suggesting that many workers had to leave the upper chambers after placing them. Smyth believes these workers escaped by descending through a well, dropping a ramp stone into place behind them. He also suggests that robbers might have later used this well to reach the upper chambers. The robbers broke through the ramp stone, leaving a jagged hole, as it had been set in plaster.

However, the architect Mr. Dupré offers a different theory. He argues that the well itself was made by robbers and was the first successful attempt to reach the upper chambers from the underground chamber, which was the only open area of the Pyramid at the time. Dupré points out that the well is rough and irregular, unlike the precise design of the rest of the Pyramid. The well's size also makes it unlikely that it was dug downward; it must have been carved from below, with the nearby grotto providing ventilation for the thieves. It seems unlikely that the Pyramid's builders would have left a broken ramp stone and a gaping hole in their otherwise perfect gallery. If the well is indeed a robbers' tunnel, this could explain why the Pyramid was empty when Caliph al-Mamoun entered and why the coffer lid was missing. A thorough inspection of the unfinished underground chamber—possibly the robbers' base of operations—might reveal traces of their presence or show where they stored the rubble from their digging. It remains unclear how the robbers entered the underground chamber, but it seems unlikely that they used the descending passage.

One intriguing feature in the Queen's Chamber is a niche in the north wall. Muslim guides often describe it as a shrine, but the niche's shape, with its walls sloping inward like those in the Grand Gallery, suggests it may have been intended as a passage. Attempts to explore the niche have been unsuccessful, but Dupré believes it may hide a secret entrance. If the well did not exist at the time, the workers may have exited the Pyramid through this hidden passage after placing the granite plugs in the ascending gallery.

Some Biblical scholars have offered remarkable interpretations of the Great Pyramid. They have claimed it to be Joseph's granary, even though its storage capacity is far too small to support that idea. Others have suggested it was meant to serve as the tomb for the Pharaoh from the Exodus, though his body was never recovered from the Red Sea and, therefore, couldn't have been buried there. Some even believe the pyramid stands as a lasting confirmation of the accuracy of the prophecies found in the Authorized Version of the Bible.

The Sphinx

Ignatius Donnelly suggests that the Great Pyramid follows a design from before the Great Flood, a style found in many ancient cultures around the world. In contrast, the Sphinx (Hu) is distinctly Egyptian. According to the inscription between its paws, the Sphinx is an image of the Sun God, Harmachis, carved in the likeness of the Pharaoh who ruled at the time. The Sphinx was later restored by Thutmose IV, inspired by a dream in which the god complained that the sand surrounding him caused him great discomfort. Excavators even found a broken beard of the Sphinx buried between its paws. The steps, altar, and temple between the paws were added much later, likely by the Romans, who frequently rebuilt Egyptian monuments.

The shallow indentation on the Sphinx's head, once thought to conceal a hidden passage leading to the Great Pyramid, was actually intended to support a now-missing headdress. Explorers have driven metal rods into the body of the Sphinx in an unsuccessful attempt to locate hidden chambers or tunnels. Most of the Sphinx was carved from a single stone, with only the front paws constructed from smaller stones. Measuring around 200 feet in length, 70 feet in height, and 38 feet across the shoulders, the Sphinx was carved either from native rock or from stone transported from distant quarries. Some once believed that both the Pyramid and the Sphinx were made from artificial stone formed on-site, but this idea was abandoned after studies showed that the limestone contains the remains of small sea creatures called mummulites.

The idea that the Sphinx served as the entrance to the Great Pyramid is a popular belief that has persisted, though without any real proof. P. Christian, drawing from the writings of Iamblichus, describes the theory this way: "The Sphinx of Giza marked the entrance to underground chambers where initiates faced trials. The entrance, now blocked by sand and debris, lay between the Sphinx's front legs. In ancient times, a bronze door guarded this entrance, which could only be opened by the Magi through a secret mechanism. Public respect and religious fear kept the entrance safe from intrusion. Inside the Sphinx, tunnels led to the underground chambers of the Great Pyramid, forming a maze so complex that anyone entering without a guide would inevitably circle back to where they began."

However, there is no sign of the bronze door Christian mentions, nor any evidence it ever existed. Over the centuries, the Sphinx has undergone many changes, and it is possible that any original entrance was sealed. Many believe that underground chambers still exist beneath the Great Pyramid. Robert Ballard writes, "Just as the priests of the Pyramids of Lake Moeris lived in vast underground quarters, it seems likely that the priests of Giza had similar residences. In fact, the limestone used to build the pyramids might have been excavated from these underground caverns. I am convinced that exploring beneath the Pyramid will reveal important clues about its purpose. A diamond drill capable of reaching a few hundred feet would be needed to investigate both the solidity of the Pyramid and any hidden spaces beneath it."

Ballard's theory raises an important architectural question. The Pyramid's builders were too skilled to place over five million tons of stone on anything but a solid foundation. If there are underground chambers, they must be small and well-supported, much like the chambers inside the Pyramid, which occupy only a tiny fraction of its total volume.

The Sphinx was likely created for symbolic purposes under the direction of the priesthood. Some theories suggest that the Sphinx once had a uraeus, or serpent symbol, on its forehead that served as the pointer of a giant sundial. Others believe both the Pyramid and the Sphinx were used to track time, the seasons, and the precession of the equinoxes. If the Sphinx was built to block access to a hidden passage leading to an underground temple within the Pyramid, its symbolic meaning would be fitting. However, compared to the majesty and scale of the Pyramid, the Sphinx seems relatively insignificant.

Today, the face of the Sphinx, which still shows traces of the red paint it was originally covered with, is heavily damaged. Its nose was broken off by a devout Muslim who feared it might lead people toward idol worship. The repairs now required to keep the head from collapsing suggest that the Sphinx could not have survived the same vast stretches of time as the Pyramid.

To the Egyptians, the Sphinx symbolized both strength and intelligence. Its androgynous form reflected the belief that initiates and gods contained both masculine and feminine energies. Gerald Massey explains, "This is the secret of the Sphinx. The Egyptian sphinx is male in the front and female in the back. The image of Sut-Typhon follows the same pattern, with horns and a tail—male at the front and female at the back. Pharaohs, too, wore the tail of a lioness or cow behind them, representing the union of both sexes within themselves. Like the gods, they embodied the complete dual nature of existence."

Despite its symbolic importance, many researchers have dismissed the Sphinx, choosing instead to focus on the greater mystery of the Pyramid.

The Pyramid Mysteries

The word "pyramid" is often thought to come from the Greek word pyr, meaning fire, symbolizing the divine flame that gives life to all beings. John Taylor believed the word referred to a "measure of wheat," while C. Piazzi Smyth suggested it meant "a division into ten" in Coptic. Ancient initiates saw the pyramid shape as a perfect symbol for both their hidden teachings and the institutions created to spread this wisdom. Pyramids and mounds were thought to represent the Holy Mountain, a sacred place believed to stand at the center of the earth.

John P. Lundy compared the Great Pyramid to Mount Olympus, saying its underground passages were like the winding paths of Hades.

The square base of the Pyramid symbolizes that the foundation of wisdom rests on nature's unchanging laws. Albert Pike wrote that the Gnostics built their knowledge on a square whose corners represented Silence, Profundity, Intelligence, and Truth. The four sides of the Great Pyramid align with the cardinal directions: north and south, which represent cold and heat, and east and west, which stand for light and darkness. The base also represents the four material elements from which the physical body is formed. Rising from each side is a triangle, symbolizing the divine being that dwells within all material forms. If each base line is treated as a square from which spiritual power rises, the total of the lines on the four sides (12) and the squares of the base (16) is 28, a sacred number. Adding the three sets of seven that represent the sun (21) gives 49, the square of seven, which symbolizes the universe.

The twelve zodiac signs are represented by the twelve edges of the Pyramid's four triangular faces. Within each face is one of the four creatures from the vision of Ezekiel, turning the entire structure into a representation of the Cherubim. The three main chambers of the Pyramid correspond to the heart, the brain, and the reproductive system—key spiritual centers in human beings. The Pyramid's triangular shape also mirrors the posture used in ancient meditation practices. According to the Mysteries, divine energy descended from the gods onto the Pyramid's tip, which was compared to the roots of an inverted tree, with branches spreading downward along the Pyramid's sides, radiating wisdom throughout the world.

No one knows the exact size of the Pyramid's capstone, and although many believe it once existed, it is now missing. It's common for builders of sacred structures to leave them unfinished, as a reminder that only God is complete. If the capstone did exist, it would have been a miniature pyramid, with a smaller version of itself on top, continuing infinitely. This capstone represents the entire structure in miniature. Similarly, the Pyramid can be seen as a symbol of the universe, with the capstone representing humanity. Within each person, the mind is the capstone of the body, the spirit is the capstone of the mind, and God is the final capstone of the spirit. Just as a rough stone is shaped into a perfect capstone, the Mysteries transform a person into the living apex through which divine energy flows into the world below.

W. Marsham Adams called the Great Pyramid the "House of the Hidden Places" because it symbolized the secret wisdom that predated Egyptian civilization. The Egyptians linked the Pyramid to Hermes, the god of wisdom and knowledge, also associated with the planet Mercury. Connecting Hermes with the Pyramid emphasizes that the structure was a temple dedicated to the Invisible and Supreme Deity. It was not built as a tomb, observatory, or lighthouse, but as the first temple of the Mysteries—a place that guarded the truths at the heart of all knowledge and science. The Pyramid perfectly represents the microcosm (the small world) and the macrocosm (the larger universe). According to secret teachings, it was also considered the tomb of Osiris, the black god of the Nile, who symbolizes a form of solar energy. His tomb represents the universe, where Osiris is both buried and crucified on the cross of material existence.

Through the hidden passages and chambers of the Great Pyramid, the enlightened ones of ancient times made their journey. They entered as ordinary men and emerged as gods. The Pyramid was known as the "womb of the Mysteries," a place of "second birth," where wisdom lived just as God lives within the hearts of people. Deep within its recesses dwelled a mysterious figure called "The Initiator" or "The Illustrious One." This being, dressed in blue and gold and holding the sevenfold key of Eternity, was the lion-faced teacher, the Holy One, and the Master of Masters. He never left the House of Wisdom, and no one saw him unless they had first gone through the trials of preparation and purification. It was in these sacred chambers that Plato, the philosopher with the broad brow, encountered ancient wisdom personified in the Master of the Hidden House.

Who was this Master who lived within the Pyramid, whose many chambers symbolized the worlds of the universe? Only those who had been "born again" could see him. He alone knew the deepest secrets of the Pyramid, but now he has left, and the sacred halls are empty. No longer do hymns of praise echo through the corridors. No one now passes through the elements or walks among the seven stars. The "Word of Life" is no longer given to the worthy by the lips of the Eternal One. All that remains visible to the world is an empty shell— an outer symbol of an inner truth—and people call this House of God a tomb.

The Master of the Secret House, the Sage Illuminator, revealed the techniques of the Mysteries to new initiates. He showed them how to recognize their guardian spirit and taught them how to free their spiritual essence from the physical body. At the height of their transformation, he shared the Divine Name—the secret and unspoken title of the Supreme Deity. With this knowledge, the initiate became like a pyramid within his soul, where others could find their own spiritual awakening.

In the King's Chamber, the initiate underwent the ritual of the "second death." There, after being symbolically crucified upon the cross of the solstices and equinoxes, he was placed in the great stone coffer. The King's Chamber had a strange and deathly cold that seemed to reach into the bones. This sacred space acted as a gateway between the physical world and the higher realms of Nature. While the initiate's body rested in the coffer, his soul, like a human-headed hawk, soared through the celestial realms. In these realms, he saw the truth of eternal Life, Light, and Truth and understood that Death, Darkness, and Sin were mere illusions. In this way, the Great Pyramid served as a gateway through which the ancient priests allowed a few to reach spiritual completion.

If someone strikes the coffer in the King's Chamber, the sound it makes does not match any known musical scale. This unique tone may have been part of what made the King's Chamber the ideal place to perform the highest rites of the Mysteries.

Modern science and theology know little about these ancient rituals. Scholars look at the Great Pyramid and wonder what motivated such immense labor. But if they paused to reflect, they might realize that only one thing could inspire such effort: the soul's deep desire to understand, to know the truth, and to exchange mortal limitation for divine knowledge. People today say the Great Pyramid is the most perfect building ever made, the origin of weights and measures, the first Noah's Ark, and the source of alphabets, languages, and even scales for measuring temperature and humidity. Few realize, however, that it is also a gateway to the Eternal.

Though the modern world may hold countless secrets, the ancient world held one—and that one was greater than all others. The many secrets of today lead to death, sorrow, selfishness, greed, and destruction, but the one secret of the past brings life, light, and truth. A time will come when the ancient wisdom will once again guide humanity's religious and philosophical search. The collapse of rigid dogmas is near. The "Tower of Babel," with its confusion of languages, was built from bricks of mud held together by slime. But from the ashes of dead creeds, the ancient Mysteries will rise like a phoenix. No other institution has ever fulfilled humanity's spiritual needs as completely as the Mysteries. Since their destruction, no religious system has emerged that someone like Plato could fully embrace. The development of the human spirit is as precise a science as astronomy, medicine, or law. Religion was created for this very purpose, and from it arose philosophy, science, and logic as tools to achieve this divine goal.

The Dying God will rise again! The hidden chamber in the House of Secrets will be rediscovered. The Pyramid will once more stand as a symbol of strength, renewal, aspiration, resurrection, and transformation. As one civilization after another is buried beneath the sands of time, the Pyramid will remain as a visible reminder of the eternal connection between divine wisdom and the world. One day, the ancient hymns of enlightenment will again echo through its halls. The Master of the Hidden House will wait in the Silent Place for those who, leaving behind the false ideas of dogma, seek only Truth and will not settle for anything less than the real thing.

Isis, the Virgin of the World

The study of Hermetic symbolism often begins with the figure of the Saitic Isis, a version of the goddess from the city of Sais. Her temple bore the famous inscription: "I, Isis, am all that has been, that is, or shall be; no mortal man has ever lifted my veil." According to Plutarch, some ancient authors believed Isis was the daughter of Hermes, while others thought she was the child of Prometheus. Both were known for their divine wisdom, though her connection to them may be symbolic rather than literal. Plutarch also interpreted the name Isis to mean wisdom. In Anacalypsis, Godfrey Higgins traced her name to the Hebrew word Iso and the Greek word zoo, meaning "to save." Other scholars, like Richard Payne Knight, suggested her name had Northern origins, possibly from Scandinavian or Gothic languages, where it is pronounced Isa, meaning "ice" or "frozen water."

This goddess, known by many names, represented fertility across various ancient religions. She was sometimes called the "goddess with ten thousand names" and, over time, was transformed in Christian tradition into the Virgin Mary. Although Isis was believed to have given birth to all living things—especially the sun—legend says she remained a virgin.

In The Golden Ass, Apuleius includes a description of Isis where she declares her divine attributes: "I am Nature, the mother of all things, ruler of the elements, first among the gods, queen of the dead, and leader of the celestial beings. The entire world honors me with different names and rituals. The Phrygians call me Pessinuntica, the Mother of the Gods. The Athenians name me Cecropian Minerva, the Cypriots call me Paphian Venus, and the Cretans know me as Diana.

The Sicilians worship me as Proserpine, and the Eleusinians as Ceres. Others call me Juno, Bellona, Hecate, or Rhamnusia. In Ethiopia, Egypt, and among the Arii, where the sun's light is strong, I am known by my true name: Queen Isis."

Some historians, like Le Plongeon, believe that the story of Isis has historical roots among the Mayans of Central America, where she was known as Queen Moo, and her brother-husband Osiris was represented as Prince Coh. According to this theory, Queen Moo fled to Egypt after Prince Coh's death, where she was accepted as queen and given the name Isis. However, the global presence of Isis in so many myths suggests that she was likely more of a symbolic figure than a real person.

Sextus Empiricus claims that the Trojan War was fought over a statue of the moon goddess, not for the mortal Helen, as commonly believed. Some authors have even tried to connect figures like Isis, Osiris, Typhon, and Thoth to the descendants of Noah's son, Ham. But since the story of Noah is more of a cosmic allegory about the renewal of life, it is unlikely that these Egyptian deities were ever real historical figures.

According to Robert Fludd, the sun embodies life, light, and heat—qualities that energize the three realms of existence: the spiritual, intellectual, and physical worlds. This is summarized by the phrase, "From one light, three lights," which reflects the sun's role in bringing life and vitality to the earth. Osiris, therefore, symbolizes the life-giving power of the sun, though not the sun itself. His symbol was an open eye, representing the "Great Eye" of the universe—the sun—while Isis symbolized the receptive force of Nature.

Modern science has shown that everything, from stars to atoms, follows a pattern of positive centers surrounded by negative bodies that depend on the central life force. This allegory is echoed in the story of Solomon and his many wives, where Solomon represents the sun, and his wives are the planets and moons orbiting it. In The Song of

Solomon, the dark maid of Jerusalem symbolizes Isis, representing the nurturing force of Nature that gives life after being energized by the sun.

The ancient year consisted of 360 days, with five extra days set aside as the birthdays of five gods and goddesses—Osiris being born on the first day, and Isis on the fourth. Typhon, the spirit of destruction, was born on the third day and is often represented as a crocodile or a mixture of crocodile and pig. Isis stood for wisdom, while Typhon symbolized arrogance and pride—traits that block understanding and truth.

The story continues with Osiris, symbolizing the sun, bringing knowledge to Egypt and traveling to other lands to spread enlightenment. Meanwhile, his brother Typhon plotted against him. Like the Norse trickster Loki, Typhon gathered conspirators and devised a plan to trap Osiris. He commissioned a beautifully decorated chest, perfectly sized to fit Osiris's body. During a banquet, Typhon invited the gods to lie inside the chest, promising to give it to whoever fit inside perfectly. When Osiris tried it, Typhon sealed the chest with molten lead and cast it into the Nile, where it floated out to sea. According to Plutarch, this event occurred on the seventeenth day of the month Athyr, when the sun was in Scorpio—a symbol of betrayal. This story also parallels the moment when Noah entered the ark to escape the flood.

Plutarch also says that the Pans and Satyrs, which are nature spirits and elementals, were the first to find out that Osiris had been killed. As soon as they discovered this, they raised an alarm, and from this event, we get the word "panic," which means fear or amazement felt by many people. Isis found out about her husband's death from some children who saw the killers running off with the box that held his body. She immediately dressed in mourning clothes and began her search for him.

Eventually, Isis discovered that the chest had floated to the shores of Byblos. There, it got stuck in the branches of a tree that quickly grew around it in a miraculous way. The king of that land was so amazed by the tree that he ordered it to be cut down and turned into a pillar to hold up the roof of his palace. When Isis arrived in Byblos, she was able to get her husband's body back, but Typhon stole it again. This time, he cut Osiris's body into fourteen pieces and scattered them across the earth. In despair, Isis began gathering the parts of her husband but could only find thirteen. The missing piece, the phallus, had fallen into the Nile River and been swallowed by a fish, so Isis made a replacement out of gold.

Later, Osiris's son killed Typhon in battle. Some Egyptians believed that the souls of gods went to heaven, where they became stars. They thought the soul of Isis shined from the Dog Star, while Typhon became the constellation of the Bear. However, it is unclear if this belief was widely accepted. In Egyptian art, Isis is often shown wearing a headdress shaped like the empty throne of her dead husband, which became her symbol during certain periods. The headdresses worn by Egyptians carry deep symbolic meaning, representing the spiritual energy around divine beings, much like halos and auras in Christian art. Frank C. Higgins, a well-known Masonic expert on symbols, noted that the way some Egyptian gods and pharaohs wore their headpieces at a backward tilt mirrored the tilt of the earth's axis. The clothing, jewelry, and ornaments of ancient priests symbolized the spiritual energy radiating from the human body. Modern science is starting to rediscover some of the lost knowledge from Hermetic philosophy. One of these discoveries is the ability to measure a person's mental, spiritual, and physical state by observing the streams of barely visible electric energy that flow from the surface of their skin throughout their life. (For more details on how this energy can be seen using a scientific process, see The Human Atmosphere by Dr. Walter J. Kilner.)

Isis is sometimes symbolized with the head of a cow, and in some cases, the whole animal represents her. In Norse mythology, the first gods were said to be licked out of ice blocks by a mother cow named Audhumla, who symbolized natural nourishment and fertility because of her milk. Isis is also depicted as a bird in some representations. She often holds the crux ansata, a symbol of eternal life, in one hand, and a flowered scepter representing her authority in the other.

Thoth Hermes Trismegistus, known as the founder of Egyptian knowledge and one of the wisest figures in history, passed down the ancient secrets that are still preserved today through myths and legends. These stories and symbols hide instructions for spiritual, mental, moral, and physical transformation, which is often referred to as the "Mystic Chemistry of the Soul," or alchemy. These sacred truths were shared with those initiated into the Mystery Schools but kept hidden from the general public. People who couldn't understand the deeper meaning of these teachings ended up worshiping the statues and symbols that represented these hidden truths. The wisdom and secrecy of Egypt are perfectly captured in the image of the Sphinx, which has kept its secrets safe for countless generations of seekers.

The mysteries of Hermeticism contain great spiritual truths that remain hidden from most of the world because of ignorance. The keys to these ancient teachings are all symbolized by the figure of the Virgin Isis. She is depicted veiled from head to toe, revealing her wisdom only to those who have earned the right to stand in her presence. These worthy few can uncover the hidden knowledge of nature and confront the deeper reality of the divine directly.

The descriptions of the symbols associated with the Virgin Isis in this text are mainly drawn from a free translation of the fourth book of Bibliotèque des Philosophes Hermétiques, titled "The Hermetical Signification of the Symbols and Attributes of Isis," with extra notes added by the writer to explain and clarify the ideas. Statues of Isis were decorated with images of the sun, moon, stars, and other symbols connected to the earth, which she was believed to rule as the guardian spirit of Nature itself. Many statues of the goddess have been found with their original symbols intact, showing the respect and status she held. Ancient philosophers viewed her as a symbol of Universal Nature, the source of all creation. She was often depicted as a partly nude woman, sometimes pregnant, and sometimes covered in a flowing robe, usually in green or black. In some cases, her clothing was a mix of black, white, yellow, and red.

Apuleius described her in great detail: "Her long hair flowed down her neck in soft, loose strands, and a crown made from many flowers rested on her head. In the center of this crown was a round object that looked like a mirror, or more like a bright, glowing light, representing the moon. Vipers, coiled like plowed furrows, wound around the crown on both sides, and ears of corn extended upward. Her robe, made from the finest linen, shimmered with many colors—white like light, yellow like crocus flowers, and rosy red. However, the part of her clothing that stood out most was a black robe that glittered darkly. It draped across her right side, rose over her left shoulder, and gathered at the front, looking like the center of a shield. The ends of this robe hung in graceful folds, with delicate tassels at the edges. Stars were scattered across the embroidery, and in the middle of these stars, the full moon shone brightly, radiating light like fire. A crown made of flowers and fruits of all kinds ran along the edge of the robe, moving with each graceful motion. In one hand, she held a bronze rattle called a sistrum, which made a sharp, triple sound as it shook. In the other hand, she carried a long, narrow vessel shaped like a boat, with the head of an asp rising from the handle, its neck swollen as if ready to strike. Her immortal feet were wrapped in shoes woven from palm leaves, symbolizing victory."

The green in her robe represents the plants that cover the earth, symbolizing Nature's clothing. The black color stands for death and decay, which lead to new life. This idea reflects the saying: "Unless someone is born again, they cannot see the kingdom of God" (John 3:3). The white, yellow, and red represent the three main colors used in alchemy, following the blackness that symbolizes decay and transformation. The name "Isis" was also used for one of the secret medicines of the ancient world, which shows that this description has connections to chemistry. Her black robe symbolizes the moon's dependence on the sun, as the moon has no light of its own but reflects the sun's light, energy, and life-giving power. Isis also represents the greatest achievements of ancient wisdom—like the Philosopher's Stone, the Elixir of Life, and the Universal Medicine.

Other symbols related to Isis are just as fascinating, but it's impossible to list them all since the Egyptian Hermetists often used them interchangeably. Isis is sometimes shown wearing a hat made from cypress branches, symbolizing her mourning for her dead husband, as well as the physical death that all living things must undergo to achieve new life or rebirth. At times, her head is decorated with a crown of gold or a wreath of olive leaves, which show her power as the queen of the world and ruler of the universe. The golden crown also represents the fiery energy of the sun, which gives life to all beings by maintaining the balance of the elements. This ongoing cycle of energy is symbolized by the musical sistrum she carries, which also represents purity.

A serpent woven through the olive leaves on her head, biting its own tail, symbolizes how the energy from the sun becomes tainted by earthly corruption. This energy must undergo purification through seven stages, called "planetary circulations" or "flying eagles" in alchemical terms, to restore it to its healing power. The sun's energy is seen as a kind of medicine for human illnesses. These seven stages are symbolized in different rituals, such as the seven circuits made by Masons around their lodge, the Jewish priests' seven marches around Jericho, and the Muslim priests' seven rounds around the Kaaba in Mecca. From the crown of gold rise three horns of plenty, which represent the abundance of Nature's gifts, all coming from one source—the heavens, symbolized by the head of Isis.

In this image, ancient thinkers describe the forces that sustain the three kingdoms of nature: minerals, plants, and animals (including humans). At one ear, the moon, and at the other, the sun represent two essential forces—one active, the other receptive, like father and mother. Isis, who symbolizes Nature, uses these two celestial bodies to spread her power across the realms of animals, plants, and minerals. On her neck, there are symbols of planets and zodiac signs, showing that heavenly forces influence the growth and destiny of all living things. These forces guide everything under the moon and shape smaller worlds that reflect the larger universe.

In her right hand, Isis holds a small ship with a spinning wheel as its mast. At the top of the mast is a water jug with a snake-shaped handle, full of venom. This shows that Isis guides the fragile ship of life through the storms of time. The spinning wheel represents how she spins and cuts the thread of life. These symbols also suggest that Isis brings moisture to everything in nature, protecting life from the sun's heat by keeping things hydrated with moisture from the air. Water helps plants grow, but this life-giving moisture often carries poison caused by decay. To make this moisture pure, it must encounter Nature's invisible cleansing fire. This fire refines, perfects, and re-energizes the substance, turning it into a healing power that can renew all life.

The snake sheds its skin every year, symbolizing the renewal of the spirit after material life. The earth also renews itself every spring when the sun returns to the northern lands. In her left hand, the symbolic Virgin carries a sistrum and a square cymbal, which produces the key-note of Nature (Fa) when struck. Sometimes, she also holds an olive branch, representing the harmony she brings to nature with her renewing power. Through death and decay, she brings forth new life in endless cycles. The square shape of the cymbal, rather than the usual triangle, shows that all things are transformed according to the balance of the four elements.

Dr. Sigismund Bacstrom believed that if a doctor could balance earth, fire, air, and water, and bring them together into the Philosopher's Stone, represented by a six-pointed star or two interlocking triangles, they could heal any disease. Dr. Bacstrom also believed the universal fire or spirit of Nature was present in everything: "It does all and is all." Through attraction, repulsion, movement, heat, evaporation, drying, thickening, and fixing, this spirit shapes matter and reveals itself in creation. Anyone who understands these natural laws and uses them wisely becomes a true philosopher.

From Isis's right breast, a cluster of grapes emerges, and from her left, an ear of corn or wheat, golden in color. This shows that Nature provides food for plants, animals, and people, nourishing all life. The golden color of the wheat suggests that within sunlight or spiritual gold lies the essence of life itself. Around the upper part of her body is a belt with mysterious symbols. This belt is held together at the front by four golden plates, arranged in a square, symbolizing the four elements—earth, air, fire, and water—that create everything. Stars also appear on this belt, symbolizing the influence of both sunlight and darkness. Isis is identified with the constellation Virgo, where she is depicted with a serpent under her feet and a crown of stars on her head. In her arms, she holds a sheaf of grain and, at times, the young Sun God.

The statue of Isis was placed on a pedestal made of dark stone, decorated with the heads of rams. Beneath her feet were several poisonous snakes. This shows that Nature has the power to remove harmful substances and cleanse all impurities caused by earthly decay. The rams' heads represent that the best time for life to begin is when the sun moves through Aries. The snakes under her feet symbolize Nature's ability to preserve life and cure illness by getting rid of impurities and decay.

This idea reflects the wisdom of ancient philosophers, who expressed it with these sayings:

Nature contains Nature,

Nature delights in her own nature,

Nature surpasses Nature,

Nature can only be corrected through her own nature.

Thus, when thinking about the statue of Isis, it is important to consider the deeper meanings behind the symbols. If we do not, the Virgin's message will remain a mystery.

A golden ring on her left arm holds a cord, which extends to a deep container filled with glowing coals and incense. This shows that Isis, as a symbol of Nature, carries with her the sacred fire, which was always kept burning by temple priestesses called vestal virgins. This flame represents the pure, eternal spirit of Nature—the essence of life itself. The oil that never burns away, known as the balsam of life, is often mentioned by wise thinkers and in religious texts, symbolizing the fuel that sustains this everlasting flame.

From her right arm hangs another thread, connected to a pair of scales. This represents Nature's precision in balancing all things, as she weighs and measures them perfectly. Isis is often shown as a symbol of justice, reflecting Nature's unwavering consistency. The World Virgin is sometimes depicted standing between two tall pillars, known in Freemasonry as Jachin and Boaz. These pillars represent the idea that Nature creates by balancing opposites. Isis, as a figure of wisdom, stands between these opposites, showing that true understanding is found in balance and that truth often appears hidden between conflicting ideas.

The golden shine in her dark hair represents how her power, although connected to the moon, comes from the sun's light, giving her a reddish glow. Just as the moon reflects the sun's light, Isis is portrayed like the Virgin in Revelation, bathed in the brightness of the sun. The writer Apuleius describes a vision in which he saw the goddess Isis rising from the ocean. The ancient people understood that life began in water, and modern science agrees. In Outline of History, H.G. Wells explains how early life filled the oceans, but the land above the tide was barren and lifeless. Later, he writes, "Wherever the shoreline ran, there was life, and that life existed through water, in water, and with water as its essential element."

The ancients believed that the seeds of life came from warm, moist vapor. The veiled figure of Isis symbolizes this vapor, which carries the life force from the sun, shown by the child she holds in her arms. Since the sun, moon, and stars appear to sink into the sea when they set, and the water absorbs their light, people believed the sea was the source of life's seeds. These seeds were thought to be formed through the combined influence of the celestial bodies. That is why Isis is sometimes shown as being pregnant.

The statue of Isis was often shown with a large ox that was black and white. The ox symbolized either Osiris, connected to Taurus, the bull in the zodiac, or Apis, a sacred bull linked to Osiris because of its special patterns and colors. In Egyptian culture, bulls were used for hard labor, reminding people that Nature works patiently to keep all living things healthy and alive. Alongside Isis, the figure of Harpocrates, the God of Silence, is often shown with a finger held to his mouth, signaling that the secrets of the wise must be kept from those who are not ready to understand them.

The Druids of Britain and Gaul knew much about the mysteries of Isis and worshiped her through the symbol of the moon. However, Godfrey Higgins believed it was wrong to see Isis as identical to the moon itself. Instead, the moon was used to represent her because it controls water. The Druids saw the sun as the father and the moon as the mother of all creation, and through these symbols, they honored the power of Universal Nature.

Sometimes, the figure of Isis stands for mystical and magical practices such as necromancy, spell-casting, and miracle-working. One myth tells of how Isis used her magic to make Ra, the powerful God of Eternity, reveal his secret, sacred name. This name is thought to be like the Lost Word of Masonry, which gives those who know it power over unseen and higher beings. The priests of Isis mastered these hidden forces of Nature, practicing things like hypnotism and mesmerism long before the modern world understood them.

Plutarch described what it takes to follow Isis, saying: "Just as a beard or rough clothing does not make a philosopher, neither do frequent shavings or wearing linen make someone a true follower of Isis. Only the one who listens, learns the stories of these gods properly, and seeks out the hidden meaning behind them, guided by reason and wisdom, is a true servant of this goddess."

During the Middle Ages, the troubadours of Central Europe kept the legends of Isis alive in their songs. They wrote poems about the most beautiful woman in the world, though her true identity was rarely known. She was Sophia, the Virgin of Wisdom, whom philosophers throughout history have sought to understand. Isis represents the mystery of motherhood, which ancient people saw as the greatest example of Nature's wisdom and proof of divine power. To those seeking truth today, Isis symbolizes the Great Unknown, and only those who uncover her mysteries can truly understand life, death, birth, and renewal.

Mummification of The Egyptian Dead

Servius, commenting on Virgil's Æneid, notes that "the wise Egyptians carefully embalmed their bodies and placed them in catacombs so that the soul would stay connected to the body for a long time, preventing it from wandering off too soon. On the other hand, the Romans, with the opposite goal, burned the bodies of their dead on funeral pyres, hoping the soul would quickly return to the original, universal element." (From Prichard's An Analysis of the Egyptian Mythology.)

There are no complete records revealing the Egyptians' secret beliefs about how the soul, or consciousness, was connected to the body. However, it seems likely that Pythagoras, who was initiated into the Egyptian temples, shared parts of these teachings when he introduced the idea of metempsychosis, or the soul's migration from one body to another. The common idea that Egyptians mummified their dead to preserve the body for a future physical resurrection does not align with modern understanding of their philosophy about death. In the fourth book of On Abstinence from Animal Food, Porphyry explains that the Egyptians purified the dead by removing the internal organs and placing them in a separate chest. He also shares a prayer, translated from Egyptian by Euphantus, which says:

"O sovereign Sun, and all you Gods who give life to humans, receive me and bring me to the eternal Gods to dwell with them. For I have faithfully honored the gods my parents taught me to worship during my life. I also showed respect for those who gave me life. As for other people, I have neither killed anyone nor cheated anyone of anything entrusted to me. I have committed no serious wrong. If I have done anything wrong by eating or drinking what was forbidden, the fault lies not with me but with these." (Here, the speaker points to the chest containing the organs.)

The Egyptians believed that removing the organs, which were seen as the source of cravings, purified the body by freeing it from their harmful influence.

Early Christians took their scriptures so literally that they preserved bodies by soaking them in salt water, believing this would ensure the spirit could return to a whole and intact body on the day of resurrection. They avoided embalming or removing internal organs, fearing that doing so would stop the soul from returning to the body. Instead, they buried their dead without using the Egyptians' complex mummification practices.

In Egyptian Magic, S.S.D.D. offers an interesting theory about the hidden purpose behind mummification. He writes, "It seems likely that only those who had reached a certain level of initiation were mummified. To the Egyptians, mummification prevented reincarnation, which was only required for souls that had failed the initiation tests. Those with the strength and wisdom to enter the Secret Adytum did not need to reincarnate. Their bodies were preserved as a kind of talisman or material anchor for the soul to return to earth when needed."

In its early stages, mummification was reserved for Pharaohs and members of the royal family, who were believed to share some of the qualities of Osiris, the divine king of the underworld, who was also mummified.

The Sun, A Universal Deity

Worship of the sun was one of the earliest and most natural ways people expressed their faith. Many modern religious beliefs are just more complicated versions of this simple, original idea. Early humans, recognizing the life-giving power of the sun, honored it as a representative of the Supreme Being. Albert Pike explains the origin of sun worship in Morals and Dogma by saying: "To them [early people], he [the sun] was the inner fire within all things, the fire of Nature. As the source of life, warmth, and energy, the sun was seen as the power behind all creation. Without him, there could be no movement, no life, and no shape to anything. He seemed vast, eternal, and always present. People felt a deep need for his light and creative force, and nothing frightened them more than his absence. His kindness and life-giving energy made him a symbol of Good. The BRAHMA of the Hindus, MITHRAS of the Persians, and ATHOM, AMUN, PHTHA, and OSIRIS of the Egyptians, along with the BEL of the Chaldeans, the ADONAI of the Phoenicians, and the ADONIS and APOLLO of the Greeks, were all forms of the sun. These gods represented the renewing power of life, the energy that keeps the world alive and refreshed."

Throughout ancient times, people built altars, temples, and mounds to honor the sun. Many of these sacred places still stand today, including the pyramids of Yucatan and Egypt, the snake mounds of the American Indians, the Zikkurats of Babylon and Chaldea, the round towers of Ireland, and the great stone circles in Britain and Normandy. Even the Tower of Babel, which the Bible says was built to reach God, may have actually been an observatory to study the stars.

Both pagan and early Christian priests and prophets knew a lot about astronomy and astrology. Their teachings often make more sense when viewed through the lens of these ancient sciences. As people learned more about the movements and patterns of the stars and planets, they began incorporating astronomical ideas into their religious beliefs. Gods were given homes among the stars, with different planets being named after these deities. The fixed stars were arranged into constellations, and the sun and planets were believed to travel through these constellations, along with the moons that orbited some of the planets.

The Solar Trinity

The sun, as the most important of the heavenly bodies visible to ancient astronomers, was linked to the highest gods and became a symbol of the supreme authority of the Creator Himself. From reflecting on the sun's powers and qualities, the idea of the Trinity, as we understand it today, was born. The concept of a Triune God is not unique to Christian or Jewish beliefs but appears in many of the world's great religions, both ancient and modern. The Persians, Hindus, Babylonians, and Egyptians all had their own versions of the Trinity. In each case, the Trinity represented three aspects of one Supreme Intelligence. In modern Masonry, God is represented by an equilateral triangle, with each side symbolizing one of the primary aspects of the Eternal Being, who is also shown as a small flame, called Yod (ˈ) by the Hebrews. Jakob Böhme, a German mystic, referred to the Trinity as "The Three Witnesses," saying that through these three aspects, the invisible divine becomes known in the physical world.

The idea of the Trinity is easy to understand when we observe the daily journey of the sun. Since the sun symbolizes all light, it has three distinct stages: rising, midday, and setting. Philosophers saw these phases as representing the three stages of life: growth, maturity, and decline. Between the soft light of morning and evening lies the brilliant peak of midday. God the Father, the Creator, is represented by the sunrise, and His color is blue, like the morning sky veiled in mist. God the Son, the radiant one who reveals His Father's glory to the world, is represented by the midday sun, shining brightly like a lion with golden hair. His color is yellow, and His power is eternal. God the Holy Ghost corresponds to sunset, when the sun rests briefly on the horizon, clothed in fiery red, before disappearing into the night. This symbolizes the soul's journey into darkness, only to rise again with the dawn.

For the Egyptians, the sun was a symbol of immortality because it dies each night but rises again every morning. Beyond its daily path, the sun also has an annual journey, moving through twelve sections of the sky called the zodiac, spending thirty days in each. Additionally, the sun follows a third path known as the precession of the equinoxes, slowly moving backward through the zodiac at a rate of one degree every seventy-two years.

Robert Hewitt Brown, a 32nd-degree Mason, explains the sun's yearly journey through the zodiac this way: "As the sun moves through the signs of the zodiac, it is said to take on the qualities of each sign or to triumph over it. In Taurus, the sun becomes a bull and was worshiped as Apis by the Egyptians and as Bel, Baal, or Bul by the Assyrians. In Leo, the sun becomes a lion-slayer like Hercules, and in Sagittarius, it takes the form of an archer. In Pisces, the sun appears as a fish—Dagon of the Philistines or Vishnu, the fish-god of the Hindus."

A close study of ancient religions shows that their priests served solar energy and that the highest god was often a personification of the sun. After thirty years of research into the origins of religion, Godfrey Higgins concluded that "All the gods of ancient times ultimately trace back to the solar fire, either as the god itself or as a symbol of a higher creative power."

Egyptian priests often wore lion skins during their ceremonies because the lion was a symbol of the sun. The sun is especially honored in the constellation of Leo, which it rules. At one point in history, Leo was considered the keystone of the heavens. Hercules, another solar figure, performed twelve heroic tasks, just as the sun completes twelve essential tasks during its journey through the zodiac each year. Like the Egyptian priests, Hercules wore a lion's skin as a belt. Samson, the Hebrew hero, also symbolizes the sun. His name reflects his solar nature, and his struggles with the Nubian lion and the Philistines (representing forces of darkness), as well as his feat of carrying away the gates of Gaza, all reflect aspects of the sun's journey and power.

Many ancient cultures had more than one sun god, with different gods and goddesses reflecting parts of the sun's energy. The gold decorations used by priests in various religions refer to solar energy, as do the crowns of kings. Ancient crowns often had pointed rays extending outward to resemble the sun, though later designs either bent these points inward or gathered them at the top under a globe or cross. Many ancient prophets, philosophers, and leaders carried scepters with the sun symbol at the top, surrounded by rays. All earthly kingdoms were seen as reflections of the heavenly kingdom, with the sun as the supreme ruler, the planets as his council, and all of nature as his subjects.

Many gods have been linked to the sun. The Greeks believed that Apollo, Bacchus, Dionysos, Sabazius, Hercules, Jason, Ulysses, Zeus, Uranus, and Vulcan either embodied visible or hidden aspects of the sun. In Norse mythology, Balder the Beautiful was seen as a sun god, and Odin was also connected to the sun, especially because of his single eye. In Egypt, deities like Osiris, Ra, Anubis, Hermes, and the mysterious Ammon shared similarities with the sun. Isis was considered the mother of the sun, and even Typhon, known as the Destroyer, was thought to be a form of solar energy. The Egyptian sun myth eventually centered around a mysterious god named Serapis. The Central American gods Tezcatlipoca and Quetzalcoatl, while mainly associated with the winds, were also linked to the sun.

In Freemasonry, the sun holds deep symbolic meaning. One of the sun's representations is Solomon, whose name, SOL-OM-ON, translates to "Supreme Light" in three different languages. Hiram Abiff, also known as CHiram by the Chaldeans, is another figure connected to the sun. His story, including his attack and death at the hands of the Ruffians, contains solar symbolism, which is explored further in The Hiramic Legend.

George Oliver, D.D., provides a clear example of the role the sun plays in Freemasonry's symbols and rituals in his Dictionary of Symbolical Masonry. He writes: "The sun rises in the east, and the east is where the Worshipful Master stands. Just as the sun is the source of all light and warmth, the Worshipful Master must inspire and energize the brethren in their work. For the ancient Egyptians, the sun was a symbol of divine providence."

The priests in ancient mysteries wore many symbols representing solar power. The gold sunbursts embroidered on the robes of Catholic priests today reflect this same idea, showing that the priest acts as a messenger of Sol Invictus, the Unconquered Sun.

Christianity And The Sun

For reasons they believed to be necessary, those who recorded the life of Jesus chose to portray him as a solar deity. The historical figure of Jesus faded into the background, and almost all the important events described in the four Gospels align with the movements, phases, or functions of the celestial bodies.

Among the many stories Christianity borrowed from ancient pagan traditions is the tale of the beautiful, blue-eyed Sun God. His golden hair flows over his shoulders, and he is dressed entirely in pure white.

In his arms, he holds the Lamb of God, symbolizing the spring equinox. This radiant figure is a blend of Apollo, Osiris, Orpheus, Mithras, and Bacchus, as he shares qualities with each of these pagan gods.

Greek and Egyptian philosophers divided the sun's journey through the year into four parts, each represented by a different figure. At the winter solstice, the Sun God appears as a newborn baby, having mysteriously escaped the forces of darkness trying to destroy him during winter's cold. Since the sun is weak at this time of year, it is shown with no golden rays, or hair, except for a single thin strand symbolizing the survival of light through winter's darkness. Because the sun's birth happens in Capricorn, it was often depicted as being nursed by a goat.

By the spring equinox, the Sun God becomes a beautiful youth with golden hair falling in curls over his shoulders, his light shining across all of creation, as Schiller described. During the summer solstice, the sun is shown as a strong, bearded man in the prime of life, representing the peak of nature's strength and fertility. By the autumn equinox, the sun appears as an old man with bent posture and white hair, slowly fading into the darkness of winter. These four stages mark the sun's twelve-month journey, during which it triumphantly passes through the twelve zodiac signs. In autumn, the sun enters the house of Virgo, symbolized by Delilah in the story of Samson, where its rays are cut and it loses its power. In Masonic symbolism, the harsh winter months are represented by three figures who try to destroy the God of Light and Truth.

The arrival of the sun was celebrated with joy, while its departure was a time of sorrow and mourning. This brilliant and radiant sun, the true light "which lighteth every man who cometh into the world," was seen as the ultimate benefactor, the one who brought life to everything, fed the hungry, calmed storms, and rose from death to restore life. This Supreme Spirit of love for humanity and generosity is recognized by Christianity as Christ, the Redeemer of worlds, the Only Begotten of the Father, the Word made Flesh, and the Hope of Glory.

The Birthday of The Sun

The pagans celebrated December 25th as the birth of the Solar Man. They rejoiced with feasts, processions, and offerings at temples. This marked the end of winter's darkness and the return of the sun's light to the Northern Hemisphere. It was believed that the old Sun God had destroyed the house of the Philistines (representing the forces of darkness) to make way for the new sun, born that day from the earth alongside symbolic creatures of the underworld.

An anonymous scholar from Balliol College, Oxford, explains in Mankind: Their Origin and Destiny that "The Romans also had a solar festival, celebrated with games in the circus, to honor the birth of the sun god. It took place eight days before the Kalends of January—December 25. Servius, in his commentary on the Æneid (Book 7, verse 720), mentions that the sun is considered 'new' on December 25. During the time of Leo I, some church leaders even stated that Christmas was made special less by the birth of Jesus and more by the return, or 'new birth,' of the sun." On the same day, the Romans celebrated the birth of the Invincible Sun (Natalis Solis Invicti), as shown in the Roman calendars from the reigns of Constantine and Julian. This title, 'Invictus,' was the same one the Persians gave to their god Mithra, whom they believed was born in a grotto. Christians later depicted Christ's birth in a stable in a similar way.

The same scholar also writes about the Catholic Feast of the Assumption and its link to astronomy. "Eight months after the sun god's birth, he moves into the eighth sign of the zodiac and absorbs the celestial Virgin into his light. She disappears in his glow and glory. This event, which occurs each year in mid-August, gave rise to a festival. In this festival, it is believed that the Virgin Mary leaves behind her earthly life to join her son in heaven. The ancient Roman calendar of Columella mentions the disappearance of the constellation Virgo around this time, stating that the sun enters Virgo thirteen days before the Kalends of September. The Catholic Church celebrates the

Assumption, or the reunion of the Virgin with her Son, on this date. This feast was once called the 'Passage of the Virgin,' and ancient texts like the Library of the Fathers contain descriptions of it. The Greeks and Romans also marked the disappearance of Astraea, the Virgin goddess, on the same day."

This Virgin mother, who gives birth to the Sun God, reflects the ancient Egyptian goddess Isis. An inscription on the Temple of Sais honors Isis with the words, "The fruit I have brought forth is the sun." While early pagans connected the Virgin with the moon, they also understood her as a constellation. Most ancient cultures believed she was the mother of the sun, and although the moon couldn't hold this role, the sign of Virgo could. According to Albertus Magnus, "We know that the constellation of the Virgin rose on the horizon at the moment we mark as the birth of our Lord Jesus Christ."

Some Arabian and Persian astronomers called the three stars in Orion's belt the Magi, who traveled to honor the newborn Sun God. The same author from Mankind: Their Origin and Destiny adds: "At midnight, the constellation of the Stable and the Ass, located in Cancer, rises to the meridian. The ancients called this Præsepe Jovis. Meanwhile, the northern stars forming the Bear were known as Martha and Mary or the coffin of Lazarus." These examples show how much ancient pagan symbolism was carried into Christianity, even though the deeper meanings have been lost over time. The Christian Church continues to follow many of these ancient customs, often giving shallow explanations when asked about their origins, unaware that each religion builds on the secret teachings of the one that came before it.

The Three Suns

The ancient sages believed that, just like human nature, the sun could be divided into three different forms. Mystics taught that every solar system has three suns, which reflect the three main centers of life in a person. These are known as the three lights: the spiritual sun, the intellectual or soular sun, and the material sun. In Freemasonry, these are symbolized by three candles. The spiritual sun represents the power of God the Father, the soular sun carries the life of God the Son, and the material sun is the means through which God the Holy Spirit is revealed. Mystics also divided human nature into three parts: spirit, soul, and body. The physical body is sustained by the material sun, the spirit is enlightened by the spiritual sun, and the soul is redeemed through the true light of the soular sun. The alignment of these three suns in the sky was one explanation for why planetary orbits are elliptical instead of perfectly circular.

The pagan priests viewed the solar system as a Grand Man and compared its three main centers of energy to the human body's brain, heart, and reproductive system. In the story of Jesus' Transfiguration, there are three tabernacles: the largest in the center representing the heart, and smaller ones on either side representing the brain and the generative system. The idea of three suns may also be connected to a natural phenomenon that has been observed throughout history. In the fifty-first year after Christ, three suns were seen in the sky at once, and two suns appeared in both the sixty-sixth and sixty-ninth years. William Lilly recorded twenty similar sightings between 1156 and 1648.

Hermetists believed that, just as the physical sun is the greatest benefactor of the material world, there is also a spiritual sun that provides for the invisible and divine aspects of nature—both human and universal. Paracelsus, a great philosopher, wrote: "There is an earthly sun, which gives all heat, and anyone with sight can see it; even the blind can feel its warmth. There is also an Eternal Sun, the source of all wisdom. Those with awakened spiritual senses will see this sun and know it exists, but even those who have not yet reached spiritual awareness can still feel its power through their inner sense, called Intuition."

Some Rosicrucian scholars gave special names to the three forms of the sun. They called the spiritual sun Vulcan, the soular sun Christ, and the material sun Jehovah, the Demiurge of the Jews. In this context,

Lucifer represents the intellectual mind without the guidance of the spiritual mind, making it the "false light." This false light is eventually overcome and transformed by the true light of the soul, referred to as the Second Logos or Christ. The secret process of turning the false, intellectual light into the enlightened mind of Christ is one of the core mysteries of alchemy, symbolized by the transformation of base metals into gold.

In The Secret Symbols of The Rosicrucians, Franz Hartmann describes the sun in alchemical terms as: "The symbol of Wisdom. The center of power, the heart of all things. The sun is a source of energy and a storehouse of power. Every living being contains within itself a center of life that can grow into a sun. In the heart of one who is spiritually reborn, divine power, awakened by the Light of the Logos, grows into a sun that illuminates the mind." In a note, Hartmann adds: "The physical sun is the reflection of the invisible spiritual sun. The spiritual sun is to the realm of Spirit what the physical sun is to the realm of Matter, but the material sun draws its power from the spiritual one."

Most ancient religions agreed that the physical sun was not a true source of power but acted as a reflector. The sun was sometimes shown as a shield carried by a Sun God, such as Frey, the solar deity of Scandinavia. This physical sun reflected the light of the invisible spiritual sun, which was the real source of life, light, and truth. The physical universe is receptive, meaning it displays the results of hidden causes that come from the spiritual realm. In this way, the spiritual world is the realm of causes, the material world is the realm of effects, and the intellectual or soul world serves as the bridge between the two. Christ, representing the higher intellect and soul, acts as "the Mediator," saying: "No man cometh to the Father, but by me."

Just as the sun is central to the solar system, the spirit is central to the human body. A person's organs and functions are like planets orbiting this inner sun, depending on its energy for life. The spiritual power within humans is divided into three parts, known as the threefold human spirit. All three are radiant and transcendent, and together they form the Divinity within man. The lower nature of man—his physical body, emotions, and mental faculties—reflects this inner Divinity and brings its light into the material world.

The three parts of man's lower nature are symbolized by an upright triangle, while his threefold spiritual nature is symbolized by an inverted triangle. When these two triangles come together to form a six-pointed star, they represent the unity of the spiritual and material worlds. This symbol, known as "the Star of David," "the Signet of Solomon," or "the Star of Zion," illustrates how humanity connects both Nature and Divinity.

A person's animal nature is connected to the earth, their divine nature to the heavens, and their human nature bridges the two as a mediator.

The Celestial Inhabitants of The Sun

The Rosicrucians and the Illuminati described angels, archangels, and other celestial beings as small suns, acting as centers of radiant energy surrounded by streamers of a powerful force called Vril. These streaming forces are the source of the common belief that angels have wings. Instead of physical wings, these beings have corona-like fans of light that allow them to move through the subtle, non-physical realms.

True mystics agree that angels and archangels are not shaped like humans, as they are often portrayed. Human forms would be useless in the ethereal worlds where these beings exist. Scientists have long debated whether other planets, such as Mars, Jupiter, Uranus, and Neptune, could support life. Many argue that creatures with human-like bodies could not survive in these environments. However, this view overlooks Nature's law that life always adapts to its surroundings. Ancient thinkers believed that life originated from the sun and that all living things absorb solar energy to grow and later release it as plants and animals. One idea suggested that the sun acts as a parent to the planets, with each planet connected to the sun by invisible cords that provide life and nourishment.

Some secret groups have taught that the sun is inhabited by beings whose bodies are made of radiant spiritual energy, similar to the glowing substance of the sun itself. These beings are not harmed by the sun's intense heat because their bodies are perfectly in tune with the sun's powerful vibrations. They resemble small suns, usually a bit larger than a dinner plate, though some more powerful beings are much larger. Their color matches the golden-white light of the sun, and they emit four long streamers of Vril energy that are always in motion. These beings also pulse or ripple, which causes the streamers to vibrate.

The most powerful and radiant of these beings is the Archangel Michael. All the beings that live on the sun and share his qualities are known today by Christians as "archangels" or "spirits of the light."

The Sun in Alchemical Symbology

Gold is connected to the sun and is often thought of as sunlight in solid form. When alchemical writings mention gold, they could be referring to either the physical metal or the sun, which is the source and spirit of gold. Sulfur, with its fiery nature, was also associated with the sun.

Since gold symbolized the spirit and base metals represented a person's lower nature, some alchemists were known as "miners." They were shown with tools like picks and shovels, digging through the earth in search of precious metals—symbolizing the search for noble qualities buried under materialism and ignorance. The diamond, hidden within black carbon, reflected this idea. The Illuminati used the image of a pearl inside an oyster, lying deep in the sea, to represent spiritual power. In this way, a seeker of truth became like a pearl diver, diving into the ocean of material illusion to find wisdom, which initiates called "the Pearl of Great Price."

When alchemists said that every living and non-living thing in the universe held the seeds of gold, they meant that even a grain of sand had a spiritual essence because gold represented the spirit within all things. A Rosicrucian saying explains this idea: "A seed is useless and powerless unless it is placed in its proper matrix." Franz Hartmann added to this idea, saying: "A soul cannot grow or evolve without the right kind of body, because the physical body provides the materials needed for development." (See In the Pronaos of the Temple of Wisdom.)

The goal of alchemy was not to create something from nothing but to nurture the seeds that were already present. Alchemical processes did not generate gold from scratch but instead helped the hidden seeds of gold to grow and thrive. Everything that exists has a spirit—a seed of the divine within it. Regeneration is not about placing something new where it did not exist before. Instead, it is about unfolding the divine essence already present in a person so that this inner divinity can shine like the sun and illuminate everyone it touches.

The Midnight Sun

Apuleius, describing his initiation, said: "At midnight I saw the sun shining with a splendid light." The idea of the midnight sun was part of the mysteries of alchemy. It symbolized the inner spirit within a person shining through the darkness of their physical body. It also referred to the spiritual sun in the solar system, which mystics could see just as clearly at midnight as at noon, as the material earth could not block the rays of this divine sun. Some believed that the mysterious lights illuminating the Egyptian temples during the night were reflections of the spiritual sun, gathered and projected by the magical abilities of the priests. The strange light seen ten miles underground by I-AM-THE-MAN in the Masonic allegory Etidorhpa (Aphrodite spelled backward) may also symbolize this mystical midnight sun from ancient rites.

Primitive ideas about the struggle between Good and Evil were often tied to the cycle of day and night. In the Middle Ages, black magic was practiced at night, and those who followed the Spirit of Evil were known as black magicians, while those who served the Spirit of Good were called white magicians. Black and white were linked to night and day, and many mythologies referred to the never-ending battle between light and darkness.

In Egyptian mythology, the demon Typhon was part crocodile and part hog, both animals known for their earthy, crude nature. From ancient times, living creatures have feared darkness, while only a few use it as cover for their activities—these animals were often linked with the Spirit of Evil. As a result, animals like cats, bats, toads, and owls became associated with witchcraft. In some parts of Europe, people still believe that black magicians take the form of wolves at night to roam and destroy, which led to the stories of werewolves.

Snakes, because they live underground, were also connected to the Spirit of Darkness. Since the conflict between Good and Evil revolves around the generative forces of Nature, winged serpents became symbols of the transformation of human instincts into higher, spiritual forces. The Egyptians often depicted the rays of the sun ending in human hands. Masons may find this symbolism connected to the "Paw of the Lion," a grip that symbolizes the power to raise things to life.

Solar Colors

The idea of three primary and four secondary colors is only a surface-level understanding. Since ancient times, it has been known that there are seven primary colors, not three. However, the human eye can only clearly recognize three of them. While green can be created by mixing blue and yellow, there is also a pure green that exists on its own and is not a mixture. This becomes clear when the light spectrum is broken apart using a prism. Helmholtz discovered that the secondary colors in the spectrum cannot be separated into primary colors. For example, when orange light passes through a second prism, it does not split into red and yellow; it stays orange.

Colors like blue, yellow, and red symbolize consciousness, intelligence, and force. These meanings are reflected in their therapeutic effects: blue is calming and has electrical properties, yellow is energizing and refining, and red creates heat and excitement. Minerals and plants also affect people according to their colors. For instance, yellow flowers tend to produce medicines that have effects similar to yellow light or the musical note "mi." An orange flower, associated with orange light, corresponds to musical tones like "re" or the chord of "do" and "mi."

The ancients connected the human spirit with the color blue, the mind with yellow, and the body with red. Heaven was seen as blue, the earth as yellow, and the underworld—or hell—as red. The fiery imagery of the underworld represents the nature of its intense, destructive energy. In the Greek Mysteries, red symbolized the irrational side of human nature, tied to uncontrolled passions and desires. In India, some gods—often forms of Vishnu—are shown with blue skin to represent their divine nature, beyond the physical world. In esoteric teachings, blue is considered the true, sacred color of the sun, while the sun's yellowish-orange appearance results from its rays passing through the material world, which distorts their original color.

In the early Christian Church, colors held deep symbolic meanings, and strict rules guided their use. However, since the Middle Ages, these meanings have been largely forgotten as people began to use colors carelessly. In their original symbolism, white or silver represented life, purity, joy, and light; red stood for Christ's suffering, the blood of saints, divine love, and warfare; blue symbolized the heavenly realm and spiritual contemplation; yellow or gold signified glory, fertility, and goodness; green reflected youth, growth, and prosperity; violet conveyed humility, deep love, and sorrow; and black represented death, destruction, and humiliation. Early church art even used the colors of clothing and decorations to show if a saint had been martyred and the nature of the work they did to earn sainthood.

Beyond the colors visible in the spectrum, there are many more wavelengths of color that humans cannot see—some are too low, while others are too high to register with the human eye. It is staggering to consider how little humanity understands about these hidden aspects of light and space. Just as people once explored unknown continents, in the future, they will explore these unseen realms of light, color, sound, and consciousness, using tools specifically designed for that purpose.

The Zodiac and Its Signs

It is difficult today to fully understand how deeply the study of the planets, stars, and constellations influenced the religions, philosophies, and sciences of ancient times. The Magi of Persia were called "Star Gazers" for good reason, and the Egyptians were highly regarded for their skill in calculating the movements and power of celestial bodies and how these influenced the destinies of both individuals and nations. Ancient astronomical observatories have been discovered all over the world, though modern archaeologists often do not understand the true purpose behind these structures. Although ancient astronomers did not have telescopes, they still made impressive calculations using instruments carved from granite or shaped from brass and copper. In India, similar instruments are still used today, showing a high level of accuracy. For example, the observatory in Jaipur, Rajputana, contains enormous stone sundials that remain functional. In Peking, China, there is a famous observatory with large bronze instruments, including a simple telescope made from a hollow tube without lenses.

The pagans believed the stars were living beings that could influence the fate of individuals, nations, and races. Even the early Jewish patriarchs thought that celestial bodies took part in human affairs. This belief is reflected in the Bible, such as in the Book of Judges: "They fought from heaven, even the stars in their courses fought against Sisera." The Chaldeans, Phoenicians, Egyptians, Persians, Hindus, and Chinese all had zodiacs with many similarities, and various experts credit each of these cultures with the origins of astrology and astronomy. The Central and North American Indians also developed their own understanding of the zodiac, although their signs and patterns differed in some ways from those used in the Eastern Hemisphere.

The word "zodiac" comes from the Greek word ζωδιακός (zodiakos), meaning "a circle of animals," or, as some believe, "little animals." This name was given by ancient astronomers to a band of fixed stars about sixteen degrees wide that appeared to encircle the earth. Robert Hewitt Brown, a 32nd-degree Mason, explains that the Greek word "zodiakos" comes from zo-on, which means "an animal." He also points out that the word is derived from ancient Egyptian roots: zo, meaning "life," and on, meaning "a being."

The Greeks, and later other cultures influenced by them, divided this zodiacal band into twelve sections, each one sixteen degrees wide and thirty degrees long. These sections were called the Houses of the Zodiac. The sun, during its yearly journey, passed through each of these houses in turn. Star groups within these sections were imagined to form creatures, many of which were part animal. Because of this, these star groups became known as the Constellations or Signs of the Zodiac.

A common theory about the origin of these zodiac signs suggests that shepherds, watching their flocks at night, entertained themselves by imagining the shapes of animals and birds among the stars. However, this theory seems unlikely unless the "shepherds" were actually the priest-shepherds of ancient times. It is also doubtful that the signs of the zodiac came directly from the star groups they now represent. It is more likely that the animals connected to the twelve houses are symbolic of the different qualities and strengths of the sun as it moves through each part of the zodiac.

Richard Payne Knight writes on this subject: "The symbolic meanings given to certain animals were based on specific qualities that these animals represented. These meanings were not difficult to discover, as they came naturally from the mind's way of thinking. However, the star groups named after these animals do not actually resemble them. These animals were chosen as symbols to represent certain parts of the sky, which were probably dedicated to personified qualities that the animals symbolized." (The Symbolical Language of Ancient Art and Mythology.)

Some experts believe that the zodiac originally had ten houses, or "solar mansions," instead of twelve. In ancient times, two different systems were used to measure months, years, and seasons—one based on the sun and the other on the moon. The solar year was made up of ten months, each lasting thirty-six days, plus five extra days dedicated to the gods. The lunar year had thirteen months of twenty-eight days, with one day left over. During that time, the solar zodiac was thought to have ten houses, each covering thirty-six degrees.

The first six signs in the twelve-sign zodiac were seen as favorable because the sun traveled through them while passing over the Northern Hemisphere, bringing warmth and light. The Persians believed that these six signs symbolized the 6,000 years during which Ahura-Mazda ruled the universe in peace and harmony. The remaining six signs were considered unfavorable since the sun traveled through them while in the Southern Hemisphere, bringing winter to the Greeks, Egyptians, and Persians. These six signs represented the 6,000 years of suffering and hardship caused by the Persian evil spirit, Ahriman, who tried to overthrow Ahura-Mazda.

Those who believe the zodiac originally had ten signs suggest that Libra (the Scales) was added later. They argue that Virgo and Scorpio were once a single sign that was divided to create Libra, establishing "the balance" between the northern and southern signs. (See The Rosicrucians, Their Rites and Mysteries by Hargrave Jennings.) On this subject, Isaac Myer wrote: "We think that the zodiacal constellations were originally ten, representing a great androgynous being or deity. Later, they were changed, splitting into Virgo and Scorpio, making eleven signs. From Scorpio, Libra—the Balance—was created, completing the current twelve-sign zodiac." (The Qabbalah.)

Each year, the sun completes a journey through the zodiac and returns to the same spot where it started at the spring equinox. However, the sun falls slightly behind its previous position every year. Each zodiac sign covers thirty degrees, and since the sun loses about one degree every seventy-two years, it takes around 2,160 years to move backward through one full sign. This gradual shift through all twelve signs of the zodiac takes about 25,920 years to complete, although experts sometimes disagree on the exact numbers. This backward motion is known as the precession of the equinoxes. In this long cycle, called the Great Solar or Platonic Year, each constellation takes its turn occupying the position of the spring equinox for roughly 2,160 years before giving way to the previous sign.

Throughout history, people have symbolized the sun using the constellation it occupied during the spring equinox. For nearly 2,000 years, the sun has crossed the equator in the sign of Pisces (the Two Fishes) at the spring equinox. Before that, for about 2,160 years, it crossed in Aries (the Ram). Even earlier, the equinox was in Taurus (the Bull). The bull likely became associated with this constellation because ancient people used bulls to plow their fields, and this activity took place during the time when the sun entered Taurus.

Albert Pike describes how the Persians revered Taurus and used astrological symbols to reflect this respect: "In Zoroaster's cave of initiation, the Sun and Planets were depicted above, made from gems and gold, along with the zodiac. The Sun was shown rising from behind the Bull." In the constellation Taurus, there is also a star cluster known as the "Seven Sisters," or the Pleiades, which Freemasons refer to as the Seven Stars found at the top of the Sacred Ladder.

In ancient Egypt, during the period when the spring equinox was in Taurus, the Bull Apis was considered sacred to the Sun God. The Egyptians worshiped the Sun God through the bull, believing that the god's presence filled this constellation when the sun crossed into the Northern Hemisphere. This belief gave rise to the saying that the celestial Bull "broke the egg of the year with his horns."

Sampson Arnold Mackey, in his book Mythological Astronomy of the Ancients Demonstrated, makes two interesting observations about the bull in Egyptian symbolism. Mackey suggests that the movement of the earth, known as the shifting of the poles, has changed the positions of the equator and the zodiac. He believes that, originally, the zodiac was aligned at right angles to the equator, with the sign of Cancer positioned at the north pole and Capricorn at the south pole. Mackey thinks the Orphic symbol of the serpent coiled around the egg represents the motion of the sun under these conditions. He uses examples such as the Labyrinth of Crete, the word "Abraxas," and the magic formula "abracadabra" to support his theory. About "abracadabra," Mackey writes:

"But the gradual disappearance of the Bull is cleverly remembered in the vanishing series of letters, perfectly representing an important astronomical event. For ABRACADABRA means 'The Bull, the only Bull.' When broken down, the phrase reads: Ab'r-achad-ab'ra—'Ab'r,' meaning 'the Bull,' and 'achad,' meaning 'the only.' Achad is also a name for the Sun, given to it because it shines alone—it is the only star visible when it appears. The remaining 'ab'ra' completes the phrase: 'The Bull, the only Bull.' The way the letters are repeated, with one removed at each step until none remain, is a simple yet effective way of preserving the memory of this fact. The name of Sorapis, or Serapis, given to the Bull in this ritual confirms it beyond doubt. The word 'abracadabra' disappears in eleven decreasing stages, just like in the figure. Remarkably, a serpent with eleven coils wraps around a three-headed figure, placed beside Sorapis. The eleven coils form a triangle similar to the one created by the eleven diminishing lines of the word abracadabra."

Nearly every religion shows traces of astrology. The Old Testament, shaped by Egyptian culture, contains many astrological and astronomical symbols. Most of Greek and Roman mythology can be linked to groups of stars. Some scholars believe the original twenty-two letters of the Hebrew alphabet were inspired by star patterns, with stars forming consonants and planets or celestial lights serving as vowels. These combinations spelled out words, which, if read correctly, revealed future events.

The zodiac marks the path of the sun through the constellations, creating the changes in the seasons. Ancient calendars were based on the equinoxes and solstices, with the year starting at the spring equinox on March 21, when the sun crosses the equator going north. The summer solstice, marking the sun's most northerly point, was celebrated on June 21. After that, the sun began moving back toward the equator, crossing it again at the autumn equinox on September 21. The sun reached its southernmost point on December 21, the winter solstice.

Four zodiac signs are permanently associated with the equinoxes and solstices. Although the signs no longer align perfectly with their original constellations, modern astronomers still use them for calculations. The spring equinox is linked with Aries (the Ram), a fitting choice, as the Ram leads the zodiac. Long before Christianity, pagans revered this constellation. Godfrey Higgins writes: "This constellation was called the 'Lamb of God.' It was also known as the 'Savior' and believed to save humanity from sin. It was honored with the title 'Dominus,' or 'Lord,' and was called the 'Lamb of God which taketh away the sins of the world.' Devotees would repeat the words in prayer: 'O Lamb of God, that taketh away the sin of the world, have mercy upon us. Grant us Thy peace.'" The Lamb of God refers to the sun, which is said to be reborn each year in the Northern Hemisphere when it enters Aries, though due to a shift in the zodiac, the sun now rises in Pisces.

The summer solstice is connected with Cancer (the Crab), which the Egyptians symbolized with the scarab beetle. This beetle was sacred in Egypt and represented eternal life. The crab fits the symbolism because, after passing through Cancer, the sun appears to move backward, retracing its path along the zodiac. Cancer also represents creation and birth, as it is ruled by the moon, the Mother of all life and the protector of nature's life forces. Diana, the Greek moon goddess, was known as the Mother of the World. Regarding the worship of feminine or maternal principles, Richard Payne Knight writes:

"By attracting and lifting the ocean's waters, the moon naturally seemed to rule over moisture. It was also believed to have a powerful effect on women's bodies, making it appear to govern nutrition and passive reproduction. Because of this, the moon was said to have received her nymphs—her helpers or symbolic forms—from the ocean. The moon was often symbolized by the sea crab, an animal that can shed injured limbs and regrow them. This regeneration connects the crab to the idea of life cycles, making it a fitting symbol for the maternal principle of Nature. For pagans, this maternal force was recognized as the origin of all life, and the moon became its natural home.

The autumn equinox takes place in the constellation of Libra (the Scales). At this point, the scales tip, and the sun begins its journey into winter. Libra was placed in the zodiac to represent the power of choice, allowing humans to weigh one option against another. Long ago, when the human race was still developing, people were like angels who did not know good or evil. They became aware of good and evil when the gods planted the seeds of mental awareness in them. Through their experiences, humans developed knowledge that not only restored them to their former state but also gave them unique individual intelligence. Paracelsus explained: 'The body comes from the elements, the soul from the stars, and the spirit from God. All that the mind understands comes from the stars—not the physical stars but the spiritual beings behind them.'

The winter solstice occurs in Capricorn, known as the House of Death. In winter, life in the Northern Hemisphere reaches its lowest point. Capricorn is depicted as a creature with the upper body of a goat and the tail of a fish. During this time, the sun's power is weakest, but after passing through Capricorn, the sun begins to grow stronger. In Greek mythology, it was said that Jupiter, the Sun God, was nursed by a goat. John Cole offers a different interpretation of Capricorn in A Treatise on the Circular Zodiac of Tentyra, in Egypt: 'The Goat rising from the fish symbolizes the rise of Babylon's towering buildings from the marshes. The two horns of the Goat represent the two cities, Nineveh and Babylon—one on the Tigris River and the other on the Euphrates—but both ruled by a single power.'

It takes about 2,160 years for the sun to move backward through one zodiac sign, a period known as an age. These ages are named after the sign the sun passes through at the spring equinox each year. This is why we refer to the Taurian Age, the Aryan Age, the Piscean Age, and the Aquarian Age. During each of these ages, religious worship reflects the qualities of the zodiac sign associated with it. The sun is believed to take on the personality of each sign, just as a spirit takes on a body. These twelve signs are like the jewels in the sun's breastplate, with its light shining through each one in turn.

This system helps explain why certain religious symbols appear during specific times in history. For example, during the Taurian Age, the sun was connected to Apis, the sacred bull, and the Bull became a symbol of Osiris. (For more details about how astrological ages relate to the Bible, see The Message of the Stars by Max and Augusta Foss Heindel.) During the Aryan Age, the Lamb became sacred, and priests were called shepherds. At this time, sheep and goats were sacrificed, and a scapegoat was chosen to carry away the sins of Israel.

In the Piscean Age, the Fish became the symbol of divinity. The Sun God is said to have fed the masses with two fish. In the frontispiece of Ancient Faiths by Inman, the goddess Isis is shown with a fish on her head. The Indian god Krishna, in one of his incarnations, was thrown from the mouth of a fish. Jesus is also called the Fisher of Men. John P. Lundy explains: 'The word Fish is an abbreviation for the full title, Jesus Christ, Son of God, Savior, and Cross. As St. Augustine said, "If you join together the first letters of the five Greek words, Ἰησοῦς Χριστὸς Θεοῦ Υἱὸς Σωτήρ (Jesus Christ, Son of God, Savior), they spell ΙΧΘΥΣ, which means Fish. In this word, Christ is symbolized because He was able to live in the depths of this world without sin."' (Monumental Christianity). Many Christians honor Friday, a day sacred to the Virgin (Venus), by eating fish instead of meat. The fish was one of the earliest symbols of Christianity, and when drawn in the sand, it served as a secret sign that identified one Christian to another.

Aquarius is known as the Sign of the Water Bearer, symbolized by the man carrying a jug of water mentioned in the New Testament. This figure is sometimes shown as an angelic being, thought to be androgynous, either pouring water from a vessel or carrying it on the shoulder. In some Eastern traditions, the water vessel alone is used as the symbol. Edward Upham, in History and Doctrine of Buddhism, describes Aquarius as a pot with a color between blue and yellow, calling it 'the single house of Saturn.'

When the planet Uranus was discovered by Herschel, the second half of Aquarius was assigned to it. The water flowing from Aquarius's urn is often called 'the waters of eternal life.' Like all zodiac signs, Aquarius represents one of the ways the sun shapes human worship of the divine."

There are two main systems of astrological philosophy. One is the Ptolemaic system, which is geocentric. In this view, the earth is considered the center of the solar system, with the sun, moon, and planets revolving around it. Though astronomically incorrect, the geocentric model has proven reliable when applied to the material nature of earthly things over thousands of years. A close study of the works of great occultists and their diagrams shows that many of them were familiar with another way of organizing the heavenly bodies.

The second system is called the heliocentric model, which places the sun at the center of the solar system, with the planets and their moons orbiting around it. However, since this system is relatively new, there hasn't yet been enough time to fully study or catalog how its aspects affect people and events. Geocentric astrology focuses on earthly concerns, while heliocentric astrology aims to understand higher intellectual and spiritual aspects of life.

An important detail to remember is that when ancient astrologers said the sun was in a particular zodiac sign, they meant that the sun was casting its light into that sign from the opposite one. For example, when the sun is said to be in Taurus, it is actually in the opposite sign, Scorpio, sending its rays toward Taurus. This difference led to two branches of philosophy: the geocentric, which is outward and material, and the heliocentric, which is inward and spiritual. While ordinary people worshipped the outward reflection of the sun in Taurus (symbolized by the Bull), the wise revered the sun's true position in Scorpio, represented by the Scorpion or the Serpent, symbols of hidden spiritual knowledge.

Scorpio has three symbols. The most common is the Scorpion, which the ancients called the "backbiter," symbolizing deceit and perversion. Another symbol is the Serpent, which represents wisdom. The rarest symbol is the Eagle, which reflects Scorpio's highest spiritual nature. While the stars in the Scorpio constellation resemble both a bird and a scorpion, the Eagle—known as the king of birds— symbolizes the highest potential of Scorpio, rising above the earthly nature of the scorpion. Since Taurus and Scorpio are opposite signs, their symbols are often connected. As E. M. Plunket explains in Ancient Calendars and Constellations: "The Scorpion (Scorpio) joins Mithras in his battle with the Bull, and the spirits of the spring and autumn equinoxes are always present in both joyful and sorrowful forms."

The Egyptians, Assyrians, and Babylonians, who viewed the sun as a Bull, saw the zodiac as a series of furrows plowed by a celestial Ox dragging the sun behind it. This connection explains why people offered sacrifices of bulls and paraded decorated oxen through the streets, accompanied by temple priests, musicians, and dancers. However, the wisest among them, who wore the Serpent symbol of Scorpio (the Uræus) on their foreheads, did not participate in these rituals, seeing them as more appropriate for the general population.

The sun is often shown with its rays forming a shaggy mane, connecting it to the lion. Robert Hewitt Brown, a 32nd-degree Mason, explains the link between the constellation Leo and the summer solstice: "On June 21, when the sun reaches the summer solstice, the constellation Leo, only 30 degrees ahead, seems to lead the way, helping lift the sun to the top of the zodiac's arc. This connection between Leo and the sun's return to power explains why the ancients revered this constellation. Astrologers called Leo the 'sole house of the sun,' and taught that the world was created when the sun was in this sign. Both the Egyptians and Mexicans worshipped the lion. The chief Druid of Britain even held the title of Lion." (Stellar Theology and Masonic Astronomy.)

When the Aquarian Age fully begins, the sun will be in Leo, according to the distinction between geocentric and heliocentric astrology. At that time, secret spiritual traditions will once again include initiation rites known as the "Grip of the Lion's Paw," which symbolizes raising the soul to a higher state. (This will be like the story of Lazarus rising from the dead.)

The age of the zodiac is highly debated. It is a major mistake to say that it originated only a few thousand years before the Christian Era. The zodiac must be old enough to date back to a time when the signs and symbols perfectly matched the positions of the constellations, which reflected the sun's activity throughout each of the twelve months. One author, after years of study, believed the idea of the zodiac to be at least five million years old. It is likely that the knowledge of the zodiac came from ancient civilizations like Atlantis or Lemuria. About ten thousand years before the Christian Era, a destructive period began when knowledge was suppressed, and many records, monuments, and artifacts were destroyed. Only a few relics, such as copper knives, arrowheads, and cave carvings, remain as silent proof of those lost civilizations. Some massive structures, like the mysterious monoliths on Easter Island, also serve as evidence of lost knowledge, arts, and people. Humanity is incredibly old. Modern science measures human history in tens of thousands of years, but occult teachings believe it spans millions. There is an old saying that "Mother Earth has shaken many civilizations from her back," and it is reasonable to believe that astrology and astronomy may have existed millions of years before the first white man appeared.

The ancient occultists had a profound understanding of evolution. They saw all life as existing in different stages of growth. They believed that grains of sand were evolving into human consciousness (though not in physical form), that humans were becoming planets, that planets were becoming solar systems, and that solar systems were becoming cosmic chains. Each step in this process continued endlessly. At one stage between the formation of a solar system and a cosmic chain, the solar system transforms into a zodiac. The zodiac's houses, in turn, became the thrones of twelve celestial rulers, or in some cases, ten divine orders. Pythagoras taught that the number ten, which forms the basis of the decimal system, was the most perfect number. He symbolized it with the lesser tetractys—an arrangement of ten dots forming an upright triangle.

The early astronomers divided the zodiac into twelve houses and chose the three brightest stars in each constellation to serve as rulers of each house. They further divided each house into three sections, each containing ten degrees, which were called decans. Each decan was split in half, creating seventy-two smaller sections, each covering five degrees. The Hebrews assigned a celestial spirit or angel to each of these sections, and this system led to the Qabbalistic tradition of seventy-two sacred names. These names correspond to the seventy-two decorations—such as flowers, knobs, and almonds—on the seven-branched candlestick of the Tabernacle, and to the seventy-two representatives chosen from the Twelve Tribes of Israel.

The only two zodiac signs not mentioned earlier are Gemini and Sagittarius. Gemini is usually represented by two children, who, according to ancient myths, hatched from eggs—perhaps the same eggs that the Bull broke with its horns. The myths of Castor and Pollux, along with Romulus and Remus, may have evolved from the stories of these celestial twins. The symbol of Gemini has changed over time. The Arabians once used a peacock as its symbol. Two bright stars in the constellation of Gemini still bear the names Castor and Pollux. Gemini was also associated with phallic worship, and the two pillars or obelisks found in front of temples and churches carry the same symbolism as the twins.

Sagittarius is symbolized by a centaur—a creature with the body of a horse and the upper body of a human. The centaur is typically shown holding a bow and arrow, aiming into the stars. Sagittarius represents two ideas. First, it symbolizes the spiritual development of humanity, as the human form rises from the animal body. Second, it represents ambition and aspiration, since the centaur aims its arrow high into the sky, just as humans aim for higher goals beyond their current reach.

Albert Churchward, in The Signs and Symbols of Primordial Man, explains the importance of the zodiac in religious symbolism: "The division here [is] into twelve parts—the twelve signs of the zodiac, the twelve tribes of Israel, the twelve gates of heaven mentioned in Revelation, and the twelve portals in the Great Pyramid that must be passed through to reach the highest degree. Likewise, there are twelve Apostles in Christianity and twelve original and perfect points in Masonry."

The ancients believed that the idea of man being made in God's image should be taken literally. They thought of the universe as a vast organism similar to the human body, with every part of the cosmic structure reflected in humanity. One of the most valuable lessons given to new initiates was the "law of analogy," which taught that everything in the universe mirrors aspects of human nature. Because of this belief, studying the stars was considered sacred, as the movements of the celestial bodies were seen as the active presence of the Infinite Father.

The Pythagoreans were often unfairly criticized for spreading the idea of metempsychosis, the transmigration of souls. However, the version shared with the general public was meant to hide a deeper truth. Greek mystics believed that the spiritual part of a person came into material life from the Milky Way, which they called the "seed ground of souls." This descent happened through one of the twelve gates of the zodiac. Each soul was thought to take on the qualities of the zodiac sign it entered through. For example, a soul that entered through Aries was described as being born into the nature of a ram, while one that came through Taurus would carry the qualities of the celestial bull. In this way, all human souls were symbolized by the twelve creatures of the zodiac, each representing the traits needed to incarnate in the physical world.

This belief in transmigration didn't apply to the physical body but to the immaterial spirit that journeys among the stars, evolving by taking on the forms of the sacred zodiac animals over time.

In the Third Book of the Mathesis by Julius Firmicus Maternus, we find an account of how the heavenly bodies were aligned at the beginning of the material universe: "According to Æsculapius and Anubius—who received the secrets of astrology from the god Mercury—the cosmic arrangement at the moment of creation was as follows: The Sun was placed in the 15th degree of Leo, the Moon in the 15th degree of Cancer, Saturn in the 15th degree of Capricorn, Jupiter in the 15th degree of Sagittarius, Mars in the 15th degree of Scorpio, Venus in the 15th degree of Libra, Mercury in the 15th degree of Virgo, and the Horoscope was positioned in the 15th degree of Cancer. Based on this arrangement, they believed that human destinies were aligned with these original positions, as detailed in the book by Æsculapius called Μυριογενεσις (which means 'Ten Thousand Births' or 'Countless Births'). According to this book, nothing in the destinies of individuals can conflict with the original structure of the universe."

The seven stages of human life are each guided by one of the planets. Infancy is ruled by the moon, childhood by Mercury, adolescence by Venus, maturity by the sun, middle age by Mars, old age by Jupiter, and the final stage of life—decrepitude and death—is governed by Saturn.

The Bembine Table of Isis

A manuscript by Thomas Taylor includes this interesting statement: "Plato was initiated into the 'Greater Mysteries' when he was 49 years old. His initiation happened in one of the underground chambers of the Great Pyramid in Egypt. The ISIAC TABLE served as the altar where the wise Plato stood, receiving knowledge that was always within him, but the Mysteries awakened and brought it to life. After three days in the Great Hall, Plato met the Pyramid's Hierophant, a figure only seen by those who completed the three days, three levels, and three dimensions. The Hierophant gave Plato the highest spiritual teachings, each with its own special symbol. After staying three more months in the halls of the Pyramid, Plato was sent into the world to serve the Great Order, following in the footsteps of Pythagoras and Orpheus."

Before Rome was looted in 1527, no records mentioned the Mensa Isiaca (or Tablet of Isis). At that time, a locksmith or metalworker came into possession of the Tablet and sold it at a high price to Cardinal Bembo, a famous historian and antiquarian of the Republic of Venice, who later became the librarian of St. Mark's. After Bembo's death in 1547, the Tablet ended up with the House of Mantua, where it stayed in their museum until 1630, when soldiers under Ferdinand II captured the city. Many believed the soldiers destroyed the Tablet to collect the silver it contained, but this assumption was wrong. The Tablet was taken by Cardinal Pava, who gave it to the Duke of Savoy, who later presented it to the King of Sardinia. When France conquered Italy in 1797, the Tablet was moved to Paris. In 1809, Alexandre Lenoir mentioned it in his writings, saying it was on display at the Bibliothèque Nationale. After peace was restored, the Tablet was returned to Italy. Karl Baedeker, in his Guide to Northern Italy, noted that the Tablet was placed in the middle of Gallery 2 in the Museum of Antiquities in Turin.

In 1559, Æneas Vicus of Parma made a precise replica of the original Tablet, and the Chancellor of the Duke of Bavaria gifted one of these copies to the Museum of Hieroglyphics. Athanasius Kircher described the Tablet as "five palms long and four wide." W. Wynn Westcott stated its dimensions as 50 by 30 inches. The Tablet was made of bronze, decorated with enamel and silver inlays. Fosbroke adds: "The figures are engraved shallowly, and silver threads outline most of them. The bases where the figures sit or recline, which are left blank in prints, were originally made of silver and later torn away" (see Encyclopædia of Antiquities).

Those who know the basics of Hermetic philosophy will recognize the Mensa Isiaca as a key to Chaldean, Egyptian, and Greek theology. Father Montfaucon, a knowledgeable Benedictine, admitted that he could not fully understand the Tablet's symbols. He even doubted the symbols had any real meaning and criticized Kircher for making things more confusing than the Tablet itself. Laurentius Pignorius published an essay in 1605 with a reproduction of the Tablet, but his cautious explanations showed he didn't truly grasp the meaning behind the symbols.

In 1654, Kircher tackled the mystery in his Œdipus Ægyptiacus. After years of research into ancient secret teachings, and with help from other scholars, he made significant progress in understanding the Tablet. However, the ultimate secret still eluded him, as noted by Eliphas Levi in his History of Magic. Levi wrote: "The learned Jesuit guessed that the Tablet contained the key to sacred alphabets, but he couldn't fully explain it. The Tablet is divided into three parts: at the top are the twelve houses of heaven, at the bottom are the different types of work done throughout the year, and in the middle are twenty-one sacred signs representing letters of the alphabet. At the center is a seated figure of the pantomorphic IYNX, a symbol of universal existence, similar to the Hebrew letter Yod, which all other letters evolved from. Surrounding the IYNX is the Ophite triad, matching the Three Mother Letters in Egyptian and Hebrew alphabets. To the right are the Ibimorphic and Serapian triads; to the left are the Nepthys and Hecate triads, which represent opposites such as action and rest, solid and changeable, fire that gives life, and water that creates growth. When these triads join with the center, they form groups of seven. A group of seven also lies at the center. These three groups of seven represent the complete structure of the three worlds and the original alphabet's letters, with one extra sign added, like a zero following the digits one through nine."

Levi's suggestion seems to imply that the twenty-one figures in the center of the Tablet represent the twenty-one major cards, or trumps, of the Tarot deck. If that's true, then perhaps the controversial zero card symbolizes the crown of the Supreme Mind. This crown might be shown by the hidden triad at the top of the throne in the middle of the Tablet. The first creation from this Supreme Mind could be represented by a magician or juggler, with symbols of the four lower worlds arranged on a table before him: a rod, a sword, a cup, and a coin. In this interpretation, the zero card stands apart from the others—it serves as the fourth-dimensional source from which all the other cards emerge and into which they ultimately combine. The circle or cipher on the card would support this idea since it symbolizes the higher realm that gives rise to the lower worlds, powers, and letters.

In 1887, Westcott gathered the few theories available from various scholars and published a rare book that gives the only detailed English description of the Isiac Tablet. This was the first proper English description since Humphreys translated Montfaucon's poor interpretation in 1721. While explaining why he avoided sharing what Levi seemed to believe should remain hidden, Westcott summarized his understanding of the Tablet: "Levi's diagram, which explains the Tablet's mystery, divides the Upper Region into the four seasons, each connected to three Zodiac signs. He also included the four-letter sacred name, the Tetragrammaton, linking Jod with Aquarius (also known as Canopus), He with Taurus (or Apis), Vau with Leo (or Momphta), and the final He with Typhon. This matches the Cherubic symbols: Man, Bull, Lion, and Eagle. The fourth symbol is either a Scorpion or an Eagle, depending on whether it represents good or bad intentions. In the Demotic Zodiac, a Snake takes the place of the Scorpion.

"In the Lower Region, he links the twelve simple Hebrew letters with the four parts of the horizon. See Sepher Yetzirah, chapter 5, section 1.

"The Central Region belongs to the powers of the Sun and the planets. In the middle, we see the Sun labeled as Ops, and below it lies a Solomon's Seal, positioned above a cross. This Seal is made of two overlapping triangles—one light and one dark—forming a complex symbol for Venus. Around the upright dark triangle, representing Fire, he placed the three dark planets: Venus, Mercury, and Mars. Around the inverted light triangle, representing Water, he placed the three light planets: Saturn, Luna, and Jupiter. Water, in turn, symbolizes female power, the passive principle, and figures like Binah and the Sephirotic Mother and Bride in the Kabbalah (see Mathers' The Kabbalah). Ancient planetary symbols contain a cross, a solar disc, and a crescent: Venus's symbol is a cross beneath a Sun disc; Mercury's is a disc with a crescent above and a cross below; Saturn's is a cross with its base touching the crescent's peak; and Jupiter's is a crescent connected to the left side of a cross. Each of these symbols holds deep meaning. Levi's original plate switched Serapis and Hecate but left Apis noir and Apis blanc unchanged—possibly because he associated Bes's head with Hecate.

"Having placed the twelve simple letters in the lower section, the seven double letters must align with the planetary region in the center. The great triad—A.M.S.—the three mother letters representing Air, Water, and Fire, surround the central Iynx or Yod. These are also connected to the Ophionian Triad: two Serpents and the Lion-like Sphinx. Levi's use of 'Ops' at the center refers to both the Roman goddess Ops, the spirit of the Earth, and the Greek figure Rhea or Cybele, often depicted as a goddess riding in a lion-drawn chariot. Cybele is crowned with towers and holds a key." (See The Isiac Tablet.)

In 1809, Alexandre Lenoir published an essay in French about the Tablet. While the essay is creative and original, it adds little useful information. Lenoir argued that the Tablet was either an Egyptian calendar or an astrological chart. Most writers since 1651, including Montfaucon and Lenoir, either relied heavily on Kircher's work or were strongly influenced by him. A full translation of Kircher's original article—eighty pages of 17th-century Latin—has been made for this book. The double-page illustration at the beginning of this chapter is an exact reproduction of Kircher's engraving from the Museum of Hieroglyphics. The small letters and numbers on the figures were added by Kircher to help explain his commentary and will also be used here for clarity.

Like many ancient religious and philosophical artifacts, the Bembine Table of Isis has sparked much debate. In a footnote, A. E. Waite, unable to distinguish between the true nature and the supposed origin of the Tablet, echoed J.G. Wilkinson's views. Wilkinson, another respected scholar, claimed: "The original [Table] is extremely late and can roughly be called a forgery." On the other hand, Eduard Winkelmann, a scholar of great depth, defended the Tablet's authenticity and age. A careful study of the Mensa Isiaca reveals one key fact: even if the person who made the Tablet wasn't Egyptian, they were a highly advanced initiate with deep knowledge of Hermetic philosophy."

Symbolism of The Bembine Table

This short explanation of the Bembine Table comes from Kircher's writings, with some added information from the Chaldean, Hebrew, Egyptian, and Greek mystical texts. The design of Egyptian temples was highly symbolic, with each room's layout, decorations, and tools holding deeper meanings, as seen in the hieroglyphics covering them. Next to the altar, which was usually in the center of each room, there was a pool filled with Nile water, which flowed in and out through hidden pipes. The temples also contained images of gods arranged in connected groups, along with magical inscriptions. These temples used symbols and hieroglyphics to teach new students the sacred knowledge of the priestly class.

The Tablet of Isis began as a table or altar, with symbols that priests used to teach secret knowledge. Different gods and goddesses had their own dedicated tables. The materials used for these tables varied depending on the importance of the deity. Tables for Jupiter and Apollo were made of gold, while those for Diana, Venus, and Juno were of silver. Other superior gods had marble tables, while lesser deities had tables made of wood. Tables were also crafted from metals linked to the planets associated with these gods. Just as a banquet table holds food for the body, these sacred altars held symbols that nourish a person's spiritual nature.

Kircher introduces the Tablet by saying: "It reveals the structure of the threefold world—archetypal, intellectual, and physical. The Supreme God is shown expanding from the center to the edge of a universe made of both living and non-living things, all energized by a single divine force called the Father Mind, represented by a three-part symbol. The Tablet also presents three groups of three from the Supreme One, each showing an aspect of the original three-part divinity. These groups are called the foundation of everything. The Tablet explains how divine beings assist the Father Mind in governing the universe. In the upper panel, we see the rulers of the worlds, with their fiery, airy, and physical symbols. In the lower panel, we find the Fathers of Fountains, who maintain the natural principles and laws. There are also gods of the celestial spheres and wandering spirits, shown as male and female figures facing their superior god."

The Mensa Isiaca is divided into three horizontal sections or panels, which may represent the layout of rooms where the Isiac Mysteries were taught. The middle panel is split into seven smaller sections, and the bottom panel has two gates, one on each side. The entire Tablet has forty-five important figures and many smaller symbols. These forty-five figures are arranged into fifteen groups of three, with four groups in the upper panel, seven in the middle, and four in the lower section.

Kircher describes these groups: "The figures differ in eight important ways: by their shape, position, gestures, actions, clothing, headwear, staffs, and the symbols around them—whether flowers, plants, letters, or animals." These eight ways of representing the figures' hidden powers are reminders of the eight spiritual senses that can help people understand their higher selves. Buddhists express this idea with a wheel that has eight spokes and follow the noble eightfold path to raise their consciousness. The decorative border around the three main panels is filled with symbols, including birds, animals, reptiles, humans, and mixed creatures. Some interpretations suggest this border represents the four elements, with the creatures symbolizing elemental beings. Others see the border as representing the archetypal realms, showing patterns of forms that later appear in the material world. The four flowers in the corners of the Tablet are sacred symbols because they always turn toward the sun, representing the part of human nature that seeks its Creator.

According to the Chaldeans' secret teachings, the universe is divided into four levels: archetypal, intellectual, sidereal, and elemental. Each level influences and reflects the others, with higher levels guiding lower ones, and lower levels responding to the higher. The archetypal level corresponds to the intellect of the Divine Trinity. In this eternal and spiritual realm, all lower forms of life—everything that exists, has existed, or will exist—are contained as original patterns or divine ideas. These archetypes are shown in the Tablet as a series of hidden symbols.

In the center section of the Table is the Spiritual Essence—a being that contains all forms and serves as the source of everything. From this essence come nine groups of energies, each forming a triad: the Ophionic, Ibimorphous, and Nephtæan Triads. This idea is like the Qabbalistic concept of the Sephiroth, where nine spheres emerge from Kether, the Crown. The twelve cosmic rulers—the Mendesian, Ammonian, Momphtæan, and Omphtæan Triads—are responsible for spreading creative forces and are shown in the upper section of the Table. These rulers act according to divine patterns formed in the highest sphere, where the archetypes reside. Archetypes are abstract forms in the Divine Mind that guide the actions of all lower beings.

In the lower part of the Table are the Father Fountains—four triads called the Horæan, Pandochæan, Thaustic, and Æluristic. These beings guard the great gates of the universe, ensuring that the influences from the higher rulers flow properly into the lower worlds. Egyptian teachings emphasize that goodness is the foundation of everything, present to some degree in all things. Everything strives for goodness because it is the source of all causes. Goodness spreads itself naturally, existing in all things, since nothing can give what it does not have. The Table shows that God exists within everything and that everything exists within God; it suggests that all parts are connected, and each reflects the whole. In the intellectual world, there are spiritual versions of everything found in the physical world, so the lowest things reflect the highest, and physical forms reveal spiritual truths. For this reason, Egyptians made images of material things to symbolize higher, invisible powers. They assigned the qualities of eternal gods to these material images to show that the physical world is just a reflection of divine reality. Everything in the hidden, spiritual realm becomes visible through nature.

The Archetypal and Creative Mind first expresses itself through the Paternal Foundation, and then through secondary gods called Intelligences. It spreads its power from the highest realms to the lowest in a continuous flow. Egyptians used the symbol of sperm to represent the spiritual spheres because each contains all the life that comes from it. Both the Chaldeans and Egyptians believed that every effect remains connected to its cause and constantly seeks to return to it, just as a lotus flower turns toward the sun. Through the Paternal Foundation, the Supreme Intellect created light first—the angelic world. From that light came the stars, and from the stars came the four elements and the physical world. In this way, everything exists within everything else, according to its nature. Physical elements are connected to the stars, just as the stars are connected to angels, and angels to God. Therefore, everything exists within the divine world, the angelic world, and the physical world all at once. Just as a seed contains a tree waiting to grow, the universe is God unfolding into physical form.

Proclus explains: "Every divine quality flows into all of creation and shares itself with all lower beings." One way the Supreme Mind expresses itself is through the power of reproduction, which it grants to all living things. Each being—whether a soul, a heavenly body, a plant, or a stone—reproduces according to its type, but all depend on the one creative power in the Supreme Mind. This life-giving force takes different forms depending on what it flows through. In minerals, it becomes physical existence; in plants, it creates life; and in animals, it produces awareness. It gives motion to the stars, thought to humans, intelligence to angels, and essence to God. All forms share the same substance, and all life draws from the same energy, existing together within the Supreme One.

Plato first introduced these ideas, and his student Aristotle explained them this way: "We believe this physical world is a reflection of another, greater world. If this world is alive, then the higher one must be even more alive. Beyond the stars, there are other heavens, more brilliant and immense than these, and they are not separated by space like the heavens we know. These higher realms are spiritual, not physical. There is also a kind of earth there, not made of lifeless matter, but filled with living creatures and natural things, just like here, but of a better kind. There are plants, rivers, and animals, but all of them are nobler than the ones we know. There is air full of eternal life. Although the life there is similar to ours, it is greater because it is unchanging, intellectual, and eternal. If someone asks how such things can exist without physical bodies, the answer is that they exist in a pure state, created directly by the First Cause without taking on material form. They are like mind and soul—they do not experience decay or destruction. Everything there is full of energy, strength, and joy, living a perfect life, all coming from one source and sharing the same nature. These beings are like perfect scents, sounds, colors, and tastes, each keeping its true form without mixing or corrupting each other. Unlike physical beings, they are simple and do not multiply but remain exactly as they are."

At the center of the Table is a large, covered throne with a seated female figure representing Isis, referred to here as the Pantomorphic IYNX. G.R.S. Mead defines the IYNX as "a transmitting intelligence," while others see it as a symbol of Universal Being. Above the goddess's head, the throne is topped with a triple crown, symbolizing the Triune Divinity—the three-part God known by the Egyptians as the Supreme Mind. This divine triad is described in the Sepher ha Zohar as "hidden and unknowable." In Qabbalism, the Tree of the Sephiroth is divided into two parts: the invisible upper part with three aspects and the visible lower part with seven. The three invisible Sephiroth are Kether (the Crown), Chochmah (Wisdom), and Binah (Understanding). These higher aspects are too abstract for humans to understand, but the seven lower spheres can be grasped by human thought. The seven triads in the central panel of the Table represent these lower Sephiroth, all coming from the hidden triple crown above the throne.

Kircher explains: "The throne shows how the three-part Supreme Mind spreads through the three worlds. From these three unseen realms comes the physical universe, which Plutarch called the 'House of Horns' and the Egyptians called the 'Great Gate of the Gods.' The top of the throne is surrounded by serpent-shaped flames, symbolizing that the Supreme Mind is full of eternal life and light, untouched by the physical world. The Table illustrates how the Divine Fire of the Supreme Mind reaches all creatures through the force of Nature, symbolized by the World Virgin, Isis, called here the IYNX, or the Universal Idea containing all forms." Plato used the word Idea to describe eternal forms that exist without matter. These immaterial forms serve as the patterns that the divine power used to shape the physical world.

Kircher describes the 21 figures in the central panel as seven key triads, each linked to a higher world. These triads originate from the invisible flame of the triple crown. The first is the Ophionic or IYNX Triad, which belongs to the fiery, intellectual realm called Aetherium. Zoroaster described this realm as ruled by strict forces. The second, called the Ibimorphous Triad, relates to the ethereal world of moisture. The third, the Nephtæan Triad, governs fertility. These three triads represent the intellectual and ethereal worlds connected to the Father Foundation.

The remaining four triads belong to the material worlds. Two of these triads relate to the heavens: the Osiris-Isis Triad, symbolized by two bulls (representing the Sun and Moon), and another pair of heavenly rulers. The other two triads are connected to the sublunary and underground realms: the Hecatine Triad and the Serapæan Triad. These complete the seven worlds governed by the Genii—the spiritual powers that rule the natural universe. Psellus quotes Zoroaster, saying: "The Egyptians and Chaldeans taught that there are seven physical worlds, governed by spiritual powers. The first is pure fire; the next three are ethereal; the final three are material. The last, called the terrestrial world, lies beneath the Moon and is full of darkness." Together with the invisible crown, these make up the eight worlds.

Plato believed that philosophers needed to understand how the seven circles under the first circle were arranged, according to the Egyptians. The first triad, connected to fire, represents life. The second triad, related to water, is ruled by the Ibimorphous gods. The third, linked to air, is governed by Nephta. From fire, the heavens were formed; from water, the earth; and air served as the mediator between them. The Sepher Yetzirah teaches that these three elements give rise to the seven directions: height, depth, east, west, north, south, and the Holy Temple at the center. The Holy Temple, shown as the great throne of Nature's spirit at the center of the Tablet, is the home of the seven powers that rule the world.

Psellus writes: "The Egyptians worshipped a triad of faith, truth, and love, along with seven fountains. The Sun, as the fountain of matter, rules over all; other fountains include those of the archangels, the senses, judgment, lightning, reflection, and mysterious characters." The Egyptians connected these fountains with specific planets. The Sun represents the solar world, the Moon governs the archangelic world, and Saturn rules the world of the senses. Jupiter is linked to judgment, Mars to lightning, Venus to reflection, and Mercury to the world of symbols. All of these meanings are reflected in the figures of the central panel of the Tablet.

The upper panel of the Table features the twelve signs of the zodiac, arranged into four groups of three. In each group, the central figure represents one of the four fixed zodiac signs: Aquarius (S), Taurus (Z), Leo (C), and Scorpio (G). These signs are known as the Fathers. In the secret teachings of the Far East, these four figures—the man, the bull, the lion, and the eagle—are called the winged globes or the four Maharajahs, who stand at the four corners of creation. The four cardinal signs—Capricorn (P), Aries (X), Cancer (B), and Libra (F)—are referred to as the Powers. The four mutable signs—Pisces (V), Gemini (A), Virgo (E), and Sagittarius (H)—are called the Minds of the Four Lords. This arrangement explains the meaning behind the winged globes in Egyptian symbolism. The four central figures

(Aquarius, Taurus, Leo, and Scorpio, known as the Cherubim by Ezekiel) represent the globes, while the cardinal and mutable signs on either side form the wings. Thus, the twelve zodiac signs can be symbolized as four globes, each with two wings.

The Egyptians also depicted the celestial triads as a globe (the Father) with a serpent (the Mind) and wings (the Power) extending from it. These twelve forces shape the world and give rise to the microcosm, which represents both the twelve sacred animals in the universe and the twelve parts of the human body. In an anatomical sense, the twelve figures in the upper panel can represent the twelve convolutions of the brain, while the twelve figures in the lower panel correspond to the zodiacal organs and members of the body. Each part of the human body is controlled by one of the twelve zodiac signs, demonstrating that humans are formed from these twelve sacred animals.

There is also a deeper meaning behind the relationship between the twelve figures in the upper and lower panels. This connection reveals one of the most hidden ancient secrets: the relationship between two zodiacs—the fixed zodiac and the movable zodiac. The fixed zodiac is described as a massive dodecahedron, with its twelve surfaces representing the outer boundaries of abstract space. From each surface, a great spiritual power flows inward, becoming one of the celestial hierarchies of the movable zodiac, which consists of stars that appear to move in the sky. Inside the movable zodiac, planetary and elemental bodies are located. The connection between these two zodiacs is reflected in the human respiratory system: the fixed zodiac represents the atmosphere, the movable zodiac represents the lungs, and the subzodiacal spheres correspond to the body. The energies of the twelve divine powers of the fixed zodiac are "inhaled" by the cosmic lungs (the movable zodiac) and distributed throughout the material universe. The cycle is completed when the lower world's negative energies are "exhaled" into the fixed zodiac, where they are purified by the divine nature of the twelve celestial hierarchies.

The Table can be interpreted in many ways. If the border of the Table is seen as the source of spiritual energy, then the throne in the center represents the physical body, with human nature seated on it. In this view, the entire Table symbolizes the aura around a person, with the border representing the outer shell of the auric field. If the throne symbolizes the spiritual realm, the border represents the elements, and the surrounding panels depict the different worlds or planes that come from the divine source. If the Table is viewed in physical terms, the throne represents the reproductive system, and the Table reveals the process of creation in the material world. From a physiological perspective, the central throne corresponds to the heart, the Ibimorphous Triad symbolizes the mind, the Nephtæan Triad represents the reproductive system, and the surrounding symbols represent the organs and body parts.

From an evolutionary perspective, the central gate represents both the entrance and exit point of existence. It also illustrates the process of initiation, where a person, after passing through various trials, reaches the presence of their own soul, which only they can fully understand. If we interpret the Table in terms of cosmogony, the central panel represents the spiritual realms, the upper panel symbolizes the intellectual worlds, and the lower panel corresponds to the physical worlds. The central panel can also represent the nine invisible worlds, with the figure labeled "I" representing physical nature—the footstool of Isis, the Spirit of Universal Life.

In alchemical terms, the central panel holds the metals, while the border represents the alchemical processes. The figure seated on the throne is the Universal Mercury, also called the "stone of the wise." The flaming canopy above the throne symbolizes Divine Sulfur, and the cube beneath it represents elemental salt.

The three triads in the central panel, also known as the Paternal Foundation, represent the Silent Watchers—the three hidden aspects of human nature. The two panels on either side symbolize the four lower aspects of human nature. There are 21 figures in the central panel, a number sacred to the sun, which consists of three primary powers, each with seven attributes. By Qabbalistic reduction, 21 becomes 3, symbolizing the Great Triad.

It is likely that the Table of Isis is connected to Egyptian Gnosticism. A Gnostic papyrus in the Bodleian Library refers to twelve Fathers, beneath whom are twelve Fountains (see Egyptian Magic by S.S.D.D.). The lower panel of the Table represents the underworld, emphasized by two gates: the great gate of the East and the great gate of the West. According to Chaldean theology, the sun rises and sets through these gates in the underworld, where it travels during the night. Plato, who studied for thirteen years under the Magi Patheneith, Ochoaps, Sechtnouphis, and Etymon of Sebbennithis, infused his philosophy with Egyptian and Chaldean teachings about triads. The Bembine Table visually represents Platonic philosophy, summarizing ancient teachings about the creation and structure of the universe. The best guide to understanding the Table is Commentaries on the Theology of Plato by Proclus. Additionally, many references to these principles can be found in the Chaldean Oracles of Zoroaster.

Hesiod's Theogony offers the most detailed account of the Greek creation myth. The Orphic version of the creation story has influenced many philosophies and religions, including Greek, Egyptian, and Syrian traditions. A key symbol in Orphic mythology is the cosmic egg, from which Phanes emerged into the light. Thomas Taylor explains that the Orphic egg corresponds to the mixture of limit and the limitless, as described by Plato in Philebus. Additionally, the egg is the third Intelligible Triad and represents the auric body of the Demiurge, or the creator god, who shapes the lower universe.

Eusebius, citing Porphyry, states that the Egyptians believed in a single intellectual creator of the world, whom they called Cneph. They depicted him as a figure with dark blue skin, holding a girdle and a scepter, wearing a crown with a feather, and shown with an egg emerging from his mouth. (See An Analysis of the Egyptian Mythology.) Although the Bembine Table is rectangular, it symbolizes the Orphic egg of the universe and everything within it. In esoteric teachings, the highest spiritual goal is to break the Orphic egg, which represents the spirit's return to Nirvana—the absolute state described by Eastern mystics.

In The New Pantheon, Samuel Boyse includes three illustrations of different parts of the Bembine Table. However, his work does not provide any significant new insights. In The Mythology and Fables of the Ancients Explained from History, the Abbé Banier discusses the Mensa Isiaca in detail. After examining the interpretations of Montfaucon, Kircher, and Pignorius, Banier concludes: "I believe it was a votive table, dedicated to Isis by a prince or private individual in gratitude for a favor they thought she granted them."

Wonders of Antiquity

It was common for the ancient Egyptians, Greeks, and Romans to place lit lamps inside the tombs of their dead as offerings to the God of Death. Some believed that these lamps would help the deceased find their way through the afterlife. Over time, this tradition grew, and instead of only using real lamps, people began placing small terracotta models of lamps in the tombs. Some of these lamps were protected inside circular containers, and there are reports of finding the original oil perfectly preserved after more than 2,000 years. Evidence shows that many of these lamps were still burning when the tombs were sealed, and some claimed they were still burning when the tombs were opened centuries later.

The idea that ancient priests could create lamps with fuel that renewed itself as it burned caused much debate among medieval scholars. Some believed these lamps could burn for centuries, though only a few suggested they could burn forever. W. Wynn Westcott noted that more than 150 writers had discussed this topic, while H.P. Blavatsky counted 173. Some argued that the so-called everlasting lamps were tricks used by clever pagan priests, but many others believed the lamps were real. Some even thought the Devil himself created these lamps to deceive people and lead them astray from true faith.

Athanasius Kircher, a respected Jesuit scholar, offered different opinions on these lamps. In his book Œdipus Ægyptiacus, he suggested: "Not a few of these ever-burning lamps were the work of devils... All the lamps found in the tombs of pagans were placed there as part of false worship, not because they could burn forever, but likely because the Devil set them there to encourage belief in a false religion." Though Kircher acknowledged that some trusted scholars accepted the existence of these lamps, he later dismissed the whole idea as impossible, comparing it to myths about perpetual motion and the Philosopher's Stone. However, he also presented another theory: "In Egypt, there are large deposits of asphalt and petroleum. What if these priests connected underground oil reserves to lamps with asbestos wicks through hidden pipes? How could such lamps not seem to burn forever?" Kircher believed this explained the mystery behind the so-called eternal lamps.

Montfaucon, in his Antiquities, agreed with Kircher's later conclusion. He thought that the stories of perpetual lamps in temples were based on clever mechanical tricks. He also noted that when some tombs were opened, smoke-like fumes sometimes escaped, making it seem as though something had been burning inside. When explorers later found lamps scattered on the ground, they assumed these were the source of the fumes.

There are many interesting stories about the discovery of ever-burning lamps in different parts of the world. One such tale comes from a tomb along the Appian Way, opened during the papacy of Paul III. Inside the sealed vault, explorers found a lamp still burning after nearly 1,600 years. According to a report by someone present at the time, the body of a young girl with long golden hair was found floating in a mysterious clear liquid, perfectly preserved, as if she had just died. The vault contained many objects, including several lamps, and one of these lamps was still lit. However, when the door was opened, the draft blew out the flame, and the lamp could not be relit.

Kircher included an inscription in his work, supposedly found in the tomb: "TULLIOLAE FILIAE MEAE" ("To my daughter Tulliola"). However, Montfaucon argued that this inscription never existed and added that, although there was no solid evidence, many believed the body found in the tomb belonged to Tulliola, the daughter of Cicero.

Ever-burning lamps have been discovered in many places across the world. Records from regions like the Mediterranean, India, Tibet, China, and South America tell of lamps that kept burning without needing any fuel. The following examples are selected from various discoveries made over the years.

Plutarch described a lamp that burned over the door of a temple to Jupiter Ammon, and the priests claimed it had remained alight for centuries without fuel. St. Augustine also mentioned a perpetual lamp in an Egyptian temple dedicated to Venus. He said that neither wind nor water could extinguish it, though he believed it was the work of the Devil. During the reign of Emperor Justinian, a lamp was discovered in Edessa or Antioch. It was placed in a niche above the city gate and protected from the weather. The date on the lamp showed that it had been burning for over 500 years before soldiers destroyed it.

In the early Middle Ages, a lamp was found in England that had been burning since the third century AD. The tomb it was found in was thought to belong to the father of Constantine the Great. Another example, the Lantern of Pallas, was discovered near Rome in 1401. It was found in the tomb of Pallas, the son of Evander, who was mentioned in Virgil's Æneid. The lamp, placed near the head of the body, had burned steadily for more than 2,000 years. In 1550, a marble vault was opened on the island of Nesis in the Bay of Naples. Inside, a lamp was still burning, though it had been placed there before the start of the Christian era.

Pausanias wrote about a beautiful golden lamp in the temple of Minerva that burned for an entire year without needing more fuel or even having the wick trimmed. Every year, they held a ceremony to refill the lamp, which also served as a way to mark the passage of time. According to the Fama Fraternitatis, when the tomb of Christian Rosencreutz was opened 120 years after his death, it was brightly lit by a perpetual lamp hanging from the ceiling.

Numa Pompilius, an ancient King of Rome and a powerful magician, was said to have caused an eternal light to burn in the dome of a temple he built in honor of a nature spirit. Another story tells of a mysterious tomb found in England with an automaton that moved when certain floor stones were stepped on. Since the Rosicrucian debate was popular at the time, many believed this tomb belonged to a Rosicrucian initiate. A farmer stumbled upon the tomb, which was brightly lit by a lamp hanging from the ceiling. As the farmer moved, his weight pressed the floor stones, triggering a mechanical figure in heavy armor. The figure stood, struck the lamp with an iron baton, and destroyed it, ensuring that the secret of the lamp's flame would never be discovered. How long the lamp had burned is unknown, but it was believed to have been many years.

There are also accounts of lights found in sealed tombs near Memphis and in Brahmin temples in India. However, these lights extinguished as soon as they were exposed to air, and their fuel evaporated. It is now believed that the wicks of these lamps were made from woven asbestos, which alchemists called "salamander's wool." The fuel was likely a product of alchemical experiments. Kircher once tried to extract oil from asbestos, believing that since asbestos was fireproof, the oil would provide an indestructible fuel. After two years of failed experiments, he concluded that the task was impossible.

Several ancient formulas for making the fuel of these lamps still exist. H.P. Blavatsky reprinted two of these recipes in Isis Unveiled from older works by Tritenheim and Bartolomeo Korndorf. One of these formulas will help give a basic understanding of the process:

"Sulphur. Burnt alum, 4 ounces; turn them into flowers until reduced to 2 ounces. To this, add 1 ounce of powdered Venetian borax. Pour highly purified spirit of wine over the mixture and let it soak. Then remove the liquid and pour in fresh spirit. Repeat this process until the sulphur melts like wax on a hot brass plate, without producing any smoke. This will serve as the fuel.

Now, prepare the wick in the following way: Gather fibers or threads of asbestos until you have a bundle as thick as your middle finger and as long as your little finger. Place these fibers in a Venetian glass, covering them with the purified sulphur mixture you prepared earlier. Set the glass in hot sand for twenty-four hours, keeping the heat high enough for the sulphur to bubble the entire time.

Once the wick is fully coated with the sulphur mixture, place it in a glass shaped like a scallop shell, making sure part of the wick stays above the surface of the prepared sulphur. Set the glass back on the hot sand and melt the sulphur until it grips the wick firmly. When you light this lamp, it will burn with a steady, never-ending flame. You can place this lamp anywhere you like, and it will continue to burn without going out."

The Greek Oracles

The worship of Apollo included the creation and upkeep of places where the gods could communicate with people and reveal the future to those worthy of such knowledge. Many ancient Greek stories tell of talking trees, rivers, statues, and caves inhabited by spirits like nymphs, dryads, or demons, who gave prophetic messages from these places. Some Christian writers claimed that these prophecies were tricks from the Devil to mislead people. However, they could not deny the reality of oracles since their own sacred texts referenced similar events. If the glowing onyx stones on the high priest's robe in Israel could show the will of Jehovah, then it was possible that a black dove, temporarily given the ability to speak, could deliver oracles in the temple of Jupiter Ammon. Similarly, if the witch of Endor could summon the spirit of Samuel to give Saul a prophecy, then a priestess of Apollo could call upon her god to predict Greece's future.

Among the most well-known ancient oracles were those of Delphi, Dodona, Trophonius, and Latona. The oracle of Dodona, with its talking oak trees, was the oldest. While the origins of oracular prophecy remain unclear, it is known that many caves and openings used as oracles were considered sacred even before Greek civilization developed.

The oracle of Apollo at Delphi is one of the ancient world's enduring mysteries. Alexander Wilder believed that the name Delphi came from delphos, meaning "womb," chosen because the cave and its vent resembled a womb. The original name of the oracle was Pytho, which came from the legend of the serpent Python. According to the story, the serpent emerged from the slime left behind by a great flood that wiped out humanity, except for Deucalion and Pyrrha. Apollo climbed Mount Parnassus, fought the serpent, and threw its body into the cave. From that point on, the Sun God, also known as the Pythian Apollo, gave prophecies from the cave. Apollo shared the honor of being Delphi's patron god with Dionysus.

Though defeated, the spirit of Python remained at Delphi to serve Apollo. The fumes rising from the cave were believed to come from Python's decaying body, and the priestess, known as the Pythoness or Pythia, inhaled these fumes to connect with Apollo. The Greeks believed Delphi was the navel of the world, symbolizing that the Earth was like a living being, and the connection between oracles and the navel held deep meaning in the ancient Mysteries.

The origin of the oracle is likely much older than the story of Apollo and Python suggests. The priests may have created this tale to explain the oracle's power to people they did not think deserved the real, hidden truth. Some say a priest from Hyperborea discovered the Delphic cave, but records show that the cave had been considered sacred for as long as history remembers. People traveled from all over Greece and nearby regions to ask the spirit inside the cave for guidance. The priests and priestesses guarded the cave closely, serving the spirit that gave prophecies to humanity.

The story of the oracle's discovery goes like this: Shepherds tending their flocks on Mount Parnassus noticed that their goats acted strangely when they wandered near a large crack on the mountain's side. The goats jumped and made odd noises unlike anything heard before. Curious, one shepherd approached the vent, which released strange fumes. As soon as he inhaled the vapors, he was overcome with a wild, prophetic excitement. He danced, sang, mumbled strange words, and began predicting future events. Others who approached the vent had the same experience. The fame of the place spread, and people came from far and wide to breathe the fumes and glimpse the future.

Some visitors could not control themselves, and, with the strength of madmen, broke free from those trying to hold them back. Many jumped into the vent and died. To prevent further accidents, a wall was built around the opening, and a prophetess was appointed to communicate with the oracle on behalf of those seeking answers. According to later stories, a golden tripod carved with images of Apollo as the serpent Python was placed over the vent. A specially designed seat was set on the tripod to help keep the priestess steady while she inhaled the vapors, preventing her from falling during her trance. Around this time, the story began to spread that the fumes came from the decaying body of Python, possibly revealed by the oracle itself.

In the beginning, young virgin maidens were chosen to serve the oracle. They were called Phœbades or Pythiæ and became part of the famous Pythian priesthood. It is likely that women were selected because their emotional and sensitive nature made them more responsive to the "fumes of enthusiasm." Three days before giving a prophecy, the priestess underwent a purification ritual. She bathed in the Castalian well, fasted, and drank only from the sacred Cassotis fountain, whose water was brought into the temple through hidden pipes. Before sitting on the tripod, she also chewed leaves from a sacred bay tree.

Some claim the water she drank was drugged to induce visions, or that the priests knew how to produce a gas that caused an intoxicating effect, which they channeled into the cave through underground pipes. However, neither theory has been proven, nor do they explain the remarkable accuracy of the oracle's predictions.

When the young prophetess completed her purification, she was dressed in sacred clothing and led to the tripod, where she sat surrounded by the fumes rising from the open fissure. As she inhaled the vapors, her behavior changed dramatically, as if another spirit had taken over her body. She began to struggle, tear at her clothes, and cry out in strange sounds. After a time, she grew calm, and an air of majesty seemed to come over her. Sitting stiffly with her eyes focused on a distant point, she began to deliver her prophecy. These prophecies were often spoken in hexameter verse, though the words were sometimes confusing or difficult to understand. Every movement she made and every sound she uttered was carefully recorded by five holy men, called the Hosii, who were lifelong scribes selected from the descendants of Deucalion.

Once the prophecy was given, the spirit left her, and the priestess began to struggle again. She was then carried to a room where she could rest until the intense state passed.

In his essay The Mysteries, Iamblichus explained how the spirit of the oracle—thought to be a fiery demon or Apollo himself—took control of the priestess: "Whether the prophetess receives the god's message through fiery vapors rising from the cave, or whether she becomes sacred to the god by sitting on the tripod, she fully surrenders to the divine spirit and is filled with the god's presence. When fire rises from the cave and surrounds her, she becomes illuminated by its brilliance. Sitting on the seat of the god, she aligns with his stable prophetic power. Through these two steps, she becomes entirely possessed by the god, who then speaks through her."

One of the most famous visitors to the Delphic oracle was Apollonius of Tyana, accompanied by his student Damis. After making offerings, Apollonius was crowned with a laurel wreath and given a branch of laurel to carry. He passed behind the statue of Apollo at the entrance of the cave and entered the sacred space. The priestess, also wearing a laurel crown with her head wrapped in white wool, gave him a prophecy. Apollonius asked if his name would be remembered by future generations. The priestess said it would, but it would be spoken of with slander. Angered by her words, Apollonius left the cave. However, time proved the prophecy true, as early Christian writers labeled him the Antichrist. (For more on this story, see Histoire de la Magie.)

The priestess's messages were passed on to philosophers of the oracle, whose job was to interpret their meaning. These interpretations were then given to poets, who translated the messages into beautiful odes and songs, making them accessible to the public.

Snakes were an important part of the Delphic oracle. The base of the priestess's tripod was formed from the twisted bodies of three large serpents. Some sources say the young priestesses were made to stare into the eyes of a snake to enter a trance-like state, allowing them to speak with the god's voice.

In the early days, the Pythian priestesses were always young maidens, often in their teens. However, after a series of assaults on these young women, a new rule was made that only women over fifty could serve as the mouthpieces of the oracle. These older women dressed as young girls and followed the same rituals as the first priestesses.

Originally, the oracle gave prophecies only every seventh year on Apollo's birthday. But as more people came seeking answers, the priestess began delivering prophecies once a month. The exact times and questions for these consultations were decided by lottery or by a vote among the people of Delphi.

The influence of the Delphic oracle on Greek culture was immense. As James Gardner explained: "The oracle's words exposed many tyrants and predicted their downfall. It saved many lives and guided countless people along the right path. The oracle promoted useful institutions and encouraged progress. It supported moral virtue and helped advance civil liberty." (See The Faiths of the World.)

The oracle of Dodona was overseen by Jupiter, who gave prophecies through oak trees, birds, and brass vases. Many writers have noted the similarities between the rituals at Dodona and those of the Druid priests in Britain and Gaul. The famous oracular dove of Dodona would perch on the branches of the sacred oaks. There, it not only spoke in Greek about philosophy and religion but also answered questions from people who had traveled long distances to consult the oracle.

The "talking" trees stood together in a sacred grove. When the priests needed answers to important questions, they would undergo solemn purification rituals before entering the grove. There, they called upon the god believed to dwell within the trees. After the priests asked their questions, the trees responded with human voices, giving the answers they sought. Some say that only one tree, an oak or beech at the center of the grove, spoke. Since Jupiter was believed to reside within this tree, he was sometimes called Phegonæus, meaning "the one who lives in a beech tree."

One of the most fascinating parts of the Dodona oracle was the use of "talking" vases or kettles made of brass. These were so well-designed that, once struck, they would continue to ring for hours. Some accounts describe a row of these vases, which would vibrate in unison if one were struck, creating a loud, overwhelming noise. Other sources mention a large vase placed on a pillar, with a second column nearby holding a statue of a child with a whip. The whip had several cords tipped with small metal balls. As the wind blew through the open building, the balls would strike the vase, creating sound. The priests carefully listened to the number and strength of the impacts and interpreted the vibrations to deliver prophecies.

When the original priests of Dodona, called the Selloi, mysteriously disappeared, three priestesses took over the oracle's duties. These women interpreted the sounds from the vases and consulted the sacred trees at midnight. Visitors seeking the oracle's wisdom were required to bring offerings and make donations.

Another well-known oracle was the Cave of Trophonius, located on the side of a hill with an entrance so small that it seemed impossible for anyone to fit through it. After making an offering at the statue of Trophonius and putting on sacred clothing, the visitor climbed the hill to the cave, carrying a cake of honey. Sitting at the edge of the opening, the visitor lowered their feet into the cave. Suddenly, they were pulled entirely into the cavern, which those who entered described as being about the size of a large oven. After the oracle's message was delivered, the visitor was ejected from the cave, usually in a delirious state, with their feet coming out first.

Near the cave were two fountains that bubbled from the earth just a few feet apart. Those about to enter the cave drank from these fountains, each of which had unique properties. The first fountain contained the Water of Forgetfulness, which caused anyone who drank it to forget their earthly troubles. The second fountain held the sacred Water of Remembrance, known as the water of Mnemosyne. This water helped those who drank it remember the visions and experiences they had while inside the cave.

Though the entrance to the cave was marked by two brass obelisks, the cave itself, hidden behind a wall of white stones and surrounded by a grove of sacred trees, did not look particularly impressive. However, there is no doubt that those who entered the cave had strange and intense experiences. After leaving the cave, visitors were required to write down everything they saw and heard during their time in the oracle. The prophecies came in the form of dreams and visions, often accompanied by severe headaches. Some people never fully recovered from the effects of the delirium they experienced.

The priests interpreted the visitors' disjointed descriptions of their visions according to the specific question that had been asked. It is likely that the priests used some type of unknown herb to trigger the dreams or visions, but their ability to interpret these experiences was so precise it seemed almost supernatural. Before anyone could consult the oracle, they had to offer a ram as a sacrifice to the spirit of the cave. Using a form of divination called hieromancy, the priests determined whether the sacrifice was acceptable and if the time chosen for the consultation was favorable.

The Seven Wonders of The World

Many sculptors and architects of the ancient world were initiates of the Mysteries, especially the Eleusinian rites. From the beginning of time, those who worked with stone and wood have belonged to a sacred order guided by divine inspiration. As civilization spread, cities were built and abandoned, monuments were raised to heroes now forgotten, and temples were constructed for gods whose broken statues lie buried in the ruins of the nations they once inspired. Research shows that the builders and sculptors of these ancient structures were not just skilled craftsmen but masters of their art, unmatched by anyone today. The advanced knowledge of mathematics and astronomy found in ancient architecture, along with the detailed understanding of anatomy displayed in Greek statues, proves that these artisans were brilliant minds, deeply educated in the secret wisdom of the Mysteries. This tradition led to the formation of the Guild of Builders, ancestors of the modern Freemasons. When building palaces, temples, or tombs, or crafting statues for the wealthy, these initiated artists embedded the secret teachings within their work. Even now, long after their bones have turned to dust, it is clear that these early craftsmen were worthy of the honors given to Master Masons.

The Seven Wonders of the World, though seemingly built for different purposes, were actually monuments designed to preserve the secrets of the Mysteries. Each was a symbolic structure placed in a specific location, and only those initiated into the Mysteries could fully understand their meaning. Eliphas Levi pointed out a connection between the Seven Wonders and the seven planets. These wonders were built by those known as Widow's sons in honor of the seven planetary spirits. Their symbolism is connected to the seven seals in the Book of Revelation and the seven churches of Asia.

1. The Colossus of Rhodes was a massive bronze statue, about 109 feet tall, and it took more than twelve years to complete. It was created by an initiated artist named Chares of Lindus. For centuries, people believed that the statue stood with one foot on each side of the harbor entrance, allowing ships to pass between its legs, though this theory has never been proven. Unfortunately, the statue stood for only 56 years before an earthquake destroyed it in 224 B.C. Its broken pieces lay scattered on the ground for over 900 years until they were sold to a Jewish merchant, who transported the metal on 700 camels. Some say the bronze was turned into weapons, while others believe it was used for drainage pipes. The statue, with its crown of sun rays and raised torch, symbolized the Sun Man of the Mysteries—the Universal Savior.

2. The architect Ctesiphon proposed a plan to the Ionian cities in the fifth century B.C. to build a monument in honor of the goddess Diana. Ephesus, a city south of Smyrna, was chosen as the site. The temple was made of marble, and its roof rested on 127 columns, each 60 feet tall and weighing more than 150 tons. The temple was

destroyed in 356 B.C. by an act of black magic, though the blame was placed on a man named Herostratus, who was believed to be mentally disturbed. Although the temple was rebuilt, its original meaning was lost. The first temple was designed as a miniature version of the universe and dedicated to the moon, which represents the cycle of creation.

3. After being exiled from Athens, Phidias, the greatest Greek sculptor, went to Olympia in the province of Elis, where he created a colossal statue of Zeus, the king of the Greek gods. No detailed description of this masterpiece remains, though a few old coins provide some idea of how it looked. The statue's body was covered in ivory, and its robes were made of beaten gold. Zeus was said to hold a globe with a figure of the Goddess of Victory in one hand and a scepter with an eagle perched on top in the other. His head, crowned with an olive wreath, was bearded and archaic. The statue sat on a beautifully decorated throne. This monument was dedicated to the planet Jupiter, one of the seven great spirits who serve the Sun.

4. Eliphas Levi lists the Temple of Solomon as one of the Seven Wonders of the World, taking the place of the Pharos, or Lighthouse, of Alexandria. The Pharos was named after the island it stood on and was designed by Sostratus of Cnidus during the reign of Ptolemy (283-247 B.C.). It was made of white marble and stood over 600 feet tall. Even in ancient times, its construction cost nearly a million dollars. Fires were lit at its top to guide ships at sea, and the light could be seen from miles away. An earthquake destroyed the lighthouse in the thirteenth century, though remnants of it were still visible until 1350 A.D. As the tallest of the Seven Wonders, it was associated with Saturn, the Father of the gods, symbolizing enlightenment for all humanity.

5. The Mausoleum at Halicarnassus was a grand structure built by Queen Artemisia in honor of her deceased husband, King Mausolus, whose name inspired the modern word "mausoleum." The building's design came from Satyrus and Pythis, and four renowned sculptors decorated the monument. It measured 114 feet in length and 92 feet in

width and was divided into five main sections, representing the five human senses. At the top was a pyramid, symbolizing the spiritual side of humanity. The pyramid rose in 24 steps—a sacred number—and a statue of King Mausolus riding a chariot stood at its peak, with the figure measuring 9 feet 9½ inches in height. Although many attempts have been made to rebuild the mausoleum after it was destroyed by an earthquake, none have been fully successful. The monument was dedicated to the planet Mars and built by an initiate to spread wisdom to the world.

6. The Hanging Gardens of Babylon, also known as the Gardens of Semiramis, were located within the palace grounds of King Nebuchadnezzar, near the Euphrates River. These gardens were constructed in a series of terraces that formed a pyramid, with a water reservoir at the top to irrigate the plants. Built around 600 B.C., the name of the designer has been lost to history. The gardens symbolized the different planes of the unseen world and were dedicated to Venus, the goddess of love and beauty.

7. The Great Pyramid was the most important of all the temples connected to the Mysteries. Its astronomical symbolism suggests it may have been built as far back as 70,000 years ago. It served as the tomb of Osiris and was believed to have been constructed by the gods themselves. The architect is thought to have been the immortal Hermes. The Great Pyramid symbolizes Mercury, the messenger of the gods, and it stands as a universal symbol of wisdom and knowledge.

The Life and Philosophy of Pythagoras

While Mnesarchus, the father of Pythagoras, was visiting the city of Delphi on business, he and his wife, Parthenis, decided to ask the oracle whether it was safe for them to sail back to Syria. However, when the prophetess of Apollo sat on the golden tripod above the vent of the oracle, she didn't answer their question. Instead, she told Mnesarchus that his wife was expecting a son who would surpass all others in beauty and wisdom and greatly benefit humanity throughout his life. Mnesarchus was so moved by this prophecy that he changed his wife's name to Pythasis to honor the Pythian priestess. When the baby was born in Sidon, just as the oracle had predicted, they named him Pythagoras, believing he was destined for greatness.

Many strange stories surround Pythagoras's birth. Some say he wasn't just an ordinary human but a god in human form, sent to guide and teach humanity. Like other sages and saviors, his birth was said to be miraculous. Godfrey Higgins, in his Anacalypsis, draws parallels between Pythagoras and Jesus, noting that both were born in Syria— Pythagoras in Sidon and Jesus in Bethlehem. Both fathers were given prophecies about their sons being future benefactors to humanity. Both mothers were away from home when they gave birth: Mary had traveled to Bethlehem, and Pythagoras's parents had journeyed to Sidon for business. Higgins also notes that Pythasis, like Mary, had a spiritual encounter—hers was with a spirit of Apollo, who told her husband not to touch her during her pregnancy. Because of these similarities, Pythagoras was called a "son of God" and believed to be divinely inspired.

Pythagoras, one of the most influential philosophers, was born sometime between 600 and 590 B.C. He lived nearly 100 years, dedicating his life to the pursuit of wisdom. His teachings show that he was well-versed in both Eastern and Western esoteric traditions. Pythagoras traveled widely, learning from Jewish teachers about the secret traditions of Moses. The Essenes later focused on interpreting Pythagorean symbols. He was initiated into the Mysteries of Egypt, Babylon, and Chaldea. Although some say he studied under Zoroaster, it's uncertain whether his teacher was the same figure revered by the Parsees. Historians agree, however, that Pythagoras traveled extensively and studied with many masters.

After mastering the teachings of Greek philosophers and likely being initiated into the Eleusinian Mysteries, Pythagoras traveled to Egypt, where he faced many challenges before finally being initiated into the Mysteries of Isis by the priests of Thebes. From there, he journeyed to Phoenicia and Syria, where he was initiated into the Mysteries of Adonis. He then traveled to the Euphrates Valley to learn the secret knowledge of the Chaldeans near Babylon. His most important journey was to India, where he studied with the Brahmins of Elephanta and Ellora. According to Ancient Freemasonry by Frank C. Higgins, Pythagoras is still remembered in Brahmin records as Yavancharya, the Ionian Teacher.

Pythagoras is credited with being the first person to call himself a philosopher. Before him, wise men referred to themselves as sages, meaning "those who know." However, Pythagoras preferred the more humble term "philosopher," meaning "one who seeks wisdom."

When he returned from his travels, Pythagoras established a school in Crotona, a Dorian colony in southern Italy. Although people were initially suspicious of him, he soon earned the respect of leaders from neighboring colonies, who sought his advice on important matters. He gathered a small group of devoted students and taught them the secret knowledge he had gained, as well as the basics of occult mathematics, music, and astronomy—disciplines he believed formed the foundation of all arts and sciences.

At around sixty years old, Pythagoras married one of his disciples, a brilliant woman who gave him seven children. She not only inspired him during his life but also continued spreading his teachings after his death.

Like many great thinkers, Pythagoras's outspokenness earned him both political and personal enemies. One man, angry after being denied initiation into Pythagoras's school, sought revenge. He spread false information about Pythagoras, turning public opinion against him. Without warning, a group of attackers stormed the community where Pythagoras and his students lived, burning the buildings and killing the philosopher.

The stories about the death of Pythagoras differ. Some say he was killed along with his followers, while others claim that after escaping from Crotona with a small group, he and his disciples were trapped in a house that was later set on fire by his enemies. In one version, when the disciples realized they were trapped inside the burning building, they threw themselves into the flames, forming a bridge with their bodies so Pythagoras could escape. However, he is said to have died soon after, heartbroken over the failure of his efforts to enlighten humanity.

After his death, his disciples tried to keep his teachings alive, but they faced constant persecution. Today, only a little remains to honor the greatness of this philosopher. It is said that Pythagoras's followers never referred to him by name, instead calling him "The Master" or "That Man." This could be because the name Pythagoras was believed to contain a special arrangement of letters with sacred meaning. In The Word magazine, T. R. Prater wrote that Pythagoras initiated his students using a formula hidden within the letters of his name, which might explain why it was held in such high regard.

After Pythagoras's death, his school gradually fell apart, but those who had benefited from his teachings continued to honor his memory just as they had respected him during his life. Over time, Pythagoras was seen not just as a man but as a divine figure, and his scattered followers were united by their admiration for his extraordinary wisdom. In Pythagoras and the Delphic Mysteries, Edouard Schure tells a story that shows the strong bond among Pythagoras's disciples:

"One of the disciples fell ill and became poor. A kind innkeeper took care of him, and before the disciple died, he drew a mysterious symbol—most likely a pentagram—on the door of the inn. He told the innkeeper, 'Do not worry, one of my brothers will come to pay my debt.' A year later, a stranger passing by noticed the sign on the door. He told the innkeeper, 'I am a Pythagorean. One of my brothers died here. Tell me what I owe you for his debt.'"

Frank C. Higgins, in Ancient Freemasonry, gives a helpful summary of the teachings of Pythagoras:

"Pythagoras's teachings are of the greatest importance to Freemasons. His ideas reflect the combined wisdom of the leading philosophers of the ancient world and represent knowledge that everyone could agree on, free from controversy. His firm belief in the unity of God supports the idea that the supreme secret of ancient initiations was the oneness of God. The Pythagorean school functioned like a series of initiations. Students had to pass through several stages, and they were not allowed to meet Pythagoras in person until they reached the higher levels. According to his biographers, there were three degrees of initiation. The first was 'Mathematicus,' where students learned mathematics and geometry—subjects that formed the foundation of all knowledge. The second degree was 'Theoreticus,' which focused on practical applications of science. The third and final degree was 'Electus,' where students were fully illuminated and ready to absorb the deepest wisdom.

Students at the Pythagorean school were divided into two groups: the 'exoterici,' or those in the outer grades, and the 'esoterici,' who had passed the third degree and were entrusted with the secret teachings. Silence, secrecy, and absolute obedience were the core principles of this great order."

Coelum Philosophorum

Paracelsus

Part I.

Concerning The Nature And Proper- Ties of Mercury

All things are hidden within everything. One thing among them acts as the container for the rest—their physical, visible, and moveable vessel. This vessel reveals all processes of melting or liquefying. It is a living, physical spirit, and when it holds something solid or frozen inside it, those things become restless, wanting to escape. There is no proper name for this process of liquefaction, nor for where it originates. Since no natural heat can match it, it is compared to the fire of Gehenna. This kind of liquefaction is entirely different from those caused by ordinary heat or solidified by cold. Such weak transformations have no effect on Mercury, who rejects them altogether.

From this, we understand that earthly elements, in their destructive processes, cannot add to or take away from celestial powers, which are known as Quintessence or its elements. These higher forces are beyond the influence of earthly elements and cannot be controlled by them. Celestial and infernal forces do not obey the four basic elements—dry, moist, hot, or cold. None of these elements can act against a Quintessence. Each higher power holds its own abilities and operates independently, without needing to rely on the elements.

Concerning The Nature and Proper- Ties of Jupiter

Within what is visible—specifically, the body of Jupiter—the other six physical metals are spiritually hidden, though each one is concealed with varying degrees of depth and strength. Jupiter does not contain any Quintessence in its makeup but consists of the four basic elements. Because of this, it melts under moderate heat and solidifies under moderate cold. Jupiter has a natural connection with the melting processes of all other metals. The more it resembles another metal, the easier it is for them to join together. Similar things interact more smoothly and naturally than those that are very different. Something distant will not affect or influence something else strongly. Similarly, distant things are neither feared nor desired, no matter how powerful they might be.

This explains why people do not strive to reach higher realms of creation—they seem too far away, and their greatness is beyond human understanding. Likewise, lower realms are not feared, since people are distant from them and unaware of the suffering they contain. Because of this, spirits from the underworld are considered insignificant. The farther away something is, the less valuable it appears, while things close to us are given more importance. Each thing changes based on its place, becoming better or transforming according to where it belongs, as shown by many examples.

Jupiter is farther away from Mars and Venus but closer to the Sun (Sol) and Moon (Luna). Because of this, Jupiter contains more qualities similar to gold and silver. The closer it is to Sol and Luna, the more beautiful, powerful, visible, and valuable it becomes—far more so than a distant object. On the other hand, the farther something is, the less value it seems to hold, and things nearby are always favored over distant ones. As something nearby becomes clearer, what is farther away becomes hidden. As an alchemist, you must seriously consider how you can move Jupiter to a distant place occupied by Sol and Luna and bring Sol and Luna closer to where Jupiter is now. The goal is to have Sol and Luna present before your eyes in their full physical forms, just as Jupiter is.

There are practical methods for changing metals from imperfection to perfection. First, mix the metals together. Then, separate the pure parts from the impure. This process is simply one of transformation, carefully guided by proper alchemical work. Take note that Jupiter contains a significant amount of gold and some silver. If you combine it with Saturn and Luna, Luna will increase in its presence and strength.

Concerning Mars and His Properties

The six hidden metals have cast out the seventh, making it solid and giving it little power while making it heavy and hard. In doing so, they have transferred their own hardness and ability to solidify into this new body. However, they have kept their color, ability to melt, and noble qualities for themselves.

It is difficult and takes great effort to turn an ordinary man into a prince or king. But Mars, with a strong and aggressive nature, takes control and seizes the throne. Even so, he must stay alert, guarding against unexpected traps that could capture him off-guard. It is also important to consider how Mars can rise to power and take the place of the king, while Sol, Luna, and Saturn take over the role that Mars once held.

Concerning Venus and Its Properties

The other six metals have transformed Venus into an external body by giving it their color and melting properties. To fully understand this, we should use some examples to show how something obvious can become hidden, and how something hidden can be made physically visible through the use of fire. Anything that can burn can naturally change its form through fire, turning into lime, soot, ash, glass, colors, stone, or earth. This earth can, in turn, be reshaped into new metallic bodies.

If a metal is burned or weakened by rust, it can regain its flexibility and strength through the careful application of fire.

Concerning The Nature And Proper- Ties op Saturn

Saturn speaks of himself in this way: "The other six metals have cast me out as their examiner. They have pushed me away from their spiritual state and given me a physical, perishable body as my dwelling, making me into something they are not and have no desire to become. My six brothers are spiritual in nature, and whenever I am placed in the fire, they enter my body and are destroyed along with me—except for Sol and Luna. These two are purified and made more noble by my waters. My spirit is like water, softening the rigid and frozen bodies of my brothers. However, my body is drawn toward the earth, and anything that enters into me takes on the same nature, becoming part of a single unified body through us.

It would do the world little good to know, or even believe, what lies hidden within me and what I am capable of achieving. It would be more valuable for the world to discover what I can do with myself. By abandoning the complex methods of the alchemists and focusing only on what I possess within me, people could find what I am truly able to accomplish. Within me lies the cold stone, a type of water that causes the spirits of the six metals to freeze together, creating the essence of the seventh metal. This process supports the transformation of Sol and Luna."

There are two types of antimony. One is the common black variety, which purifies Sol when it is melted within it. This black antimony has the closest connection to Saturn. The second type is white and is also known as magnesia or bismuth. It shares a strong connection with Jupiter, and when mixed with the black antimony, it increases the power of Luna.

Concerning Luna And The Properties Thereof

The attempt to transform Luna into Saturn or Mars is no easier than turning Mercury, Jupiter, Mars, Venus, or Saturn into Luna with great success. It is not useful to change something perfect into something imperfect; instead, the goal is to transform the imperfect into the perfect. Still, it is important to understand what Luna is made of and where it originates. Anyone who cannot figure this out will not be able to create Luna.

So, what exactly is Luna? It is one of the seven metals, standing as the seventh. It exists externally as a physical, material substance, but within it, the other six metals are spiritually hidden. These six spiritual metals cannot exist on their own without a physical metal to contain them. Similarly, a physical metal cannot exist without these six spiritual elements. All seven metals can mix easily when melted together, but this kind of mixture is not enough to create Sol or Luna. Even when combined, each metal retains its own nature—either remaining stable in the fire or being burned away by it.

For example, if you mix Mercury, Jupiter, Saturn, Mars, Venus, Sol, and Luna into a single mass, the result will not be a transformation of the other metals into Sol or Luna. Even though they all melt together, each keeps its own essence. This is how physical mixtures work. However, when it comes to the spiritual mixture and unity of metals, it is important to understand that no separation or destruction of the spirit is truly possible. Spiritual elements cannot exist without physical bodies. Even if a body is destroyed and transformed a hundred times, the spirit within will always gain a new, more noble form. This process is the transformation of metals from one level to another—moving from a lesser form to a higher one, such as Luna. From there, the metal can be perfected into Sol, the brightest and most royal of all metals.

It is true, as mentioned before, that the six metals will always generate a seventh from within themselves, revealing it clearly in its true form.

One might ask: If Luna, like all metals, comes from the other six, what are its properties and nature? The answer is that no other metal besides Luna can be formed from the combination of Saturn, Mercury, Jupiter, Mars, Venus, and Sol. Each of these metals contributes two key qualities to Luna, making a total of twelve virtues. These twelve virtues represent the spirit of Luna, and each metal offers something unique to its composition.

Luna gains liquidity and its bright white color from Mercury, along with influences from the zodiac signs Aquarius and Pisces. It receives its whiteness and resistance to fire from Jupiter, along with traits from

Sagittarius and Taurus. From Mars, along with Cancer and Aries, Luna gets its hardness and clear, ringing sound. From Venus, along with Gemini and Libra, Luna gains the ability to solidify. From Saturn, along with Virgo and Scorpio, Luna inherits a consistent body and weight. Finally, from Sol, with influences from Leo and Virgo, Luna receives its pure, spotless nature and strong resistance to fire.

This is the essence of Luna's spiritual and physical qualities. It is a combination of the six metals and their virtues, reflecting both wisdom and the natural order of exaltation, briefly summarized for understanding.

It is also important to explain what kind of body metallic spirits take on during their initial creation through the influence of the heavens. When a miner crushes a seemingly worthless stone, he melts it down, corrupts it, and completely breaks it apart with fire. During this process of destruction, the metallic spirit takes on a new body— one that is stronger and more refined. Instead of being brittle, it becomes soft and flexible.

Then the alchemist steps in, further corrupting, breaking down, and carefully refining this metallic body. Through this process, the spirit within the metal takes on an even more perfect form, revealing itself more clearly—unless it is Sol or Luna, which are already perfected. At last, the spirit and the body of the metal become fully united. They are now protected from the effects of ordinary fire and have reached a state where they cannot be corrupted.

Concerning The Nature of Sol And Its Properties

The seventh metal, after the six spiritual ones, is Sol, which is purely fire in its nature. Outwardly, it is the most beautiful, brilliant, clear, and noticeable of all metals. It also has the heaviest and most uniform body. This is because it holds within itself the frozen essence of the other six metals, combining them into one solid form. Sol's ability to melt comes from either the heat of fire or the hidden influence of Mercury, along with the zodiac signs Pisces and Aquarius, that exist spiritually within it. We can see proof of this because Mercury blends effortlessly with Sol, almost as if in an embrace.

However, after Sol melts and the fire's heat is removed, cold takes over, causing it to harden. To make Sol solid and stable, it requires the essence of the other five metals—Jupiter, Saturn, Mars, Venus, and Luna—each of which contributes its cold nature. Because of this, Sol is difficult to keep in liquid form without the constant heat of fire. Mercury cannot provide enough heat on its own to keep Sol melted, nor can it resist the coldness of the other five metals. Mercury's natural role is simply to stay in liquid form and flow, not to harden or make anything solid.

Heat and life belong to the same nature, bringing movement and fluidity, while cold brings hardness, stillness, and the absence of life, which can be compared to death. For instance, the six cold metals—Jupiter, Saturn, Mars, Venus, Luna, and even Venus again—can only be melted by the heat of fire. Snow and ice, being cold, will only cause things to harden further. Once a metal melted by fire cools, the cold seizes it, making it solid and frozen in place.

As for Mercury, in order to remain fluid and full of life, it depends on heat, not cold. Anyone who claims Mercury lives through cold and moisture misunderstands nature and follows common but mistaken beliefs. The truth is that life comes from warmth and fire, while cold brings death. Sol's fire is pure—it is not a living fire, but it is solid and contains the colors of sulfur, a perfect blend of yellow and red.

The five cold metals—Jupiter, Mars, Saturn, Venus, and Luna—each give Sol part of their nature. They contribute solidity through coldness, color through fire, hardness through dryness, weight through moisture, and sound through brightness. Gold, which is Sol's material form, cannot be burned or destroyed by ordinary earthly fire. This is because one fire cannot burn another fire; instead, adding fire to fire only makes it stronger.

The celestial fire we receive from the Sun on Earth is not the same as the fire in heaven or the fire we know on Earth. The fire from the Sun, when it reaches us, becomes cold and frozen—it forms the body of the Sun as we experience it. Therefore, earthly fire cannot overcome the fire of the Sun. Instead, the Sun's celestial fire melts objects, like snow or ice, but is never burned itself. Fire does not have the power to burn fire, because Sol is fire—its essence dissolved in the heavens but solidified here on Earth.

Gold is in its
1 Celestial
Dissolved Essence three
2 Elementary} and Fluid fold
3 Metallic is Corporeal.

Part II

God and Nature Do Nothing in Vain

The eternal nature of all things, existing beyond time, with no beginning or end, is always at work. It operates even in places where no hope can be found. It accomplishes what seems impossible. What once appeared beyond belief or hope reveals itself as truth in a marvelous and unexpected way.

Note on Mercurius Vivus

Whatever gives a white color carries the essence of life and the qualities of light, which naturally bring life into being. In contrast, anything that produces blackness shares the nature of death, carrying the qualities of darkness and the forces that lead to death. The earth, with its cold nature, symbolizes this hardness, as it solidifies and fixes things. A house, for example, is always lifeless, but the person who lives inside it is alive. If you can understand the power of this idea, you have gained mastery.

Tested liquefactive powder: Burn the fat of verbena.

Recipe: Four ounces of saltpeter, half as much sulfur, and one ounce of tartar. Mix them and melt.

What Is to Be Thought Concerning The Congelation Of Mercury

Trying to solidify Mercury and turn it into Luna, while also refining it through great effort, is a waste of time. This process only leads to the loss of the Sol and Luna already present within Mercury. There is a much simpler and quicker way to transform Mercury into Luna, without the need for freezing or excessive labor. This method minimizes waste and saves effort, making it possible to create silver and gold with ease.

Anyone can learn this alchemical process since it is straightforward and simple. By using it, one can produce large amounts of silver and gold in a short time. Long, complicated explanations are unnecessary—most people prefer clear instructions. So, follow these steps, and you will create Sol and Luna, which will bring you wealth. Pay close attention as I explain this process briefly. Keep these instructions well in mind so that, by working with Saturn, Mercury, and Jupiter, you can produce Sol and Luna.

There is no easier or more effective method in alchemy, and it requires very little effort to master. The process for making Sol and Luna is so fast that no further books or detailed lessons are needed—writing more about it would be as pointless as documenting last year's snow.

Concerning The Receipts of Alchemy

What, then, should we say about the recipes used in alchemy, along with the many different tools and vessels? These include furnaces, glassware, jars, waters, oils, lime, sulfur, salts, saltpeter, alum, vitriol, chrysocolla, copper greens, black inks, orpiment, green vitriol, white lead, red earth, thucia, wax, lutum sapientiae (the clay of wisdom), ground glass, verdigris, soot, eggshells, crocus of Mars, soap, crystal, chalk, arsenic, antimony, red lead, elixirs, lazurite, gold leaf, sal ammoniac, calamine stone, magnesia, Armenian bole, and many other substances.

Moreover, the steps involved—such as fermentation, digestion, testing, dissolving, cementing, filtering, refining, burning, distilling, purifying, and more—fill alchemical books to the brim. Then there are the materials drawn from herbs, roots, seeds, woods, stones, animals, worms, bone dust, snail shells, other shells, and pitch. Many of these things, however, only make the work more complicated. Even if Sol and Luna could be made with them, they would slow down the process rather than help it. The truth is that the art of creating Sol and Luna is not learned from these things. Therefore, they can be ignored, as they do not help when working with the five metals to make Sol and Luna.

Someone might ask, "What is the quick and easy way to create Sol and Luna, without unnecessary effort?" The answer is that this process has already been explained clearly and thoroughly in the Seven Canons. There is no point in trying to teach it to someone who does not grasp these Canons, as it would be difficult to convince them that this knowledge can be understood, though it must be approached in a hidden way rather than openly.

The art is this: Once you have created heaven, or the sphere of Saturn, and allowed its life to flow across the earth, place upon it the planets—whichever ones you choose—ensuring that Luna plays the smallest role. Let them run their course until Saturn, or heaven, has vanished entirely. At that point, the planets will remain lifeless, with their old, corruptible forms discarded. However, they will have gained new, perfect, and incorruptible bodies.

These new bodies are the spirit of heaven. From this spirit, the planets receive new forms and life, and they continue as they did before. Take this body, born from both life and earth, and keep it. It is Sol and

Luna. Here, then, is the entire art, explained plainly and completely. If you still do not understand it, or have not practiced it, that is fine. It is better that this knowledge remains hidden and not revealed to everyone.

How To Conjure The Crystal So That All Things May Be Seen In It

To conjure means nothing more than to observe something correctly, to know what it is, and to fully understand it. A crystal is a representation of the air. Whatever appears in the air—whether it moves or stays still—also appears as a reflection or wave within the crystal or mirror. This is because air, water, and crystal are the same in terms of how we see through them. They function like a mirror, showing a reversed image of whatever is reflected within them.

Concerning The Heat of Mercury

Those who believe that Mercury is naturally cold and moist are mistaken. In truth, Mercury is warm and moist by nature, which is why it remains in a constant state of fluidity. If it were cold and moist, it would behave like frozen water, always solid and hard, requiring fire to melt it, as is the case with other metals. But Mercury doesn't need fire to become liquid. Its own natural heat keeps it fluid, giving it the ability to move freely, or "quick," meaning it cannot be killed, solidified, or frozen.

It is important to note that when the spirits of the seven metals, or however many are combined, meet fire, they compete with one another—especially Mercury. Each metal tries to display its powers and virtues, working to dominate the others through liquefaction and transformation. One metal will take on the life and properties of another, giving a new form and nature to the one it overtakes. The heat stirs the spirits or vapors of the metals to interact with each other, constantly changing one into another until they reach perfection and purity.

What, then, must be done to Mercury to remove its natural warmth and moisture, and replace them with extreme cold that will solidify, bind, and fully harden it? Follow this method: Take pure Mercury and seal it tightly in a silver container. Place this container in the middle of a jar filled with pieces of lead. Allow it to melt for twenty-four hours, or one full day. This process removes Mercury's hidden heat, adds external warmth, and introduces the coldness of Saturn and Luna, two planets with cold properties. This forces Mercury to freeze, solidify, and become firm.

It is important to understand that the cold needed to solidify Mercury is not the same as the cold we feel from snow or ice. Instead, this cold has a different quality—on the surface, there may even seem to be some warmth. Likewise, the heat that keeps Mercury fluid is not the same kind of heat we normally experience. Instead, Mercury can feel cool to the touch, which has led some scholars, who speak more than they understand, to wrongly conclude that Mercury is cold and moist. They mistakenly suggest that heat will solidify Mercury, but instead, heat makes it even more fluid, as they continue to discover at their own expense.

True alchemy, which teaches the only way to make Sol and Luna from the five imperfect metals, offers this principle: "Only from metals, within metals, by metals, and through metals can perfect metals be made." In some metals lies the essence of Luna, and in others, the essence of Sol.

What Materials And Instruments Are Required in Alchemy

All you need are a foundry, bellows, tongs, hammers, cauldrons, jars, and small refining dishes made from beech ashes. After gathering these tools, introduce the metals—Saturn, Jupiter, Mars, Sol, Venus, Mercury, and Luna. Let the process run its course, finishing with Saturn.

The Method of Seeking Minerals

The hope of finding metals within the earth and stones is very uncertain, and the effort required is immense. However, since this is the most direct way to obtain them, it should not be dismissed but highly praised. This desire to seek metals should be encouraged, just as the natural desire for marriage in youth and adulthood is accepted. Just as bees are drawn to roses and other flowers to create honey and wax, so too should people—apart from greed or selfish ambition—seek metals within the earth. Whoever does not search for them is unlikely to find them. God grants not only gold and silver to some but also poverty, hardship, and suffering.

Some people, however, are given special knowledge of metals and minerals, enabling them to discover easier ways to create gold and silver. These methods are faster than digging and smelting, allowing them to extract precious metals from their original forms. This applies not only to things found underground but also to metals refined from imperfect minerals. Gold and silver (Sol and Luna) can be made from any of the five metals—Mercury, Jupiter, Saturn, Mars, and Venus— although some are easier to work with than others. Sol and Luna can be made more easily from Mercury, Saturn, and Jupiter, while it is more difficult to create them from Mars and Venus, though it is still possible with the addition of existing Sol and Luna. For example, Luna can be produced from Magnesium and Saturn, while pure Sol can be made from Jupiter and Cinnabar.

A skilled alchemist, through careful thought and study, can perfect the transformation of metals better than by relying on the movements of the twelve zodiac signs or the seven planets. It is unnecessary to follow these celestial movements, whether they indicate favorable or unfavorable days, good or bad planetary influences. These things neither help nor hinder the process of natural alchemy. If you have a working process, you can perform the operation whenever you choose. However, if something is missing from your method or understanding, no alignment of stars or planets will make up for it.

Metals that remain buried in the earth for too long not only rust but can also transform into natural stones over time, though this is known to very few. In fact, old coins from ancient times, bearing various images, are sometimes found in the earth. These coins were originally made of metal but, through the slow transformation of nature, have turned into stone.

What Alchemy Is

Alchemy is the deliberate effort to change one type of metal into another. Each person, using their own understanding, can find the best path and discover the truth, as truth is revealed to those who pursue it with dedication. It is essential to understand both stars and stones because the spirit of all stones is linked to the stars. Sol (the Sun) and Luna (the Moon), representing celestial bodies, are also connected to a single stone. The stones of the earth originate from these celestial stones. Through fire, purification, and separation, these earthly stones are made bright and pure, much like their celestial counterparts. The entire earth is made from a mixture of materials that have solidified into a stony mass resting within the larger sphere of the universe.

Precious stones found on earth are the closest in perfection to the heavenly stones. These earthly stones possess purity, beauty, brilliance, strength, and resistance to fire, just like celestial stones. However, they are often found in rough environments, and most people mistakenly believe these stones were created exactly where they were found. They assume that these stones were simply polished and traded for their beauty, color, and value. A brief description of these stones follows:

The Emerald is a transparent green stone. It is said to improve eyesight and memory and protect purity. If the person carrying it loses their purity, the stone will lose its perfection.

The Adamant is a black crystal, also called Evax, known for bringing joy to those who carry it. It is dark, with a metallic color, and is the hardest of all stones. However, it can dissolve in goat's blood. It rarely grows larger than a hazelnut.

The Magnet is a stone made of iron that attracts iron to itself.

The Pearl is not truly a stone since it forms inside seashells. It is white and grows within living creatures, like fish or mollusks, which makes it different from typical stones.

The Jacinth is a yellow, transparent stone. Its name also refers to a flower, which legend says was once a man.

The Sapphire is a stone with a heavenly color and is considered connected to celestial qualities.

The Ruby glows with an intense red color.

The Carbuncle is a solar stone that shines as brightly as the sun itself.

The Coral is a stone that can be white or red. It forms in the sea, growing like a plant or shrub. When exposed to air, it hardens and becomes fireproof.

The Chalcedony is a stone with mixed colors, sitting between transparency and opacity, often with cloudy or liver-colored patterns. It is considered the least valuable of the precious stones.

The Topaz is known to shine at night and is found among rocks.

The Amethyst is a stone with a purple or blood-red hue.

The Chrysoprasus shines like fire at night and resembles gold during the day.

The Crystal is a transparent white stone that looks like ice. It forms from the essence of other stones through extraction and purification.

The key to understanding these stones lies in knowing their origins and connection to metals. The truth is that metals are the most refined part of common stones. They contain elements like oil, fat, and grease, but they remain impure and imperfect as long as they are mixed within the stones. To create perfect metals, these elements must be identified, separated, and extracted from the stones through a process of melting and refining. Once purified, the substance becomes a metal comparable to the stars, which are themselves like separated stones from the heavens.

Those who study metals and minerals must be guided by reason and intelligence. They should not limit themselves to exploring only the known metals buried deep within mountains. Often, valuable metals are found closer to the earth's surface, while deeper layers may not yield the same quality. Every stone—whether a large boulder or a simple rock—must be examined carefully, for even a stone that seems worthless might contain hidden value, sometimes more valuable than livestock. The place where a stone is found does not always determine its true worth, as the influence of the sky plays a role in its formation. Even common earth, dust, or sand can contain traces of gold or silver, and those who look carefully will notice this.

The Book Concerning the Tincture of The Philosophers

Paracelsus

Preface

Since you, O Sophist, insult me with false and foolish words, saying that, being from rough Helvetia, I am incapable of understanding or learning anything—and also criticize me for being a physician who travels from place to place—I have decided to write this treatise to show the ignorant and inexperienced what true arts existed in the past. I will demonstrate the value of my knowledge against yours, and yours against mine, so that future generations will know how to follow my path in this enlightened age. Look back at Hermes, Archelaus, and others from the early times—see what great philosophers and alchemists lived then. Their work proves that your so-called mentors, O Sophist, are nothing more than empty images and idols. Even if those you call fathers and saints refuse to acknowledge this, the ancient Emerald Tablet reveals more wisdom and skill in philosophy, alchemy, and magic than anything you or your followers could ever teach.

If you still cannot understand how great these treasures are, then tell me: Why did no prince or king ever succeed in conquering the Egyptians? And why did Emperor Diocletian order all the Spagyric books to be burned wherever they could be found? If the contents of those books had remained unknown, the people would have continued to suffer under his oppressive rule. Know this, O Sophist: One day, a yoke just as heavy will be placed upon you and your companions.

In the middle of this age, the authority over all arts has been given to me—Theophrastus Paracelsus, Prince of Philosophy and Medicine. I have been chosen by God to eliminate the empty, false works and misleading words of Aristotle, Galen, Avicenna, Mesva, and their followers. My teachings, which are based on the light of Nature, are solid and unchanging. Though they may seem unappreciated now, in the 1,558th year they will begin to flourish. At that time, people of all kinds—craftsmen and ordinary folk—will see proof through extraordinary signs and fully understand how unshakable the

Paracelsian Art is, no matter how hard the sophists try to maintain their flawed knowledge with the support of papal and imperial privileges.

You call me a beggar and wandering sophist, but the Danube and the Rhine rivers will speak in my defense, even if I remain silent. Your lies about me have angered many courts and princes, as well as noble orders and cities. I have a hidden treasure in a city called Weinden, part of Forum Julii, stored at an inn—a treasure so valuable that neither Leo of Rome nor Charles of Germany could buy it, no matter their wealth. Even though the symbol of the star has been applied to your names, only those who follow the divine Spagyric Art know its true meaning.

So, you worm-ridden Sophist, since you think me—a master of hidden knowledge—a foolish and wasteful quack, I now choose to explain, through this treatise, the proper way to prepare and use the famous Tincture of the Philosophers. This explanation is given to honor all who seek the truth and to ensure that those who dismiss the true arts will suffer poverty. This great secret will illuminate the final age, making up for all past losses through divine grace and the reward of true wisdom. From the beginning of the world until now, no growth of knowledge or wisdom will ever have equaled what is to come. In the end, vice will not be able to defeat virtue, and no matter how many resources evil people gather, they will not harm those who remain righteous.

The Book Concerning The Tincture of The Philosophers

I, Philippus Theophrastus Paracelsus Bombast, declare that, through Divine grace, many different paths have been taken toward discovering the Tincture of the Philosophers. In the end, however, they all reach the same goal. Hermes Trismegistus, the Egyptian, followed his own method. Orus, the Greek, used a similar approach. Hali, the Arabian, stayed committed to his process. Albertus Magnus, the German, also followed a long and complex path. While each of these philosophers advanced according to their chosen methods, they all reached the same outcome—achieving long life, which philosophers have always desired, along with the means to sustain it honorably within this troubled world.

Now, in my time, I, Theophrastus Paracelsus Bombast, Monarch of the Arcana, have been given special gifts by God so that all seekers of this ultimate philosophical knowledge must follow my example. No matter whether they are Italian, Polish, French, or German—or from anywhere else—they must imitate my path. All philosophers, astronomers, and spagyrists, no matter how renowned, must come after me. I will reveal and teach them—both alchemists and doctors—the secrets of bodily regeneration. I will show them the tincture, the hidden knowledge (arcanum), and the quintessence, which contain the foundations of all mysteries and works.

Everyone must only believe in what they have tested through fire, for it is by fire that the truth is separated from falsehood. If someone presents a theory that goes against this method of practical experimentation in alchemy or medicine, there is no reason to trust them. Only those who work in the light of Nature will see this truth, as the light of Nature is given to help us test everything. With this light, we will demonstrate, using the best methods, that those before me— who relied too much on their ideas and speculations—only harmed themselves with their foolishness. For this reason, I have seen many simple people rise to greatness through hard work, while many nobles, trusting only in their imaginations, have fallen into foolishness, thinking of "golden mountains" in their minds before they even touched the fire.

The first things you must learn are digestion, distillation, sublimation, reverberation, extraction, solution, coagulation, fermentation, and fixation. You must also gain experience using all the necessary tools, such as glass vessels, cucurbites, circulators, earthen vessels, baths, blast furnaces, and reverberatory ovens, along with materials like marble, coals, and tongs. Only through mastering these tools and processes will you succeed in alchemy and medicine.

However, as long as you cling to fantasy and opinion, relying on false books, you will never be able to achieve anything in these fields.

Concerning The Definition of The Subject and Matter of The Tincture of The Philosophers

Before I explain the process of creating the Tincture, it is important to introduce the subject properly. Up until now, this knowledge has been kept hidden by those devoted to truth. The Tincture, when understood in a Spagyric sense, is something that passes from three essences into one through the art of Vulcan—or it can remain in that state. To give it its proper name, as used by the ancients, it is often called the Red Lion, though few truly understand what it is. With the help of Nature and the skill of the alchemist, it can be transformed into a White Eagle, producing two from one. For the alchemist, these two together shine more brightly than gold itself.

If you do not understand the teachings of the Cabalists and the ancient astronomers, then you were neither destined by God for the Spagyric art, nor chosen by Nature for the work of Vulcan, nor created to speak on the subject of alchemy. The essence of the Tincture is a great treasure—like a pearl of immense value—and it is one of the most noble things on earth, second only to the revelation of the Divine and the pursuit of wisdom among men. This Tincture is the true "Lili" of both alchemy and medicine, a treasure that philosophers have sought tirelessly. Yet, because of their incomplete knowledge and lack of proper preparation, they have never achieved the full result. Through their experiments, they managed to discover only the first stage of the Tincture. But the real foundation—the one my fellow alchemists must follow—was left for me to uncover, ensuring that no false ideas would interfere with our true purpose.

With the right to do so, and based on my extensive experience, I correct the errors of other Spagyrists and separate truth from falsehood. Through my long research, I found just reasons to criticize and change many aspects of the old teachings. If I had discovered that the experiments of the ancients were better than my own, I would not have devoted myself to such difficult labor. But I willingly endured these efforts for the benefit and progress of all true alchemists.

Now that I have explained the Tincture and revealed its essence faithfully, in a way that one brother would share with another, I will move on to its preparation. After presenting the discoveries of the earliest ages, I will add my own inventions. In time, the Age of Grace will embrace my contributions, no matter which of the ancient teachers, O Sophist, you choose to follow in the meantime.

The Emerald Tablet

(Thoth the Atlantean)

Hermes Trismegistus

The Emerald Tablets Of
Thoth The Atlantean

The story behind these tablets is unusual and may seem unbelievable to modern scientists. They are said to be incredibly ancient, going back around 36,000 years before the common era. The author is Thoth, an Atlantean priest-king, who established a colony in Egypt after the destruction of Atlantis.

Thoth is credited with building the Great Pyramid of Giza, though it has been wrongly attributed to Cheops. In the pyramid, he stored his knowledge and preserved the records and tools from ancient Atlantis. Thoth ruled over Egypt for about 16,000 years, from around 52,000 to 36,000 BCE. Under his leadership, the once primitive people of Egypt rose to a high level of civilization.

Thoth had overcome death and could pass from life only when he chose, without actually dying. His great wisdom made him ruler over many Atlantean colonies, including those in South and Central America. When it was time for him to leave Egypt, he built the Great Pyramid over the entrance to the Halls of Amenti, where he placed his records and selected the most worthy people to guard his secrets.

In later times, these guardians became the priests of the pyramids, and Thoth was worshiped as a god of wisdom and the Recorder. In the age that followed his departure, the Halls of Amenti became known in legend as the underworld, where souls went after death for judgment.

Thoth's spirit continued to incarnate in human form, as described in the tablets. He returned three times, with his last appearance as Hermes, known as the "thrice-born." During this incarnation, he left behind writings known as the Emerald Tablets, a later and more simplified version of the ancient mysteries.

The tablets translated in this work are ten in total, originally placed in the Great Pyramid under the care of the pyramid priests. For convenience, the content has been divided into thirteen sections. The final two tablets contain such powerful knowledge that it is currently forbidden to release them to the public. However, the ones included here hold valuable secrets for those who are serious about seeking wisdom. They should not be read just once but studied many times, as only through careful reading can their deeper meanings be understood. A casual reading will provide glimpses of beauty, but true insight comes only through deep study.

Now, let me explain how these ancient secrets were brought back to light after being hidden for so long. Around 1,300 BCE, Egypt was in turmoil, and many priests were sent to other parts of the world. Among them were some of the pyramid priests carrying the Emerald Tablets. They used the tablets as a symbol of authority, allowing them to influence less advanced priesthoods in other regions descended from Atlantean colonies.

These priests eventually settled in South America, where they found the Mayan civilization, which had preserved much of the ancient wisdom. The priests stayed with the Mayans, and by the 10th century, the Mayan people had established themselves in the Yucatan. The Emerald Tablets were placed under the altar of a great Sun Temple.

After the Spanish conquest, the Mayan cities were abandoned, and the treasures within their temples were forgotten. It's important to understand that the Great Pyramid has always been a temple for initiation into the mysteries. Even figures like Jesus, Solomon, and Apollonius were initiated there.

The author of this translation, who is connected to the Great White Lodge that works through the pyramid priesthood, was instructed to retrieve the tablets and return them to the Great Pyramid. After many adventures, the tablets were recovered. Before returning them, permission was granted to translate and keep a copy of the wisdom they contain. This translation was completed in 1925, and only now has permission been given to release part of it to the public. Some people will doubt its authenticity, but true seekers will find wisdom within these words. If the light is already within you, the light in these tablets will resonate with your soul.

Now, let me describe the physical nature of the tablets. They are made of a bright emerald-green material, created through a process of alchemical transformation. These tablets are imperishable and immune to all natural elements, with their atomic structure remaining stable forever. In this way, they defy the natural laws of matter and ionization.

The ancient Atlantean language is engraved on their surfaces, and these inscriptions respond to focused thoughts, releasing mental vibrations that awaken understanding in the reader. The tablets are held together by hoops of a golden-colored alloy, suspended from a rod made of the same material.

The knowledge within these tablets forms the foundation of the ancient mysteries. Anyone who reads them with an open mind will greatly expand their wisdom. Read them, believe or not, but read them—and the vibrations within will awaken a response in your soul.

In the following pages, I will reveal some of the deeper mysteries hinted at in previous writings. Humanity's search for the laws that govern life has been constant, but the truth has always been hidden just beyond the veil that separates the higher realms from the material world. Those who seek knowledge must learn to look inward, for the answers lie in silence, beyond the distractions of the physical senses. Those who talk do not know, and those who know do not speak.

The highest truths cannot be spoken, for they exist beyond words and symbols. Symbols serve as keys to understanding deeper truths, but often people cannot see what lies beyond the symbols because they seem too overwhelming. If we realize that all material symbols are just representations of higher truths, we begin to develop the vision to see beyond the veil.

Everything in the universe moves according to law. The laws that govern the planets are no different from the laws that shape human life. One of the most important Cosmic Laws is the one that connects the material aspect of humanity with the spiritual. The key to this connection lies in the intellectual part of human nature, which bridges the material and spiritual worlds.

Those who seek higher knowledge must strengthen their minds and concentrate all their energy on their chosen path. The search for light, life, and love begins on the material plane, but it reaches its ultimate goal in complete unity with the universal consciousness. The material world is only the starting point; the true goal is spiritual enlightenment.

In the following pages, I will interpret the Emerald Tablets and reveal some of their hidden meanings. The words of Thoth contain many layers of truth, and these hidden meanings will become clear with thoughtful reflection. If your own inner light is awakened, the knowledge within these tablets will resonate with your soul.

TABLET 1 I, Thoth, the Atlantean, master of ancient mysteries, keeper of sacred knowledge, and mighty ruler, have lived through countless generations. As I prepare to enter the Halls of Amenti, I write down this wisdom for those who come after me. In the great city of Keor, on the island of Undal, I began this life long ago. The people of Atlantis were not like the men of today—they did not live short lives, but instead, they renewed their existence over and over through the Halls of Amenti, where the river of life flows eternally.

I have traveled down the dark path that leads to light a hundred times over, and just as many times I have returned from darkness, renewed in strength and power. Now, I leave once more, and the people of Khem (ancient Egypt) will no longer see me. But one day, I will rise again, mighty and powerful, to demand an account from those I left behind. Beware, people of Khem, if you have betrayed my teachings, for I will cast you down into the darkness from which you came.

Do not reveal my secrets to those from the North or the South, or my curse will fall upon you. Remember my words, for I will return and demand from you all that you have been entrusted with. Even from beyond time and death, I will return to reward or punish you according to how you have followed my truths.

My people were great in ancient times, far greater than the people who live now. We held knowledge that reached into the depths of the universe, uncovering wisdom from Earth's earliest days. We were wise with the knowledge of the Children of Light, who lived among us, and we drew power from the eternal fire. Among us, the greatest of all men was my father, Thotme, the keeper of the great temple and the link between the Children of Light and the people who lived across the ten islands of Atlantis. He was the voice of the Dweller of Unal, whose words the kings obeyed.

I grew up under my father's guidance, learning the ancient mysteries, and the fire of wisdom grew within me until it consumed my soul. On a great day, the Dweller of the Temple summoned me before him. Few men had looked upon his face and lived, for the Children of Light, when not in physical form, are not like the sons of men. I was chosen from among humanity to be taught by the Dweller, so that I might carry out his purposes, which were not yet born in the world.

For long ages, I lived in the temple, learning ever more wisdom until I reached the light of the great fire. The Dweller taught me the path to Amenti, the underworld where the great king sits on his throne of power. I bowed before the Lords of Life and Death, and they gave me the Key of Life. I was freed from the cycle of death and rebirth. I traveled to the stars, where space and time meant nothing, and after drinking deeply from the cup of wisdom, I looked into the hearts of men. There, I discovered even greater mysteries, and my soul was at peace.

Throughout the ages, I have watched people die and be reborn in the light of life. But as Atlantis declined, the consciousness that had once been one with me faded, replaced by lesser beings from distant stars. Following the laws of the universe, the word of the Master began to take form. The thoughts of the Atlanteans turned downward into darkness, and the Dweller awoke from his detachment, calling forth his power. Deep in the heart of the Earth, the Sons of Amenti heard his call. Using the power of the Logos, they directed the eternal fire, shifting its course.

A great flood swept over the world, shifting the balance of the Earth, and only the Temple of Light remained standing on the mountain of Undal, still rising above the water. Some among us survived the flood. The Master commanded me to gather my people and take them across the waters to the land of the barbarians who lived in caves. There, we would carry out the plan we knew so well.

I gathered my people, and we boarded the Master's great ship. As we rose into the morning sky, the Temple of Light disappeared beneath the rising waters. It vanished from the Earth until the appointed time when it would return. We fled toward the rising sun, and beneath us lay the land of the children of Khem. When we arrived, the barbarians came at us with spears and clubs, filled with rage and intent on destroying the Sons of Atlantis.

I raised my staff and directed a ray of vibration at them, freezing them in place like stones from the mountain. Then I spoke to them calmly, telling them of the greatness of Atlantis and explaining that we were messengers of the Sun. I used my knowledge of magic and science to subdue them until they bowed before me. When I released them, they groveled at my feet in fear.

We lived in the land of Khem for many long years. Following the Master's command, I eventually sent the Sons of Atlantis to distant lands, so that the wisdom of Atlantis could rise again in the future.

Through the womb of time, knowledge would once more be reborn in those who seek it.

For a long time, I lived in the land of Khem, using my knowledge to perform great works. The people of Khem grew in understanding, nourished by the wisdom I shared. To retain my power, I opened a path to Amenti, allowing me to live through the ages as a Sun of Atlantis, preserving knowledge and records. The people of Khem became strong, conquering those around them and slowly rising in spiritual strength.

Now I must leave them and descend into the dark halls of Amenti, deep within the Earth, where I will stand once more before the Dweller. Above the entrance to Amenti, I raised a gateway—only a few have the courage to cross it. Over the portal, I built a mighty pyramid, harnessing the power that defies Earth's gravity. Inside, I placed a force-chamber, creating a circular passage that reaches near the top. At the summit, I set a crystal to send a ray through time and space, drawing energy from the ether and focusing it toward the gateway of Amenti.

I built other chambers that seem empty but hide the keys to Amenti within them. Only those who dare to explore the dark realms may enter, but first, they must purify themselves through fasting. Those who seek the mysteries must lie in the stone sarcophagus within my chamber, and then the hidden truths will be revealed. Even in the depths of the Earth, I will meet them. I, Thoth, the Lord of Wisdom, will dwell with them always.

I built the Great Pyramid, designing it to align with the forces of the Earth, so it would burn with energy for eternity and stand through the ages. Inside, I placed my knowledge of magic and science, ensuring I could return from Amenti. While my body sleeps in the halls, my soul will roam freely, incarnating among humans in different forms, including as Hermes, thrice-born.

I serve as the Dweller's messenger on Earth, following his commands to guide many toward enlightenment. Now I return to the halls of Amenti, leaving behind fragments of my wisdom. Keep the Dweller's command: Always lift your gaze toward the light. In time, you will become one with the Master, united with the All. I leave now, but remember my teachings. Live by them, and I will be with you, guiding you into the light. As the portal opens before me, I descend into the night's darkness.

Deep in the heart of the Earth lie the Halls of Amenti, beneath the sunken islands of Atlantis. These halls are places for both the living and the dead, illuminated by the fire of the infinite All. In a distant past, the Children of Light observed humanity's struggle, seeing that people were bound by forces beyond them. They knew that only by breaking free could humans rise from Earth toward the Sun. The Children of Light took human form and came down to Earth, saying, "We are beings formed from the dust of space, part of the infinite All. Though we live as humans, we are not entirely like them."

They created vast spaces beneath the Earth's surface, far from where humans lived, surrounding these halls with powerful forces to protect them from harm. They built other spaces nearby, filling them with life and light from above. In these hidden places, they built the Halls of Amenti to dwell there eternally, living with endless life.

Thirty-two of the Children of Light came among humans, seeking to free them from the darkness and the forces that bound them. In the Halls of Life, a bright, flaming flower grew, expanding and driving away the darkness. At its center, they placed a powerful ray, filling all who came near with life and light. Around the flower, they arranged thirty-two thrones, where the Children of Light sat, bathed in its radiance and filled with the eternal light.

Over the ages, they placed their original bodies in these halls, reawakening them every thousand years with the life-giving light, which quickened their spirits. Though they appeared to sleep, their souls moved freely through the bodies of men, guiding and teaching them. As their bodies rested, they incarnated among humans, leading them from darkness into the light. In the Halls of Life, they kept knowledge unknown to humanity, living forever beneath the cool fire of life.

At times, they awakened from their rest, coming forth as lights among people, infinite beings among finite men. Those who rise from darkness into light are freed from the Halls of Amenti and the Flower of Life. With wisdom as their guide, they pass from among men to join the Masters of Life, free from the bonds of darkness. In the center of the radiant flower sit seven Lords from realms beyond time, guiding humanity with infinite wisdom along the path through time. Though they are silent and hidden, their power is immense, and their knowledge is endless.

Drawing from the Life force, different yet connected to the children of men. Though different, they are also One with the Children of Light. They guard and watch over the forces that bind humanity, ready to release them when the time for enlightenment arrives.

At the forefront sits the Veiled Presence, the Lord of Lords, the infinite Nine, standing above the Lords of the Cycles—Three, Four, Five, Six, Seven, and Eight—each with a purpose and unique power, guiding and shaping human destiny. They sit in strength and wisdom, untouched by time or space. Though not of this world, they are connected to it, like Elder Brothers to humanity. With wisdom, they judge and observe, watching how the Light grows within mankind.

The Dweller led me before them, and I witnessed him blend with the ONE from above. A voice came forth, saying, "Thoth, you are great among the children of men. From this moment, you are free from the Halls of Amenti, a Master of Life among men. Death will come to you only if you desire it. Drink from the well of Life for all eternity, for Life is now yours to take. Death is yours to command at will. Stay here or leave when you wish; Amenti is open to you, a Sun among men. Take Life in any form you choose, Child of the Light who has grown among humanity.

Though free, you must always labor along the path of Light. You have taken one step on the endless journey upward, but the mountain of Light stretches infinitely before you. Every step you take raises the mountain higher; each bit of progress makes the goal seem farther away. You will forever move toward infinite Wisdom, but the goal will always stay just out of reach. You are now free from the Halls of Amenti."

Thank You for Reading

Dear Reader,

We hope this timeless classic has sparked your imagination and enriched your literary journey. Now that you've turned the final page, we want to share a vision for the future of reading—one where every classic you've ever wanted to explore is at your fingertips, in a format that best suits your life.

We'd like to invite you to gain immediate, unlimited digital & audiobook access to hundreds of the most treasured literary classics ever written—along with the option to secure deluxe paperback, hardcover & box set editions at printing cost. Together, we can spark a new global literary renaissance alongside our small, independent publishing house called "The Library of Alexandria."

Thousands of years ago, the Library of Alexandria stood as a beacon of knowledge—until it was lost to history. We aim to reignite that spirit of preservation and discovery right now, in the modern age—only this time, it's accessible to all, in every language and every format.

Picture a world where every timeless classic, novel, poem, or philosophical treatise is not only available to read but also updated for today's readers—modernized, translated into any language or dialect, and ready to enjoy in any format you choose, whether that is in an eBook, audiobook, paperback, or deluxe hardcover & box set version a printing cost.

By joining our movement to rebuild the modern Library of Alexandria, you become part of an unprecedented mission to offer:

- **Unlimited Audiobook & eBook Access to the Greatest Classics of All Time**

  Instantly explore thousands of legendary works, from Plato and Shakespeare to Jane Austen and Leo Tolstoy. All are instantly ready to read or listen to, giving you a complete literary universe at your fingertips.

- **Paperback & Deluxe Editions at Printing Costs:**

  Purchase any title in a paperback, deluxe hardbound, or deluxe boxset edition at printing costs, shipped right to your doorstep. Curate your personal library of Alexandria with editions worthy of display—crafted to last, designed to captivate, and delivered straight to your door.

- **Modern translations for Contemporary Readers in all languages and dialects**

  Discover a vast selection of classics reimagined in clear, current language—no more struggling with outdated phrases or obscure references. Next to the original versions, we aim to offer translations in as many languages and dialects as possible.

  As we continue our translation efforts and add new languages, readers everywhere can connect with these works as if they were written today. By bridging linguistic divides, you're contributing to ensuring that these timeless stories become more meaningful, accessible, and inspiring for people across the globe.

- **Your Personal Library of Alexandria:**

  Over the months and years, you'll curate a unique physical archive of classics—each volume a testament to your taste, curiosity, and love of knowledge. It's not just about owning books—it's about curating a cultural legacy you'll cherish and pass down for generations to come.

- **Join a Global Literary Renaissance:**

  Your support fuels an ongoing mission: allowing us to reinvest in offering deluxe print editions (including special boxsets) at their true cost, broaden the range of available formats and translations, and extend the reach of these works to new audiences worldwide. By joining today, you're not just preserving a legacy of masterpieces; you set in motion a powerful wave of literary accessibility.

  We are more than a publisher—we're a movement, and we can't do it alone. Your support lets us scale our mission, preserving and reimagining history's greatest works for tomorrow's readers.

Become a Torchbearer of knowledge.

Thank you for picking up this book and allowing us into your literary journey. As you turn the pages, know that you're part of something larger: a global effort to keep these stories alive, share their wisdom across borders and generations, and spark a true cultural revival for the modern era.

If this resonates with you—please consider taking the next step by visiting:

www.libraryofalexandria.com

With gratitude and a shared love of knowledge,

The Modern Library of Alexandria Team

Visit:

www.libraryofalexandria.com

Or scan the code below:

www.ingramcontent.com/pod-product-compliance
Lightning Source LLC
Chambersburg PA
CBHW011352010726
47494CB00008B/2275